By David Morgan, the creator of the cult series of 2019 books.
He doesn't understand the title either.

Other books by David Morgan

The 2019 Series   www.2019books.co.uk

2019: The Beginning

The murder of a Countess starts an incredible series of events from Hong Kong and Paraguay to rural England. Why does billionaire Jessica Crowne want old documents? Who is the unseen Jerome Jones? What is the Octagon? Why do some people never age? Answers start on page one

2019: The Second Coming

Magick. Is the world changing? A mysterious man with two glamorous assistants launches an organisation promising peace and prosperity. Why do they seek an ancient golden cat? The Omasor Agency investigates, with help from Brick and Blonde, celebrity adventurers. Created from mostly natural English with no added squirrels but may contain nut residues and textual nudity.

ISBN 978-1846858932

2019: Athens 1 Atlantis 0

Atlantis fought Athens, 11,000 years ago for global domination. Their descendants intend to control the planet again using the Treasures of Poseidon and helped by the Temple Virgins, who are different to other women in interesting ways. Corruption, lust, kidnap, murder follows. Also some bad things. The Omasor Agency gets involved..

ISBN 978-0-9559767-0-4

2019: Godsplay

Selena and Chris have to travel to the universe of the gods to save Jerome Jones. A journey through many strange worlds populated by humans and the gods are amongst them, disguised as fellow inhabitants. Is it life or death? Or just a game? Fast, fun action with twists and turns everywhere.

ISBN 978-0-9559767-1-1

Amazon Bear Joiner

DAVID MORGAN

Published by

Living Designs Publishing

Campion House, Campion Terrace, Leamington Spa, CV32 4SU

www.livingdesignspublishing.co.uk

First published by Living Designs Publishing 2008

ISBN-13: 978-0-9559767-2-8

This book is for Claire

1

Nymphomaniac.

In the 23 years of his life, that hadn't been a word for John Smith to handle face-to-face. Then again, it could be commonly used in job interviews, as this was only the third applicant he had seen since placing the advert in the newspaper.

John was average height with light brown hair that tousled and he wished it didn't. It made him look like an old schoolboy. No real complaints, in many ways he was lucky. He was rich with millions in the bank. But he didn't have parents.

Both his father and mother had been professors of antiquity, archaeologists of some renown. They were always travelling to distant places, digging in some ruins or studying manuscripts. He had not seen them often during his schooldays, travelling with them just once for an eight-day excavation in Greece. Both had died when he was at university. Died prematurely, a long way from home. They had been in South America, somewhere along the Amazon and the reports said they were killed violently by a local gang.

An old family friend, Colwyn Bayers, had gone to the area to clear up the formalities. He had asked John not join him but concentrate on university. That is what his parents would have wanted. The bodies were returned. A quiet cremation and they were gone. John had no brothers or sisters and everything was left to him. Everything comprised a villa in north Cornwall, the far South West of England, with a legacy of about 20 million pounds. John's father hadn't created the wealth; all of it was inherited through the family. But he also hadn't spent it and it sat in a variety of bank accounts, generating interest payments of more money than he could use.

John had dedicated himself to his studies and completed his degree three months ago. Then he moved to the villa, completely unsure of what to do with his life. At university, he had been social but not an extrovert partygoer. Studious, but not a bookworm. Active, but not an athlete. Quite average really.

John had visited Colwyn Bayers to discuss his future. A tall, lean man with white hair that was always immaculately brushed back. Before retirement, he had also been a professor and lived in the same area. His advice had been to go into property. Set up an investment company to buy up land and houses, rent them out and then resell at a significant profit after a couple of years.

John didn't like that idea. It didn't satisfy an indefinable urge within him. A need for adventure. Some days later, he read again the novel that had been one of his favourites 10 years before. An old book set in the 1930s. 'Cadaver Wincepole, Gentleman Detective'. The next day he woke with a decision. Not as interesting as waking with a woman but longer lasting. He would be the new Wincepole and his first case would be to investigate the death of his parents.

First he needed an assistant. Wincepole had Bongo Whittler, an old school chum but John didn't know anyone from school he wanted to associate with. He placed the advertisement in a national newspaper.

'Assistant to investigator required. Fit and active. Prepared to travel anywhere. Accommodation provided. Good salary and car.'

298 application forms that he quickly stripped down to five. Four men and one woman. Now he was interviewing in his newly decorated office, one of the many spare rooms in the villa. And had prepared a set of questions. He wasn't just looking for blind loyalty, Bongo Whittler like. What he wanted was sharp, deductive powers and his questions were designed to test just that.

The first two were serious young men and they had both failed the final question. Eliza Clustbour was the third and she was very different. A fresh faced girl, just a little shorter than John. Curly, shoulder length, reddish brown hair, quick and sharp brown eyes and an expression that seem to indicate that everything amused her.

He began the interview as soon as she sat in front of his desk.

"Ms Clustbour?"

"I'm 21, clever as a badger, strong as a panda and quick as an okapi. I was born in England, degree in Rabbit Appellations. I speak several languages, know lots of stuff, don't get ratty during my periods and have the deductive capacity of a minus sign. I am unattached. I can drive, use computers and ski. My only failing as is that I'm a nymphomaniac."

That's where we came in. John decided not to comment.

"I have some questions."

"I was joking about the Rabbit Appellations degree. Actually it's in Mythology."

"Right."

She breezed through the first nine questions.

"This is the final one. You have three seconds to answer. I walk 10 miles south, 10 miles west and 10 miles north and arrived back at the same place I started. Can you tell me exactly where in the world I am?"

It took maybe half a second.

"No."

"Explain the answer."

She explained succinctly.

"Do I get the job?"

She smiled openly, no artifice.

"It's yours if you want it."

"Are you sure? I wasn't completely joking about the nymphomania. I haven't really got that, it's a medical condition. But I have got a degree of hyper sexuality. I'm not at it all the time, it's often just in my mind."

"That's reassuring."

"Shall I tell them? My first task?"

The two applicants waiting in the next room. She was sharp.

"Yes, please do that."

She was away before he finished and he noted her lithe movement and fit body. Now he has an assistant, about as unlike Bongo Whittler as you could get. John didn't have a partner. He had slept with a handful of girls at university but nothing fulfilling. He wasn't desperate to find company but didn't dislike it. Average again.

He was now residing at the villa with just the housekeepers who had been there since before he was born. Now in their early 50s, the Wormgraspers were a fixture. What had changed was their size. As a child he remembered them as an active couple, always on the move. They had gone in different directions since then. Percy was now a thin, almost stick like man with a bony, blotched, weathered face. His wife, Sue was just a mass of blubber with great rolls of flab clinging to every muscle. Strangely, they both eat the same meals. 'Real country food', Sue called it. Fried breakfasts, frozen beef burgers and chips for lunch and a dinner of fried anything, including pies, meat and fish encased in lumps of oils and butter. Followed by cream cake.

Percy was still just as active, tending the garden, cleaning rooms, repairing and maintaining. Sue spent most of the day in the kitchen, adding several extra snacks to her daily intake.

Eliza returned.

"All done, they're gone. I'll write to the first two and tell them sorry."

"I didn't ask when you could start."

"I've started. Do I have an office?"

"The next room, where you waited. There's just a table and chairs there at the moment. I was going to suggest that you decide the lay out and buy anything that you need. Just get whatever furniture you want."

"I researched your background. Lots of money. You should get me to sign a silence contract so I can't seduce you and then sell the story or use it for blackmail."

"No contract. I think I'd enjoy the notoriety."

"I wouldn't do it. Money doesn't bother me. If it did, I'd probably be bonking some old billionaire into extinction."

"Right. You also have residential rooms here. There's a suite on the second floor. The building is old but I had it completely refurbished inside when I was at university. New electrics, new plumbing, new flooring, everything."

"I'll move in today."

"Really?"

"I'm renting a flat at the moment. I'll organise the move for this afternoon, there's not a lot to bring. Mostly clothes and shoes plus a laptop computer."

"The offer is the same as for the office. Just go and get anything you like for the rooms. It's your private apartment and I've had a new lock fitted. Only you will have the keys."

"You might find it safer to lock me in at night."

John hesitated.

"And it's the same for the car. Just buy one. I'll give you a debit card. It does have a limit but hopefully you won't reach it."

"What is the limit?"

"£250,000."

"I'll try and leave at least five pounds."

"You're not serious now."

"As I said, money's not important to me. You should have asked about my family and background in the interview."

"That's personal to you."

"You lost your parents a few years ago. Mine were killed when I was nine. I have one sister, Agnes. She's six years older than me and married to an American computer whiz. Lives near Los Angeles."

"I'm sorry about your parents."

"No need. Long time ago. Agnes and I were raised by an aunt and uncle in central England. Love them still. Left to go to university at 17. The last year,

I've been travelling round the world. I have no steady relationship. Unbelievably, I was a virgin until I was 18. A few lovers although none serious. As I said, I'm a little hypersexual. I think about it a lot. I'm very choosy about partners, that's my woman side taking over."

"Right."

"What else? Well, you might remember my parents."

"The Clustbours? I'm sorry but it doesn't bring anyone to mind."

"They used different names on stage. Peter Shikk and Meli Twill. The Shikwills Consortium."

"What? Even I've heard of them. One of the biggest rock groups of the 80s. I know the story of the crash. Everyone remembers what they were doing when they heard the news."

"As I said, it's a long time ago. I just remember them as a little girl and I still love them. But no bitterness, they wouldn't want that. Nice to see them sometimes on videos but I never look back. Of course, Agnes and I inherited. I'm worth £5,435,192 as at yesterday. Not in your class."

"I understand why money doesn't bother you. Why on earth would you apply for this job?"

"The same reason as you. Any instructions or shall I get busy?"

"I didn't think anything would happen this fast. I know our first investigation but it can wait for a few days. Give you a chance to settle in."

"Okay. Then you want to find out how your parents died."

That did surprise him.

"It's worrying how you know so much."

"Simple deduction. You're only just setting up so it can't be a client. Must be something personal. I didn't see anything else in your background."

"This begins to feel like Baker Street. Do you smoke a meerschaum pipe?"

"Only in bed. Actually I don't drink, don't smoke, don't take drugs. Pretty unique with my background."

"I'm the same."

"Good. Otherwise I'd have to murder you and take over the agency."

John showed her the apartment and introduced her to the Wormgraspers. He was amazed to see how she charmed them instantly. Within a few minutes, Sue was ferrying cups of tea to her while Percy moved furniture with more enthusiasm than John had seen since he arrived. Eliza was soon on the phone arranging the move, furniture, computers and a car. He returned to the peace of his office and relaxed at his desk. He had been expecting to launch the agency in a few weeks, probably with some ex-police or army man as assistant. Now he had the bubbling, wealthy, 21-year-old daughter of two members of a famous rock group. And she was hypersexual.

He was pleased. Very pleased with his day's work.

2

Six days later. John awoke from the doze and glanced across at Eliza. She was writing in a small notebook, emanating energy like a hyperactive squirrel. They were flying first-class to Rio de Janeiro and from there would travel by chartered helicopter to the scene of his parents killing.

"Do you ever sleep?" he asked.

She grinned.

"I just need about four hours. You've been out for 69 minutes. Would you like tea, coffee or sex? I'd quite like to join this mile high club."

"Would it upset you if I chose tea?"

"No, it would just confirm you as a frigid man who needs to be released from his inhibitions. Either that or you just feel like tea."

Five minutes later he was sipping from a mug while she spoke.

"I suggest we go through the story again."

"Yes, sure. Colwyn Bayers gave us a lot of detail when we met him."

"We're talking nearly a year ago. Apparently, the wall of some ancient building was found by a river trader somewhere up the Amazon basin. That's still a rarely visited area and it was almost buried under a mass of vegetation away from all the normal routes. The trader took a couple of photos and sent them to a friend in a town not far from Rio. This man was an amateur archaeologist who had met your parents on a visit to England. He forwarded the pictures to them for advice and they saw something in them that made them travel to Brazil almost immediately. Our first problem is that we don't know what it was. Your father only told Colwyn Bayer that there was something extraordinary in the pictures."

"And as far as we know, the trader and the friend didn't have copies."

"Both are dead. They died before the bodies of your parents were discovered. The trader was found drowned and the friend was killed in a car accident. As far as we know, nothing relevant was found in their possessions."

"According to Bayer, my father and mother reached Brazil and started up the Amazon. They flew as far as you can go by helicopter and then chartered a boat. Radio contact was lost with them after two days but that's not so unusual in the area. And that was it, until a week later when one of the river men found their bodies on the bank in some backwater near a place called Comcalcinta. He brought them back to the nearest town after four days travel. Just the bodies as all their belongings were apparently taken during the attack."

"The remains were badly mutilated. Sorry if that's upsetting."

"Not now. I just want to find out."

"Understood. Another problem we have is that no one now knows where this structure is. So no photos and no location."

"Our starting point is where the bodies were found," John asserted.

"That's logical although the authorities visited the area and found absolutely nothing."

"It still must be the place to start."

"I don't agree but you're the boss," Eliza responded, sitting back with lips pursed together.

"You didn't mention sulking during the interview."

"I'm just being obedient. I solved my first mystery when I was six. My sister said she lost a book and I volunteered to find it. She had it last on the sofa and I deduced that it had got mixed up with newspapers. I went to the kitchen where we put all the old papers in a pile for garbage."

"Yes, clever."

"But the book wasn't in the pile. That left three possibilities. The least likely were that it had already been trashed or that aliens had taken it. I calculated a 90% probability for the third."

"What was that?"

"I told my sister not to be jealous of me. I wasn't competing with her. Then I asked her where she had hidden the book. She admitted that it was under the mattress of her bed. I suggested that she announced to everyone that she had found it and I hadn't been any help."

"Why tell her not to be jealous?"

"Attention. It's all about attention. You should know these things if you want to be a detective. Babies cry, toddlers fall over and pretend hurt, children talk loud and dress strange. Adults do all that and more, often with weapons. 'Please notice me', that's the message."

"Profound."

"Just streetwise. Maybe you should do more streetwalking."

"Err, yes, maybe I should. So as you're the one with the deductive talents, where do you say we should go first?"

"We should check out the two murdered men."

"Murders?"

"The one who took the photo and his friend."

"You think they were murdered? I suppose it's possible but it was a long time ago. Why start with them?"

"Simply because you can't begin at the end."

"Good suggestion. My decision then. We'll go your way this time."

"I'm not competing," she said with a cheeky grin and he couldn't stop himself smiling.

They quickly passed through customs at the airport, Eliza using her most appealing looks to undermine any officiousness. The helicopter John had chartered was waiting with the pilot already on board.

"He looks fit," observed Eliza as they approached.

A young man, with sleek dark hair to his collar and a flashing white smile. He greeted them in an American drawl.

"Okay guys, I'm ready to shift."

"Wow, you're from the States," Eliza said girlily.

John gave a wry smile. He was beginning to understand her now.

"Sure am. Stu Kimber's the name from southern Texas. Lived here for three years. Love this country."

John moved forward.

"Change of plan. We want to go first to this town."

He indicated on a map the place where his parent's friend had died.

"No problem. You're all paid-up for the week. Fuel charge at cost. I'll go where you say."

After boarding, Eliza sat in front with Stu while John took a seat in the cabin and pulled out his set of files.

Manuel Dirriganjo was the man who had sent the photos to his parents. Not really a friend but sharing a common interest. He was an accountant by occupation but harboured a fanatical interest in archaeology. Over the years, he had made innumerable contacts and everyone knew he would pay well for artefacts or information on any new discoveries. Never married, no children and had lived in the same town for almost all his life. That was about all they knew.

"About 25 minutes," Stu yelled over the engine noise.

John looked up and noticed Eliza leaning over towards the dark haired man, her hand on his shoulder. He returned to his study of the files.

They landed in a field, on the fringes of the town. From the air the settlement seemed very small, maybe just 40 or so houses.

"Hot and sticky. Do you sweat a lot?" Eliza asked as he joined her on the grass.

"No more than most."

"One friend of my parents was always twitching and perspiration dripped from him. I told him he was a sweater and a jumper. Not bad for a 7-year-old girl."

"Hope you've improved since."

"I don't sweat much. Humidity doesn't bother me."

She looked as fresh as a daisy in the clinging heat.

"Now I guess we have to find this Dirriganjo's house."

"Yes but first we need to speak to any close friends."

"I'll go with that."

"Sorry boss, just a suggestion."

"I believe in allowing my employees to express themselves within the guidelines I set."

Eliza grinned.

"You provide the aquarium and we swim around anywhere we want inside?"

"Sort of."

Her expression turned serious.

"If you see my dorsal fin flapping, it means I want to ask a question."

"Okay, that's good."

He really couldn't tell if it was.

Eliza was already walking towards a handful of men standing on a road that ran along the edge of the field.

"Hey," she shouted and jogged towards them. John reached her as the men began to fall about with laughter.

"Just told them a dirty joke in Portuguese," she remarked.

She conversed rapidly with the now sociable group. It ended with her clasping the arm of a podgy, middle-aged man and they began to walk away.

"Come on. My friend here has agreed to drive us," Eliza shouted over her shoulder.

The man led them to a battered Fuaro Pramdo. Eliza jumped in the passenger seat and John looked for a place in the back that was cluttered with mobile phone and CD boxes, chicken feathers, cigarette packets and a mass of other modern jetsam. The driver leant over and pushed the garbage to one side, clearing just enough space to allow him to sit.

The car grumbled its way through scattered buildings, many of wood but a few elegant stone built houses. Eliza continued to chat and the driver frequently turned to look at her, waving both arms to make a point. The car slewed round dangerously on the rough road surface and John found that the temperature outside was exceeded significantly in the back of the car. He was frying in his own sweat when they finally pulled up in front of a shabby bar in the centre of town. Eliza handed the driver of a pile of notes and kissed his flabby cheek before he departed.

"I assume that our man frequented this bar," remarked John.

"No. Our friend told me that his old girlfriend works here."

"Seems a bit rough. I assumed that he mixed in higher circles."

"Don't you know anything about men? The higher up the tree, the more they like sleaze, providing it's wrapped in plastic."

"Well, I'm a man and it's never attracted me."

"Yes, right. Shall we go in, boss?"

"Who's the lady?"

"Molhado. Apparently, she entertains here."

They entered a room that could have doubled as a steam bath. Smoke filled, baking hot and the grimy walls glistened with humidity. A long, stained bar on the far side with a mess of wooden tables and chairs shambled together in front. It was packed with people, chatting loudly enough to be heard over blaring music.

Eliza shouted in the ear of the nearest drinker and he pointed. John followed the direction and his eyes met a wall of flesh. A woman who bulged in all the right places and also all the wrong places. Plus all the neutral places.

"You'd only want her like Everest. Because she was there," Eliza remarked as they approached. John saw the woman's eyes fix on him and her thick lips parted in a practised invitational smile.

"You want threesome?" she enquired amiably.

"I think she could have one of those by herself," Eliza whispered.

"We want to talk privately. You'll be well rewarded," John responded in a formal tone.

"You pay some upfront first. Then go my room."

She reached out a podgy hand, palm down and John pushed a large note into it. She didn't check it. Apparently she could identify denominations with her fingers.

"Okay. Come with me."

Her room was as filthy as the bar but contained a kaleidoscope of smells, all of them stale. Molhado sat on the bed, bowing it almost to the floor while John and Eliza remained standing as a precaution against infection.

"Manuel Dirriganjo, you knew him?" asked John.

Her eyes sharpened.

"You police?"

"No, we're lawyers. He left some money to give to people he knew and you're one of them. It's taken a long time to clear up all the legal details."

"How much?"

"$5,000 American."

"I'll take it now."

"No. We need to ask you questions to confirm your identity."

"I don't have papers."

"That doesn't matter. Tell me about Manuel."

She relaxed backwards and the bed squealed for mercy.

"I knew him three years, right 'til he died. Good man. Honest and friendly."

"We can only check your story against the last few weeks before his death."

"It started when he told me he was going to have lot money. He had bought photo cheap and sent it to big man in England. Man was coming here to pay him plenty."

"What happened then?"

"I saw him after big English man arrived with wife. He said he had been given a little payment but lots money when they got back. Said they'd gone up river to look at something."

"Did he say what?" asked Eliza.

"Didn't tell. Said it was now very secret but he promised I would have big share of money when he got it."

"Did you see him again?"

Molhado looked down, deep in thought for a moment. When she lifted her head, there was something new in her eyes.

"Yes. I saw him. Day before he died. He was scared. I'd never seen him with gun but now he carried one. Even had it on the bed. He talked about leaving."

"What was he scared of?"

"Wouldn't talk about it. Just said he wished never seen photo. Then next day I hear he's dead in car crash."

"Did he ever show you the photo?"

"Never. I guessed it was something bad. Maybe blackmail job."

"Would he have kept copies of it?"

"Don't know. He was tidy man. Maybe kept something but it was long time ago."

"Can you tell us where he lived?"

John pulled out a local roadmap and she marked the location of the house.

"New people bought it soon after Manuel dead. I guess nothing of his still there. Do I get money now?"

John handed her a wad of $100 bills and her face lit up as she counted the notes.

"You good man. Want threesome now?"

"No thank you. We're in a hurry."

Back in the street, Eliza turned to John.

"Need transport. I'll find something."

She moved off down the street and John followed her to a general store, still contemplating the words of the big woman. A man walked from the store towards his car, an eight-year-old Putto Ranki, and Eliza intercepted him with a help me look. Within six minutes they were driving off in the newly purchased car.

"I can drive if you can handle navigation," Eliza had said, making map reading sound the hardest job in the world.

3

Put a satellite picture of England on your screen. Zoom into central London and roll the cursor west a bit, so you're outside the concrete morass and into the tiny green bits. Scroll and zoom a bit more. That large house with the row of trees in front and the big barn behind it. Many barns in the area had been converted into residences but this one has been modified to include some unique features that only a tiny number know about.

Go inside and it appears to be an elegant, three-bedroom, single storey house. The entrance hall has vertical wooden struts embedded in the walls, giving a rustic feel. Between the second and third strut, there is a concealed door, totally invisible to even a close inspection. It leads to an elevator that goes one level down and you emerge in a modern chamber with ten chairs around a large meeting table. A kitchen and toilets lead off the room.

Two maids are now in the kitchen, preparing a tray of coffee and tea. They carry it into the main room where eight people are seated at the table. The maids leave the trays, and then depart in the elevator.

One of the people at the table stands up. An elegant, businesslike woman looking less than content.

"Does anyone here know why we've been summoned to this meeting?"

A murmur of negativity from the others who seemed to share the woman's impatience.

"Well, I need to run my company. I'm negotiating a three million dollar takeover at the moment and I can't waste my time here," she continued.

"I would appreciate your silence. Please sit."

The words didn't come from the group of people. They emerged from a series of loudspeakers that must have been hidden somewhere in the room. The speech was gravelly but precise, a result of electronic voice modification. The woman sat down.

"My apologies, Leader. I was unaware that you had personally called this meeting."

There was a slight pause before the voice continued.

"I invited you all here for a friendly chat. It is now nearly one year since my request that you locate the orb. In my view, this was not too arduous a task as you have been provided with limitless finances and personnel. May I ask if any of you has any success to report?"

Heads lowered around the table. No one responded.

"Then you must have some guide, some indication as to its whereabouts?"

The elegant woman looked up.

"I have over 350 searching, including 294 in the field. The country has been divided into sectors and we are focusing a team in each of them. They are the best investigators money can buy."

Silence. When the voice came again, it had an edge. A sharp edge.

"Money? That is totally insignificant. I can obtain unlimited wealth and care nothing for your trivial expenditure of a few million. You have wallowed in the power and wealth I have bestowed on you but have been unsuccessful in your primary task, the location of the orb. You have failed. That is my judgement."

No one responded. The eight people began to shift uneasily in their chairs.

Something moved in a corner, like a hologram that was flicking on and off rapidly. On again, this time in a different place. Suddenly, the room was alive with the movement. Then it was as if the switch had been left on. Screams filled the chamber as the first flesh was sliced. No one would hear, the soundproofing was very effective. It took some time before the screaming stopped.

One hour later, builders arrived at the house to fulfil their lucrative emergency contract. The upper building was destroyed and bulldozed flat with liquid concrete forced down the shaft until it filled the chamber below. Within fourteen days, an attractive new home covered the site.

The Joiner had limited patience.

4

The house wasn't hard to find. A large white villa set back from the road. Two men were grooming the tidy front garden.

"Tourists, I think," Eliza said as she drove through the entrance. The gardeners immediately walked across to block the driveway, holding their palms up. She stopped and was quickly out of the car.

"Isn't it beautiful, George," she called, ignoring the approaching duo.

John joined her and they gazed wide-eyed at the white building. The two men reached them, waving their hands and shaking their heads.

"Hello. We've just come to admire this lovely house," Eliza said cheerily.

The men pointed back to the entrance.

"Oh, I'm sure the owners won't mind if we have a little peek. Go and ask them, please."

She repeated the question in Portuguese but John could already see a woman walking quickly from the house.

"What do you want?" she asked icily. Expensive clothes, dark, pinned back hair and a less than friendly expression.

Eliza beamed at her.

"We saw your beautiful house from the road and I fell in love with it. Just had to have a closer look. That's all right isn't it?"

"You can look from here and then leave."

"Okay. Thank you," Eliza responded.

John saw her edge sideways, eyes fixed on the building. Then she nudged into him and he tripped over her foot.

"Oh, my dear, I'm so sorry," Eliza squealed, kneeling beside him. She pressed one hand down on his stomach while the other felt his leg.

"That feels bad. He suffers from Spindleatemis. Very fragile bones and muscles," she called to the onlookers with her face lined with concern.

"You must drive him to a doctor. Please leave now. My men will take him to the car."

The two gardeners were already carrying John and Eliza followed as they stuffed him, not too carefully, into the passenger seat.

"That didn't work," she remarked as she drove off.

"You could have broken my leg."

"You said you allow your staff freedom of expression."

"Right. Well, it wasn't productive so maybe we should head back to the helicopter."

"There was something wrong at that house."

"I didn't see it. They just didn't want visitors. For all we know it could be the home of some crime lord who is keeping nosy people out."

"The woman was English, pretending to be a local speaking English."

"I think I follow. But so what?"

"And her shoes. Did you notice?"

"Not really."

"Men never see shoes. They're a designer brand and only one shop in London sells them."

She pulled the car over and produced her mobile phone.

"What now?" John asked.

"I know the owner of the shop."

He saw her change mode and commence a girl conversation. Heard her ask about the woman. When she had finished, Eliza sat with a satisfied expression.

"Found something?"

"Yes."

"Want to share it with the boss?"

"I'm trying to think of a subtle way to make you think it was your idea."

"To do what?"

"To break into the house."

"We're not doing that."

"Okay. I'll do as you instruct then."

A silence. John knew he had to draw the line. There could only be one person in charge of his agency. What did Cadaver Wincepole say in similar circumstances? He turned to face her.

"Look, Eliza. One of us chaps has to be on top or we'd all be going in different directions. A table needs a leg and you're my leg. Apart, we're nothing but together we stand."

He hadn't expected her to burst out laughing.

"You want to sit on my leg?"

"Yes, in a metaphorical way."

"You didn't ask why."

"Okay, why?"

"Because she's the wife of Lord Ian Feltspen."

"What?"

Lord Feltspen was one of the richest property owners in England with large chunks of many major cities in his possession. His face rarely appeared in the press but his influence was immense.

"Why would his wife be staying in a little house in Brazil?" asked Eliza.

"Nothing comes to mind."

"So we need to find out."

"We're supposed to be investigating my parent's death."

"Maybe it's connected."

"There's absolutely no link between a rich lord and two academics. My parents didn't know anyone like that, only other professors and scientists."

"So you're not coming."

"The implication is that you're going anyway, whether I come or not."

"Yes."

"I'll come. Just this once. But this is the last time. After this you will do as I say."

She looked at him wide-eyed.

"Okay boss."

One a.m. The house lights were all off and they had taken a circuitous route to avoid security lights in the garden. Now they were at the side of the building.

"Could be alarmed. Let's try the back," Eliza whispered.

They circled round the rear. The doors and windows were locked and Eliza moved to a hinged cover in the ground.

"Basement," she whispered and carefully pulled it open.

An angled shaft with a wooden door at the bottom. Eliza slid down and opened it. Then she disappeared. John eased into the hole and closed the metal cover gently as he slid down. Total darkness, then a glow of light. He saw that Eliza was holding a small torch.

"Be careful not to bump into anything," he said quietly.

They cautiously made their way to a flight of stone steps and climbed up. A door at the top with a bright glow appearing around its edges. It had to be an enclosed room as the light wasn't visible outside. Eliza was already crouching by the keyhole. She pulled John down to look.

It appeared to be an office. He could see two empty desks but the rest of the room wasn't visible. No sign or sound of movement. Eliza tried the door. A slight grating noise but it opened and he followed her into the room. Four desks with a few papers neatly stacked on them. John looked at the nearest pile. Most were letters and folders concerning property deals in Brazil. He opened the desk drawer. Only one item inside. A cream laid envelope with a curious symbol on the top left. It was like three vertical zeros on top of an inverted V. Inside the envelope was a photograph. A photograph of a stone wall almost covered with vegetation. John's heart pinged. This was the picture. He stuck it in his pocket and hissed to Eliza.

"I got it. Let's get out."

She hesitated then he heard the sound. Someone talking inside the house and getting louder. They rushed back into the cellar and levered through the exit, John pushing Eliza up the sloping hole to the outer cover. She climbed out and reached down to pull him up.

"Exciting," she said, eyes gleaming in the half-light.

John didn't want to admit it but it was. The most excitement in his life. They edged round the side of the house and almost collided with a man. One of the gardeners stood there, almost as surprised as they were. Then he yelled and reached forward to grab John.

"Hit him," he heard Eliza shout but his flailing arms had no effect. Suddenly there was a dull thud and he was free. He saw Eliza drop the brick and sprinted after her as she ran through the shadowy area surrounding the house. Shouting and lights but he didn't look back. When he reached the car, she was already starting the engine.

"Helicopter. Need to get away," he gasped breathlessly.

"I obey, master."

She set off at speed. John found himself still breathing heavily. He had thought himself fit but a mixture of tension, adrenalin and exertion had drained him. He made a mental note to convert one of the rooms in his villa into a gymnasium.

"Try to get the pilot on the phone," Eliza shouted over the engine noise. She called out the number as John dialled.

"Bad news. No reply," he said, after three tries.

"Worse news behind."

He levered round in his seat. Two pairs of headlights.

"Maybe just ordinary traffic."

"Not at this speed."

He remembered what Wincepole had done.

"Let's try turning into a side road and switching off the lights. Wait for them to pass and go back the other way."

He remembered Pongo Whittler being impressed with the success of this plan.

"There are no side turnings."

"Right. Don't worry, I'll think of something. Do you know the route back?"

"I studied the maps. Can't go wrong, there's only one road."

They were approaching the town where they had met Molhado.

"We can hide somewhere here," John suggested.

"Yes boss. Move as soon as I stop."

She screeched round a corner and stopped behind a large lorry. John was out instantly and running for a narrow alley between two houses but Eliza passed him before he reached it. He affirmed the definite need for that gymnasium. As they raced down the alley he heard cars pulling up in the street and voices shouting. They were closer than he thought.

The alley led to a back street and they were facing stacks of empty beer crates.

"Quick," he shouted and she followed him behind a pile of crates against the wall. They crouched down, waiting. Just 30 seconds before four men burst out of the alley. One of the gardeners and three others who looked even bigger and meaner. They all held guns.

A short conversation and they split up, two going right down the street, one to the left and the other moved towards the crates. He was one of the three new ones. Tall and lean, with eyes flashing white in the shadows. He began to search among the crates, slowly getting closer.

Eliza squeezed her lips against John's ear.

"Get ready to run," she whispered.

At that moment, a door opened, blasting a pool of light on the scene. A thickset man emerged in vest and pants and commenced a loud argument with the stranger. It didn't last long. The butt of the gun struck the head of the man in underwear and he was down. But other lights were clicking on now and new figures began to appear on the street.

"That's our man," Eliza whispered.

John recalled the driver who had bought them to the helicopter. He was in a group coming towards the gunman who hid his weapon and ran off down the street.

Eliza ran out towards the chubby man and began to talk excitedly. John could see him nodding and then she beckoned him to join her.

"He'll take us back. I told him the gunman was trying to rape me. These are good people and they don't like that at all."

Soon after, they were standing next to the helicopter watching the man drive away.

"We haven't got a pilot," John remarked.

Eliza pointed to the cabin. Lace underwear was draped over one of the seats. She marched up to the craft and banged a fist on the cabin door. A cry inside and after a short delay, it was opened by Stu Kimber.

"What the hell?" he muttered, rubbing his eyes.

"You have no clothes on," remarked Eliza.

"What? Oh yeah."

He reached for a pair of pants and pulled them on. Behind him, a girl with long black hair was dressing rapidly.

"We need to go now," Eliza said firmly.

"Sure, okay. Just give me a second."

He hugged the girl who then grabbed her possessions and ran from the helicopter, hiding her face with her hand.

They climbed on board.

"I'll just finish dressing," the pilot mumbled.

"Now," Eliza demanded.

"Okay. You got the police after you?"

"No, gangsters. Shoot to kill."

He moved faster and they were soon in the air.

"Where to, guys?"

"Go at least 50 miles and then stop somewhere we can get a bed," John said and joined Eliza in the cabin.

He looked at her flushed face. It gleamed with excitement and her eyes were bright as diamonds under neon.

"I need a bed. This has got me really excited."

"It certainly makes the adrenalin flow."

"No, I mean excited."

"Yes, right. It was like a movie," John agreed.

"Are you on bromide?"

"That's a strange question. Isn't that what they use in the forces to keep the men passive?"

"Correct. Do the words 'I feel moist' mean anything to you?"

"Oh, I see. Yes, I'm afraid I'm a little sweaty. Sorry. I'll have a shower when we get to a hotel."

She was silent for a second.

"Let's change the subject. You don't seem comfortable in a fight."

"I did a little boxing at college. Are you a martial arts expert?"

"No. I just learned to defend myself with anything handy. Like a brick."

"I think I should convert a room at the villa to a workout place."

"Good idea. I like exercise in the morning."

5

After breakfast, the next morning, they sat in a private corner of the hotel lounge. The plan was to visit the place where the bodies of John's parents had been found. Shouldn't take too long by helicopter.

John was studying the photograph for the 50th time. The previous night, he had obtained several enlarged photocopies and mailed one of them back to his villa in England. That was a trick Wincepole had used, except he had to get his picture re-photographed. No colour copiers then. Even enlarged, the image was disappointing. It looked like an overgrown garden wall with vegetation masking two thirds of it. Not the clearest picture in the world, taken with a low resolution camera and the enlargement only increased the fuzziness. There was no indication of a location, it could have been anywhere in the Amazon Basin. The only thing of interest was the same symbol as on the envelope, a column of three circles on top of the inverted V, cut into an exposed area of pale stone wall. Comparison with the foliage indicated that the design was nearly human size.

"Any ideas, boss?" asked Eliza.

"Nothing at all. We don't even know the age of the building. Might have been constructed last year with the way things grow round here."

"The Amazon isn't a place with any great ancient history, not like the Maya or Inca. I'm surprised your parents showed any interest in a relatively modern structure."

"That's a good point. They didn't bother with anything less than 1500 years old. Maybe the building is from that time and that's why they were so intrigued," John responded.

"As far as I know, the oldest places around here date back only a few hundred years. There must be something in the picture."

"It's just a wall and plants."

"And the symbol. I recognise it."

"You do?"

"It's an ancient Egyptian hieroglyph representing rope. Phonetically, it's an H."

"Still means nothing to me," John remarked.

"As it was also on the envelope, could be the logo of a business or organisation."

"If that was Lady Feltspen at the house, it might represent some company of her or her husband."

"That's my instinct. I also believe that we're in danger now. We've burgled a house and assaulted a man. So we could have police after us as well as the hard looking bunch at the house. Don't forget Lord Feltspen is very rich. Lots of influence and he can employ as many as he wants."

"You think we were recognised?" asked John.

"They're bound to associate the burglars with the two tourists. Sooner or later, they'll put names to our faces."

A little shudder of nervousness ran through him. He hadn't allowed for being chased by people. Pulling out his mobile phone he dialled the villa in Cornwall. If the Wormgraspers saw anyone strange hanging around, he wanted to know. It rang six times before anyone answered.

"Hello, is that Sue?" he asked.

"Mr. Smith?"

This wasn't Sue Wormgrasper.

"Yes. Who are you?"

"You have been a bad boy. You have stolen something and we want it back."

"What do you mean?"

"I'm not going to repeat myself, so listen. Bring the stolen item to Comcalcinta. We will contact you there."

"I'll go as soon as I can."

He couldn't think of anything else to say.

"We will be waiting."

The line went dead.

"What's the problem?" asked Eliza, seeing the stony look on his face.

"They are at my villa."

He repeated the conversation verbatim.

"What about Sue and Percy?" asked Eliza.

"I didn't ask. Didn't want to put ideas into their heads."

"That was smart. If you'd shown concern about their welfare, they'd have used them. Of course, they may already be dead."

He paused.

"I don't want to think about that. Maybe this whole detective thing is a bad idea. I could just live very comfortably without doing anything."

"So could I but it would be a waste of our lives. You may as well take a pill and die now. I've travelled around the world for years. Nightclubs aren't exciting now, just a lot of boring posers using drugs and alcohol to forget how tedious it all is. People need a reason to live and this is fun. Every day is different and I enjoy working with you, John."

She gave an irresistible elfin smile.

"Sorry, just the inner coward coming out."

"Put him back in your trousers and be positive. They said they will meet us at Comcalcinta. That's where the bodies of your parents were found."

"Yes. Maybe they somehow knew it was our next destination."

A brief silence and then they spoke in unison.

"The pilot."

"He must have told them. No one else would know," John added.

"But now we have the big decision. Do we go or not?"

"Well, yes of course. We hand over the picture and then leave. We can start taking some less risky investigations when it's all cooled down. Unfortunately, we've got involved in something that doesn't concern my parent's death. I'm sure now that they died just as reported."

Eliza shook her head.

"John, think. You're trying to convince yourself by those arguments. Firstly, why should they let us go when we give them the photo? They could never be sure we haven't made copies. I'm absolutely certain we'll either be captured or killed."

He knew she was right again but hadn't wanted to think about the possibility. Eliza continued.

"Secondly, it's a near certainty your parents got caught up in this. I believe they were killed because they discovered something about this mystery we've got ourselves into."

"Eliza, I agree with everything you said. To be honest, I'm frightened. I just hadn't visualised getting into this sort of situation."

"If it helps, I'm scared too. But we've only got two choices. One is to work out a way to get this job sorted without being killed."

"That's the dangerous one. What's the other?" asked John.

"Collapse in a blubbery heap."

"Then I'm ready for the work out but I don't have any ideas."

"Nor me. The best thing is to look at possible actions and see where they lead. Let's say we go to the helicopter and fly to Comcalcinta."

"And the pilot is one of them."

"Yes. We pretend to go with their instructions. The picture is our only advantage. They don't know if we made copies so they'll want to find that out before killing us."

"Comforting. So we could be tortured before death," John observed unhappily.

"I'm thinking we could give them the photo and then trade the location of the copies for our lives."

"Short term. When they have them all, they'll still kill us."

"So we need to have a clever strategy," Eliza observed.

"Sounds good. What is it?"

"I don't know yet. The only other thing I can think of is to offer to join them."

John thought for a second.

"Why don't we publish the photo on the Internet? If everyone can see it, there would be no point in killing us to keep it secret," he proposed.

"A possibility."

She paused and John followed her eyes. A man was wandering over to them, looking anything but threatening. Below average height, soft, forgettable features and brownish hair. Perhaps 25 or 30. The sort that wouldn't be noticed in a crowd of more than two.

"Excuse me, I think I dropped my pen when I sat here earlier," he said in a nondescript voice.

John edged away as the newcomer crouched by the side of his chair. Then he found a ball of paper in his palm.

"Found it. Sorry to disturb you," the man said, waving a silver fountain pen. He disappeared from sight.

Cadaver Wincepole regularly had balls of paper pressed into his hand and John knew exactly what to do.

"I'll just make a list of the things we need to buy," he said, reaching into his inside pocket for a notebook. When he held it in front of him, the paper was unfolded and flattened against the pages.

'You're being watched. I am a friend. Ford Rampon. Destroy this paper.'

John wrote the words, 'this came from man with pen' in the notebook and handed it to Eliza.

"Can you just check through the list," he asked.

She read without changing expression and wrote quickly.

"I must visit the ladies before we leave," she announced, handing the book back to John as she passed. The paper had gone and she had written 'let's go with plan A'.

An hour later, they were approaching the helicopter. John had checked for anyone tailing them but no obvious sign. Perhaps the man with the pen had mistaken them for someone else. They hadn't seen him since the episode at the hotel and it all seemed ridiculous now.

Stu Kimber was lounging in front of the craft

"Hi folks. Got your call and ready to go," he announced warmly.

"How long will it take," asked John.

"Say an hour or 90 minutes max."

He didn't seem like an enemy but they had already decided to behave as if they knew nothing. Eliza and John exchanged long stories of their college days to fill the time and carefully avoided any discussion of the investigation. It was 69 minutes later when they set down on a rare clear area near the river.

Comcalcinta was a small community, mostly comprising wooden huts but with a few stone buildings. They left Stu with the helicopter and walked towards the settlement.

"Where do we go?" asked John.

"I don't think it matters. They're going to contact us soon," Eliza replied

A thin old man wearing a smart white shirt and dark trousers, sidled up to them.

"You have been wise to come. The article is in your possession?"

"We can tell you where it is," Eliza said quickly.

The man smiled with jagged yellow teeth.

"Sure, I understand. You say that so we don't kill you and take it. Now you come with me."

He led them away from the buildings and along a narrow pathway. A multitude of cuts on the vegetation indicated that the mass of branches, tendrils and leaves was kept clear only by regular pruning. This had created a sort of hazily lit tunnel that continued for over fifty metres. Then John saw bright light ahead and they emerged, blinking in the sunlight. The sight was unexpected and astonishing. A large clearing, surrounded by impenetrable forest and in the centre, a modern stone building. Two stories, white painted and equal to anything in a classy holiday resort. A recently constructed villa right in the midst of the jungle. Along the side wall were three huge generators emitting a constant hum.

"You come," called the old man and led them up to the entrance. John immediately saw the symbol above the door, the same as on the envelope and wall.

A dark suited girl opened the door and they walked in to a blast of cool, dry air. She led them to the rear of the building and they entered a huge, glass covered, air-conditioned chamber. A swimming pool on one side and four people on the other. Dominating the group was a woman in a short blue dress, seated on a velvet padded chair. The other three, a red haired girl and two men, stood attentively at her side, as if waiting for an instruction. The men moved to the new arrivals, running hand scanners over them. Then they nodded and stepped back.

"Come forward," the seated woman called.

The voice of someone used to commanding others. She had straight black hair hanging to her shoulders, dark eyes and narrow lips. Maybe mid-40s and not unattractive. Eliza advanced, wearing a bright smile.

"Hello, I'm Eliza."

The woman gazed at her for a moment.

"Yes. I sense you have a talent, girl."

"Talent? For pole dancing maybe?"

"Do not be flippant in my presence. I am saying that you have certain undeveloped paranormal powers."

"Well, thank you. And my boss?"

The woman's dark eyes moved to John and gave him what seemed like a full frontal medical. Then she gave a slight smile.

"The innocent purity of a knight. A panther in a rabbit suit. Perhaps one day you will burst out of it. You badly need a woman to help with that. You'd like to assist him, wouldn't you Romnia?"

The sultry, red haired girl smiled enticingly and John shuffled his feet.

"Look, I don't know your name and I don't know what's happening here but I've got the thing you want. All we want to do is hand it over and leave."

"My name is Mariom Wander. You will call me Ms Wander. First, you will give me the item you have stolen and then we will have an amicable discussion."

"If I simply hand it over, you could just imprison or kill us."

"That is true. I could also easily kill you if you continue to prevaricate but we will start by cutting off the girl's fingers."

She nodded and the two men moved to Eliza. One gripped her arm while the other pulled out a long knife. Eliza didn't appear too concerned.

"Start with the left. I'm right-handed and have no plans to marry."

"It's your decision, Mr Smith," Wander said.

He pulled an envelope from his pocket.

"Here it is."

Romnia moved to him and took it, her fingers caressing his hand as she did. Then she paused, running her tongue over full red lips.

"Thank you John," she murmured breathily.

She checked the photo inside, nodded and returned to stand next to Wander.

"Now that's done, we want to go," he said firmly.

"I'm sure that's what you want. However, I will not permit it. I must first be certain if you have made copies or told others."

"There's no one else to tell and I did have two copies made. They're in the envelope. I expected you'd want them. The picture is useless anyway. Just a bit of wall that could be anywhere."

"I am inclined to believe you and I therefore can't think of a good reason not to kill you now."

Eliza stepped forward.

"We have information that would be useful to you. Our proposal is that we work with you although we don't know who you are or what organisation you represent."

Wander laughed.

"People work for me not with me. All I will tell you of myself is that I represent powers and influence beyond your imagination. Nothing, absolutely nothing is beyond us."

"Okay. So how could we work for you?"

"You are not required. I do not believe you have any information useful to us. However, I can see you are clearly completely out of your depth and I feel in a generous mood."

"Then we can leave?" asked John.

"Of course not. You will be killed but not tortured. That is considerably more than you deserve for the trouble you have caused."

The two men produced guns, jostling John and Eliza out of the chamber. They were dragged down a flight of stairs into a vast basement where two other gunmen were waiting. John found himself pushed against the wall with Eliza beside him and saw the four lined up in front of them, aiming their guns.

"At least I'll die pretty," Eliza murmured as the guns were raised. John squeezed his eyes closed.

Four thudding noises from a silenced pistol that came rapidly, like automatic fire.

"Thank me later," a voice said.

John unfastened his eyelids. The insignificant man from the hotel, dressed completely in black and holding a pistol. Eliza was already hugging him.

"I said thank me later. In your case, I'll take gratitude when we're alone one night."

"It would be a pleasure for both of us," she responded.

"Follow me quickly."

He sprinted up the stairway and through a side door at the top. Within seconds they were outside the villa. Just a minute later he was leading them along a narrow track that led to a rough road where a Skinntu four-wheel drive was waiting. They jumped inside and he was away, driving smoothly over the bumpy earth road.

"You were lucky I had been watching that place and was already inside the building. You need more answers but wait until we get to my place," Ford said tersely.

An hour later he pulled in beside a compact modern house on the fringes of a small town. The journey had passed with zero conversation.

"Right. Come in and relax."

He led them into the air-conditioned house. A girl was waiting in the lounge.

"Meet my partner, Locey Sherron," Ford announced.

John met her body first. A full and perfect figure dressed in just shorts and T-shirt. A figure that would attract a group of men anywhere in the world. But the bit above wouldn't. A narrow, schoolgirls face with a flop of brownish hair that looked as if she had cut it herself, wearing a blindfold.

"Hello people," she said in a little girl voice.

After completing the introductions, she showed them to their separate bedrooms upstairs and it was 20 minutes before they returned, washed and refreshed. Eliza made her own tea while John poured a coffee and joined the others at the table. Ford settled back in his chair.

"Now I'll tell you what you're up against. You have come into contact with a most dangerous and powerful organisation. The Trysse. It's spelt T R Y S S E but pronounced 'trice'."

"All the comic books have world domination groups," remarked Eliza with a smile.

"It's not funny. They are horrid people," Locey interjected.

"What does the name mean?"

Ford shrugged.

"We don't know exactly. Let me tell you the whole story. For me, it began ten months ago. I was out with Zelda one morning, just walking along the street, when a big limousine suddenly stopped in front of me. Two men got out and told me that the person in the car had taken a liking to Zelda. I told them to get lost. Next thing, one man smashed me in the jaw and I was out. When I came to, the car and Zelda had gone."

"She was your partner?" asked John.

"No, my dog. Golden Labrador. Loved her to bits. We slept together every night. So I dedicated my life to getting her back and taking revenge on her kidnappers."

Eliza looked puzzled.

"You gave up your job for a dog? What did you do for money?"

"I was with an American government anti-fraud squad and was working undercover for two years in the stock markets. I didn't discover any criminal activity but I was rather good at the job. Made £3 million in bonuses alone."

"Okay. So what did you find out?"

"I won't go through the whole story. As a matter of routine, I'd memorised the car's number plate. From there it was simple detective work. The clues led me deeper and deeper into the web. I collected data from all over the world, press reports, countless nights of surveillance, various documents I bought or stole and that sort of thing. The structure of the organisation began to clarify but I've still not got the whole picture."

"So they are pretty big?"

"They have influence in every country in the world. Involvement in legal and illegal companies everywhere. Whenever you see big profits, you can be sure they are there. Sometimes as owners or major shareholders but never in the front line, never in the headlines. The same with the illegal stuff. They just finance and rake off a big slice of the takings. No risks."

"Wealthy, then," John remarked.

"You couldn't count it. Over time, I have identified one or two senior individuals in the Trysse and they have to be some of the richest people on the planet. You've met one, Mariom Wander."

"So do they have a purpose? Apart from making money."

"I'm not exactly sure about that. Over the last few months, they've become supporters of selected politicians and a few of them are already in power in one or two countries. With their unlimited wealth, they can do anything."

"Taking over the world, just like in the movies?"

"Films can become reality. There's something else that is also out of a script. From my research, I've become convinced that the Trysse is directed by one person. Someone unidentified in the background."

"So what is the history of this organisation?"

"That's something I can't work out. Maybe you know their symbol, three zeros on legs. All I know is that it's the Egyptian hieroglyph for rope. This Trysse organisation seems to have started in the mid 1800s but only mushroomed within the last year."

"The symbol is etched on an old wall here in Brazil," Eliza offered.

"That doesn't surprise me. I suppose it's possible that they are a sort of ancient secret society that had been dormant until just recently."

"And Locey has been with you all this time?"

The girl gave a start, like a frightened mongoose.

"Oh no, I only met Ford three months ago. He's a wonderful man. Rescued me from a living hell."

"Really?" Eliza didn't sound too sympathetic.

"Yes, I was employed as a personal maid servant to one of the big movie stars at his massive house in Florida. I was so pleased to get the job and everything was fine until the first night I was there. Then he wanted me to do something."

"I understand."

"No, I must tell you. He told me to dance for him, wearing nothing except long black leather boots with fur on the tops."

"I see. Not even a thong or bra?"

"Oh, that didn't matter. But animal fur on both boots? It was disgusting. So, of course I ran away. They chased me but Ford was watching the house at the time and he rescued me like a lovely knight in armour. He's so brave as well as clever."

"Yes, right," Eliza murmured, unimpressed.

"So the two of you are fighting this group alone?" John asked.

Ford nodded then shook his head.

"Yes and no. On two occasions, I've tried to stop certain of their financial deals going through but found that someone had beaten me to it. Then another time, I'd broken into one of their offices in Geneva. As I clambered in through a window, I saw a figure climbing out of one on the floor above. It was night and I couldn't make out any details. The person was wearing a dark bodysuit and mask and they'd gone in a few seconds."

"So there could be five of us," John observed.

"It's possible."

"Now you'd like us to decide whether to join up with you?" queried Eliza.

"Exactly. As you can see, I know a lot about the opposition and I can assure you they won't give up chasing you. You need to tell me your story first, of course."

"I'll tell you," Eliza said quickly before John could respond.

She recounted most of the events but didn't mention their personal backgrounds, only indicating that John had financial backing for his agency. She also omitted any reference to nymphomania. Ford nodded when she had finished.

"So shall we pool our resources?" he proposed.

"I've decided we will. First we'll show you the photograph. We handed over the original but made a few copies," John announced, anxious to reassert himself.

Eliza reached inside her shirt and pulled a folded paper from her bra. Ford looked disapproving.

"If you don't mind my saying, that's the first place they look. When I trained as an agent, we always checked women's underwear first. Try hiding it in your shoe or even a pocket. Apart from anything else, it avoids embarrassment from sniffer dogs."

"I'll remember," Eliza responded and handed over the still warm paper.

Ford examined it carefully.

"That's definitely the symbol. Do you know where it is?" he asked.

"It could be in the African jungle with little gorillas living next to it. Or maybe chimpanzees. They're cute," Locey observed helpfully.

"It's definitely somewhere near the Amazon," said John.

Ford smiled.

"Shouldn't be hard to find. Not hard but risky. I know exactly the area this place is located."

"Really?"

"There has been a lot of activity with a good number of the opposition travelling upriver. I recorded conversations between a few of their people before they left. They mentioned where they were going."

"What? Why didn't you say earlier?"

"Trust. I needed to be sure I could trust you. The opposition have people everywhere and they've been after me for a long time. You could have been a plant."

"A pretty rosebush?" Eliza asked.

"Or a poison ivy. I've decided that you are the real thing."

John changed the subject.

"So now we need a plan to get to this place."

"We could get a huge herd of lions and tigers then send them in to attack," offered Locey.

Ford nodded. "Good thinking but it might not be practical."

"We have a chartered helicopter but the pilot is working for them," Eliza said thoughtfully.

"I think it would be too long and dangerous to travel by the river so the air is the best way. If we take this pilot out, I could fly it," Ford remarked.

"Where exactly is this place?" John asked.

Locey went to a drawer and returned with a map that she spread across the table. Ford pointed a finger.

"Just near a little town called Bunocoto. I don't think the wall is close to the main river. More likely it's somewhere off a side stream."

"There could be leopards there with little furry cubs. I'd love to run with them through the jungle," Locey announced.

Ford looked at her.

"I doubt if we'll find lions or tigers there but anything is possible. So here's the plan. Tomorrow we sort out this pilot, take the helicopter and go to the ruins. Then maybe a lot of questions will be answered."

John nodded.

"We're ready," he said but was churning inside.

Locey was still stuck on the big cat theme.

"We need to get to bed early then. I'm thinking about tigers now, Ford. You know what that does to me."

"Yes. Busy day tomorrow," he said quickly and they disappeared upstairs in a big hurry.

"Maybe this hyper sexuality is more common than I thought. You want to sleep with me, John?" Eliza enquired.

"Well, in one way, yes."

"How many ways are there?"

"It's just that my mind is full at the moment and I'm too tensed up."

"So tigers don't do it for you?"

"Don't get me wrong. You're a very attractive woman but well, you know."

"I'll probably never offer again."

John was relieved but said the right thing.

"Don't say that. It's just my current feeling. I really do find you very enticing."

"Then I'll leave you feeling your currents and see you tomorrow."

She went upstairs alone.

6

Next morning the four of them were hiding in undergrowth, observing the helicopter. Two girls had just left the craft, leaving a dishevelled Stu Kimber who looked as if he had missed out on a nights rest.

"I'll take him," Ford muttered and disappeared into the jungle

"Ford is so courageous," breathed Locey with admiration.

A minute later, they saw him approaching from the far side. The pilot was sitting on the cabin floor, dangling his legs outside and eating something from a packet. Ford rapped a fist on the other side of the craft and Stu jumped down to investigate, only to find his legs grabbed from behind. Two blows later, he lay unconscious.

Ford piloted with Eliza as navigator, leaving John facing Locey in the cabin. She moved her legs forward so that their knees touched.

"You must be a brave man to take on these people. Do you like lions?"

"Well, yes they're lovely animals."

She beamed and placed a palm on his thigh.

"I knew it. Let me show you something."

She unbuttoned her shirt to reveal a crude, circular pendant on a chord. It had a lion's head on it.

"What do you think of that?"

She pulled the shirt wide and leant forward, exposing a substantial everything. John squirmed.

"Very nice indeed. A beautiful lion."

"You can touch it if you like."

"I'd love to but I think I should study the photograph again."

"Oh yes. I'll show you again later when we have more time."

John quickly pulled out the photograph while she buttoned up.

They landed in a small clearing to the north of Bunocoto and the other three looked to Ford who had now become their unofficial leader.

"Okay folks, let's get kitted out," he said, opening two large holdalls.

Weapons. They each put on belts fitted with silenced guns, ammunition clips and machetes. And a few electronic devices. John had never worn a gun before but pretended otherwise.

"Now which way?" Eliza asked.

"It shouldn't be difficult. We head for the river and watch for activity. With the number of people sent here by the enemy, we should be able to pick up their trail easily."

He was right. After travelling only about 50 metres, they came to a freshly cleared, wide track with wheel marks and took a parallel route through the jungle. Progress was slow but after eleven minutes, they heard the sound of a vehicle approaching from behind them. Taking cover, they watched as a jeep drove past rapidly. John recognised the passenger. Lady Feltspen. He whispered the news to his companions.

"I've heard of her husband but she's new to me as one of the enemy," Ford remarked.

They continued for another 14 minutes, hacking a pathway through the clinging tendrils and branches until the sound of machinery indicated that their objective was close. Suddenly they were at the edge of a clearing that bustled with activity. A bulldozer, shovelling a huge pile of vegetation from the site and maybe 25 people with a variety of tools, working feverishly to finish clearing the area.

There it was. The same wall as in the photograph but now part of an almost completely exposed building. A simple, rectangular single storey construction, about 50 metres long and 20 wide, made with large blocks of stone. The Trysse symbol was very clear now but otherwise there were no external markings. Simple stone blocks with a narrow entrance, just large enough to admit one person. No sign of Lady Feltspen. She must be inside.

"Are you certain there are no tigers?" Locey whispered disappointedly.

"What now, Ford?" asked John, ignoring the question.

"It'll be a problem to get in. There are too many to do anything openly. Maybe we should wait until night. Then we're going to need an ID badge. You noticed they're all wearing one."

John hadn't and looked again. Every individual has a laminated card hanging from a cord around their neck. He settled back to wait with the others.

As darkness began to fall, most of the workers left the site in the flotilla of vehicles parked on one side of the clearing. They were obviously travelling back to Bunocoto for the night. Five remained, three near the building while the other two began to patrol the perimeter of the area. John could now see a glow coming from the entrance. They must have installed lighting inside. Lady Feltspen hadn't emerged.

"Can we take all five?" Eliza whispered.

Ford shook his head.

"I can't see how. The three by the building are too far away."

"I know the way to get in. It's easy," Locey offered unexpectedly.

A few minutes later, the patrolling guard heard a noise he couldn't believe. The growl of a lion. He pushed a few steps into the jungle and found something else he couldn't believe. A voluptuous woman, dressed only in skimpy blue pants. She smiled and moved sinuously towards him. Then he had a power cut.

Four minutes later the guard reappeared in the clearing, pushing the near naked Locey in front of him with his pistol.

"Who's that?" called one of the other men and all four quickly approached.

"I got lost in the jungle," Locey exclaimed.

Unsurprisingly, her body grabbed their total attention and they failed to notice that the other guard was a new man. Until he spoke.

"Please drop your guns on the ground and do not speak," Ford said quietly, waving his pistol.

One of the men reached for his weapon but he had barely moved when Locey's fist hit him on the side of his head, just next to the temple. Within a couple of minutes, all four guards had joined their companion, bound and gagged with strips of their own clothing.

They now had five ID cards and Ford stuffed the spare one in his pocket while Locey dressed. Eliza looked at her with admiration.

"That was impressive," she said truthfully and received a delighted smile in response.

"That's really nice of you. I'm quite proud of my chest and it's great to get a compliment, especially from another girl."

"Okay, right. You're quite a fighter too."

"Oh, that. I just learned some stuff from an old boyfriend. He was a martial arts expert. You'd be amazed at some of the things he could do."

"Right people. Time to see what this is about," Ford said quietly and they followed him to the entrance.

The murmur of conversation from inside. John crouched at the side of the doorway and grabbed a look

He had expected to see Lady Feltspen but had not anticipated she would be chained to the wall. He had also half expected to see Mariom Wander and the red haired Romnia but the big surprise was a radiant, ice blue sphere that hovered hypnotically between them and the chained woman. Below it was a carved wooden box.

"You have disappointed us," Wander said grimly.

The veneer of composure had left the titled woman. She was trembling and sweat poured down her face but her eyes were painfully fixed on the sphere. It was about palm sized but the glow made it seem larger.

"I gave instructions. The guards were careless. They have all been eradicated now," she appealed.

"Let me kill her," Romnia pleaded, her eyes bright with some unknown emotion.

Wander shook her head.

"No. Observe the power of the orb, girl."

The sphere began to move back and forth, its colours changing in rhythmic patterns. Suddenly, it shot forward, hitting Lady Feltspen in the chest. Or not hitting. It seemed to transform into a liquid that covered her body completely in a glowing blue. The woman screamed. Once. Then the coating reformed again into the sphere.

Nothing remained. Lady Feltspen had disappeared. Not one particle of dust remained of her.

Romnia gave a squeal of ecstasy, her cheeks now bright red.

"A lesson, girl. A reminder to obey all my commands without question," said Mariom.

The red haired girl knelt in front of her with head bowed and then ripped her blouse apart, exposing her chest.

"Yes, I'll do anything for you. Anything at all."

Wander displayed a smile of dominance and reached towards her. Suddenly, she stopped.

"We meet again, Mariom," said Ford, leading the others inside the chamber.

Romnia rose to her feet, covering herself while Wander's expression hardened.

"Shall they be converted?" she asked.

Her question was addressed to the sphere. It remained in the same position for a second and then shot towards John. He reached up his hands and the sphere stopped as soon as it touched his skin. It didn't feel metallic but soft and warm, like clouds floating in a bright summer sky. And it was communicating. A message that passed through his skin and filled his body, his mind, his soul.

"Are you all right?"

John saw that the voice emanated from the female named Locey. She had appeal and her body was very acceptable to serve. Beside her, a man. He was known to us. Insignificant in stature but holding a certain power. Yes, we knew him well. Then the third. Another body that could meet our needs. And yet she resisted us. No creature was permitted to do that. She must be subjugated urgently. Nothing could be allowed to betray the true light and infect others with their disruptive influence. These three were not unintelligent but John felt he was now their superior. He knew what he must do but had to proceed with care.

"I'm fine," he said and smiled at Eliza's concerned expression. At that moment, the sphere curved smoothly through the air, back to a position in front of Wander.

"So what do we do now?" Locey asked.

John saw Ford eyeing him for a moment before replying.

"We'll take the orb," he said with certainty.

Wander laughed.

"You cannot do that, little man."

As if in recognition of the threat, the ball flew to the carved wooden box. The lid opened briefly and it disappeared inside, closing with a thud that reverberated around the chamber.

"That's convenient. We'll take it boxed," remarked Ford.

The wooden chest was a cube of only about fifteen centimetres or roughly six inches. Locey walked over and bent to pick it up. It didn't move. A look of puzzlement and she gripped it again with both hands. She could not lift it one millimetre.

"It won't move. Must be fixed somehow to the floor."

Locey tried to raise it again. Then she kicked it and struck it with her gun. The blow had no effect, the weapon rebounding as if it had struck reinforced steel.

"It just won't budge. Shall I shoot it open?" she shouted in annoyance.

Ford shook his head.

"First, that would be too dangerous in this confined area. The bullet could ricochet anywhere. Second, I don't think it would have any effect."

Wander smiled at him.

"I suggest you leave here now if you wish to continue living."

"Let me try," said Eliza.

She walked to the box and picked it up.

The chamber was silent for three seconds.

"How did you do that?" asked Ford, genuinely surprised.

"I just moved it sideways a little. I think it was slotted into something."

Wander was still staring at her with a mixture of disbelief and horror. Then her hand reached inside her jacket. She had barely moved before finding herself in Locey's grasp and her pockets being searched. Locey didn't produce the gun they were expecting but just a sheet of paper covered with printed text.

Ford led them from the chamber. John was the last to depart and Romnia looked meaningfully at him as he left. Not just a look but a promise of reward. The Trysse was generous to its followers.

They piled into one of the parked vehicles and Ford drove carefully but smoothly along the rough track. John was seated in the rear next to Eliza and becoming more aware of her casual attraction. A wanton appeal that should be thoroughly satisfied. He would have her body. Yes, the Joiner approved of that. Then she must adopt the rightful path or die. For now, he would be patient. Wait for the opportunity.

Within twenty minutes, they were in the helicopter. An uneventful return journey back to Ford's house and they arrived, tired but pleased with the success of the venture. All except John. He didn't feel tired and his success depended on carrying out his orders.

Ford sat down with a sigh.

"That was interesting. We have a weird blue sphere and a message that Mariom didn't want us to see."

Eliza cradled the chest in her arms.

"I don't think we should try to open this. Too dangerous," she said emphatically.

"I haven't looked at the paper but I guess it could be important," Locey said, holding up the folded sheet.

"Let me have it to study while you three freshen up," offered John.

Ford looked at him steadily.

"No. We should all look together. My shower can wait."

Taking the paper from Locey, he unfolded it and made copies using the computer scanner. Then he shared the duplicates with the others. The document was headed with the Trysse symbol followed by a page of text.

'You will be rewarded substantially for locating the first orb. I will be with you shortly to collect it in person.

Now I require you find the second. I know only that it is somewhere in central USA. My perception is that it may be more arduous to discover than the first. Some months ago, I designated agents to search for it and one of them recently communicated a message using his satellite phone. The message was recorded on my priority line that is reserved for critical contact and I therefore consider that he may well have located the orb.

Unfortunately, his words were garbled. In my judgement, this was as a result of deliberate electronic interference by others attempting to block the call. Consequently, the message is merely a series of speech fragments. My people attempted to identify the words but presented the following result, which is clearly nonsensical.

'Trees smile best. Mike speaking. Down wick. Building. Biker search. Bearing hairs here ripped.'

The agent was not heard from again and is presumed dead. I know that he was in central USA, probably Colorado and our search is therefore being concentrated in that area. You will take charge of the operation.

The third orb is in England but regrettably my people there have been unable to discover even the slightest indication as to a possible location. The Joiner arranged the permanent termination of this team and a replacement group are continuing the search. Your colleague has now assumed personal control.

Remember that it will be a truly triumphant day when all three orbs are in our possession.

You will leave for Chicago eleven a.m. Friday. I look forward to hearing of your further success in the USA.'

"It's all about balls," Locey summarised succinctly.

"We've got something. This message must be from their Leader," remarked Ford.

John leant forward.

"I don't think it's worth pursuing. This whole thing seems just a waste of time. What do we care if they collect these things? They seem harmless to me and all we're doing is attacking them. Obviously they'll try to defend themselves against us. Let's just get on with our lives and leave them to it."

A short silence.

"So you're not staying with us?" asked Eliza.

"I didn't say that. It's simply that these people seem like a normal enough group looking for their Holy Grail. If we start fighting everyone like that, we'll be taking on the whole world."

John spread his arms as he spoke.

He noticed that the woman, Eliza was observing him intently. Clearly she was an enemy who sought to undermine the coming joy and prosperity. First he must have her body and then her threat must be removed. The orb that she was holding so tightly must be recovered.

"I think we all need to sleep now. We can decide what to do tomorrow," Eliza proposed.

John assented. He didn't need sleep but tonight he could take action.

Two hours later he was approaching the door of Eliza's bedroom. The house was silent and he was satisfied that the others must be sleeping. Opening the door carefully, he entered the room. A faint beam of moonlight gave enough illumination to reveal the figure curled on the bed. She wore only brief pants. That was good. Violence should not be necessary. He expected the woman to welcome him, to want him.

He stripped off his clothes and slid onto the bed beside her. She turned sleepily towards him and he reached to pull her towards him and under his body. Her eyes opened. Strange. A quizzical look, not heavy lidded desire. Then he felt the blow on the side of his head and fell into darkness.

John awoke uncomfortably. He didn't know how long he had been unconscious. It was broad daylight and he was on Eliza's bed, naked and spread-eagled with his legs and arms tied to the four bed posts. The three enemies stood before him.

"You will die for this," he screamed.

"John, what happened?" the Locey woman asked.

"We know that. He touched the sphere," Ford observed.

"You will die for stealing the orb. We must rid ourselves of you creatures," John cried suddenly. Then his head fell back and he appeared to be in a deep sleep.

"Perhaps we should kill him? Might need to bang a wooden stake through his heart," Locey proposed.

"No. There must be a way to bring him back," Eliza responded.

Ford scratched his head.

"We could all see that he was affected. That's why we laid the trap."

"I think he's turning into a werewolf. Is there a cure?" Locey asked.

Ford shrugged.

"Maybe. It could be a weird psychological effect or possibly there's some sort of chemical coating on the sphere. I'm not a medic so it's pure guesswork"

Eliza was lost in thought for a moment. Eventually she spoke with certainty.

"Let's leave him and keep watch. I'll take first shift."

Just over an hour passed before she opened the door.

"He's still asleep. We'll know more when he wakes."

Ford gave her a long look before speaking.

"We should talk about how to get the other spheres," he suggested.

"I've given it some thought," responded Eliza.

Locey interrupted with enthusiasm.

"Me too. I think they could be prehistoric eggs with cute little baby dinosaur things inside. They're just waiting to hatch and then take over the world that they used to rule before humans and ice ages killed them off. Revenge of the raptors, if you know what I mean."

"You could just be right although there are other possibilities," nodded Ford.

Eliza continued.

"Well, these are my thoughts. The note we found is pretty explicit. There are three spheres in total. We don't know their source but the Trysse obviously need all of them and urgently. We now have one and there are two more somewhere in the USA and England. Wander has to leave for Chicago on Friday, just three days from now. That's one starting point for us. The message indicated that possession of all the three spheres will give some immense power, wealth or whatever."

Ford grinned.

"Good summary. The only other point is that the note must have come from the Leader of the Trysse. The way it's worded shows how that person dominates the organisation. My feeling is that our best plan would be to split up and cover both England and the States. First, we need to see how John is."

They walked into the bedroom and right on cue, he began to stir.

"Thanks Pongo," he murmured vaguely.

"I don't think Pongo was equipped to administer the cure," Eliza responded.

"Who the hell is Pongo?" asked Ford.

"Forget it. We just need to be sure he's okay."

Locey bent over the still bound naked body.

"What happened, John?"

"I don't know. We were in the building and a blue ball touched me. The next thing I remember was a wonderful, beautiful dream. Then I woke up."

"He could be pretending," Ford observed, unconvinced.

"John, what would Wincepole do now?" asked Eliza.

He smiled.

"First thing, he'd get some clothes on. I'm not used to being on display like this."

Eliza untied the ropes and John dressed quickly.

Ford raised his eyebrows.

"Maybe it was your tender bedside care, Eliza?"

She shrugged.

"You'll probably never know."

"Whatever. I propose that I look after the orb from now."

Eliza paused and then smiled.

"I think we should let Locey keep it tonight."

Ford returned the smile.

"Okay, I agree. Now we can go for the next one. I'm suggesting I take the USA with Locey and you guys go to England. We've got a time, date and place so you've got the tougher job."

"I'll book the flights," John responded with a new glow in his eyes.

Locey waved a hand.

"Wait. You've forgotten something."

The others looked puzzled.

"What's that?" asked Ford.

"The note said that their boss was coming to Brazil. Maybe already here."

Ford ran a hand through his hair.

"That's right. Maybe we should wait for the Leader."

The doorbell rang. A silence as they looked at each other. It rang again and Ford started downstairs.

"Okay. I open the door and you three keep out of sight, ready to help if needed. It's unlikely to be an attack. These people wouldn't just ring the bell."

They followed him downstairs and took up position each side of the door. He opened it.

A woman in her mid-fifties, smartly dressed. She was smiling but without any humour whatsoever.

"Can I help?" asked Ford.

"I'm just here with a message for all of you and John in particular."

"Go on," said Ford but found John pushing past him to stand open mouthed in front of the woman.

"The message is very simple. Leave the orb here and go back home now. Do not continue your interference. We have been gentle so far but will certainly kill you all if you persist. Make the right choice. That's all."

She turned and walked rapidly back to a car with dark windows. The driver pulled away immediately she was inside.

"Who the hell was that?" Ford asked.

"My mother," replied John, his face ashen.

Early next morning, Ford woke and saw Locey sleeping peacefully beside him. He wanted to check the orb and opened the wardrobe where she had stored it the previous night.

Not there.

"Hey, Locey. It's gone," he shouted.

She woke with a sleepy smile.

"Gone?"

"The sphere. You put it in the wardrobe last night, right?"

She was up quickly, standing beside him.

"It was definitely there. Maybe aliens have teleported it away."

"I'll call Eliza and John."

He did that and John emerged scramble haired from his bedroom.

"The sphere has gone. Where's Eliza?" Ford asked.

"Don't know. She took the other room."

Ford rushed to the door and pulled it open. No Eliza. No sign the bed had been used. He ran downstairs. A note was propped on the kitchen table.

'Taken sphere to hiding place. Safest for us all. John to meet me in England, at Birmingham airport. Extellance restaurant next Friday morning. Love Eliza.'

"She had no right to do that without discussing it first," Ford muttered.

"I think Eliza's brave. She did it to protect us," Locey remarked.

He shrugged and a bitter look crossed his face for a moment.

"Well, it's done now. She can tell me where it is when we meet up again. Still two more to find."

John sat alone in the hotel room. His flight to Birmingham was in eleven hours and he had time to relax. But that was impossible. Ford and Locey had already left for America and he would meet up with Eliza when he arrived in England.

Maybe he shouldn't go. Stay here instead and find his mother. He was still shocked at her sudden appearance. He wasn't sure, couldn't decide anything. Much too nervous and perhaps a little frightened.

A soft knock on the door. Must be room service but he couldn't remember ordering anything. He opened it and was enveloped in a soft embrace. A heavy, wet kiss that lasted long.

"I had to see you again, John," breathed Romnia, her eyes shining with passion.

"You people are trying to kill us," he stammered and tried to push her away. It wasn't a serious attempt and all the urges of his body fought it bravely.

"I'm not really with them. I'm being forced to obey their instructions. If I don't, they'll do horrible things to me."

She looked up at him, moist eyed and stunningly attractive. Her red hair flowed in curves to her shoulders, forming a perfect frame for a sensuous face. Her full red lips were slightly open and competed with the eyes for moistness. She wore a simple, knee length burgundy dress and carried a small bag over her shoulder.

"Look, I'm not sure about this. Can you tell me about my mother?"

"She has joined them. You saw the power of the orb. It can kill but also bend people to its will. Your mother is under its control but if you can get the sphere, I know how we can use it to release her."

Most parts of John were unsure and confused. The exception was his body, which was absolutely certain what it wanted to do.

"I do want my mother back but I just don't know if I can trust you, Romnia," he mumbled.

She tottered into his arms again.

"I'm sorry, I feel a little faint. Let me just lie down for a second."

He helped her to the bed and she rolled onto it. The action made her dress ride up high around her waist as she lay back, eyes half closed. She maintained a firm grip on John's hand.

"John, you're my only hope. I need you."

Romnia embraced him tightly and he was somehow pulled onto the bed next to her. His eyes were drawn irresistibly to the fully exposed legs, tanned and perfectly curved. The gaze tracked upwards to the tiny turquoise briefs, revealed in full by the errant dress. Now the battle between intellect and desire escalated into an all-out war. Lust began to infiltrate his brain, suggesting that satisfying its craving could do no harm. Why not? That was the message. Suddenly the fortress was overrun, the tower stood firm and the ram parts took complete control.

He ran his hand over her thigh and felt soft kisses on his neck as she manoeuvred her body on top. He lay flat as she knelt astride him, then saw her reach around her back to pull off the misbehaving dress. A couple of positions later and her underwear had also gone, together with most of his clothing.

"You'll help me, won't you?" she breathed from her new location underneath.

"Yes. Anything for you, Romnia."

Her fingers never stopped moving, unceasingly finding exactly the right places.

"The sphere is all we need. Please tell me it's here now."

He was in ecstatic agony. She was just doing enough but always holding him back.

"Romnia!" he groaned, his whole body shaking.

"The sphere. Is it here?" she whispered, her touch still restraining.

"No, no. One of them took it to hide somewhere. I don't know who and I don't know where."

He did know who but had found it impossible to say Eliza's name, even on this tortuous route to climax.

At last, she released him and John moaned in sweet fulfilment. Then he fell back on the bed at her side. She kissed his cheek and disappeared into the bathroom, picking up her clothes and bag on the way.

Romnia closed the door and took a phone from the bag. Her call was answered instantly.

"He doesn't have it. One of the others took it to hide. That's all he knows."

A short pause before she whispered again.

"Yes, I'm sure that's the truth. I had him totally under my control."

Another pause.

"And should I kill him now?" she asked.

A few seconds later, she ended the call.

John could barely move. The red haired woman had completely drained him and he had never experienced anything like it before. He vaguely saw her emerge, fully clothed from the bathroom but she appeared less alluring. The softness had left her face and her eyes were now hard, her lips tight and dry.

Romnia didn't speak. She glanced briefly at him, walked to the door and left.

Friday morning. John finished his late breakfast and took a gulp of coffee. His flight to Birmingham had been delayed and Eliza was waiting for him at the restaurant. He wasn't going to tell her about the session with Romnia. Her reaction was very predictable and he didn't believe anything had occurred to help them with the search.

"Ford was a bit upset you took the sphere," he remarked.

"Safest for us all."

"Well, I think it was a good idea but maybe you should have told us first."

"We'd never have agreed."

"So where did you hide it?"

"There wouldn't be any point in concealment if I tell everyone."

"Yes, I suppose so."

His eyes drifted to the window.

"You're thinking about your mother," Eliza observed.

"Sorry, I can't help it."

"It could have been an impostor who was there just to unnerve you."

"No. It was definitely her. I should know. I still think I should have stayed in Brazil."

"Look, it's just possible that one or both of your parents are alive but if that was your mother, she is under the influence of our enemy. The only way to release her is to defeat this organisation and to do that we need to be here in England."

"That sounds logical but I want to see her again."

"I think it's just as likely she'll be back in this country. Ford and Locey are heading for Chicago and our job is to find the sphere."

"Where do we start? Maybe my house in Devon?"

"I agree. That's the best place to begin. The next is Lord Feltspen."

7

Chicago airport operates like the gritty cogs of steel machinery. Mirroring the city itself, it does its job, does it well and doesn't make a big deal about it.

Ford Rampon leant back in a seat in the passenger lounge. Jeans, rough jacket and holdall. No one noticed him in the crowd. The flight from Brazil had just landed and he scanned the small crowd waiting to greet the arrivals at the exit gate. One or more of the enemy would be amongst them. He identified the probables. Two men, suited and unsmiling, headed his list. The others were a single older man, two grandparents with three kids, a couple of girls with backpacks and a middle-aged man and wife. Ford switched off the babble of noise around him and zoomed in on the group analytically. Something unusual but he couldn't quite identify it.

Locey Sherron had acquired a stewardess outfit and moved around busily doing nothing. He saw her circulating through the gathering, smiling sweetly as the passengers began to emerge. Mariom Wander, accompanied by Romnia, walked towards the gate. Then he knew. He grabbed his holdall and veered quickly past the waiting group. As he brushed through, he affixed a tiny tracker to a sleeve. Then he left, rapidly and unobtrusively. Within two minutes Locey had joined him in the car.

"You're clever. The two girls with packs. How could you tell it was them?"

"Instinct, I guess. The least likely to be waiting for Mariom. I put a tracker on one of them and we just have to hope they don't change their clothing. Where are they now?"

Locey had the monitor screen displayed on a laptop. A red dot was moving but still within the airport complex.

"They're not leaving by the main entrance," Ford muttered and began to drive the vehicle on the circuit of the car park.

"I see now. They're going through the emergency gate," shouted Locey.

Ford raced for the exit but a jam of cars blocked their route. He grunted in annoyance as the red light moved off north.

"Must have pulled strings to use that way out. These are powerful people."

Locey smiled benignly.

"All power is within us. We can be as strong as a zebra or fight like an anaconda. Everyone has the battery inside them and it just needs charging up like a rampant rhinoceros," she announced zoologically.

"Yes, right. See if you can guess their destination."

"All I can tell at the moment is that they're heading north."

Ford caught up quickly. Within fifteen minutes they were half a mile behind and keeping that distance. Mariom Wander didn't appear to be hurrying. The route curved off, running through a string of small towns.

"They've stopped in the place ahead. It's called Bleeksville," announced Locey.

Ford parked in the outskirts and they ran a check on the town through the internet satellite link. Bleeksville, population four hundred and ninety. That was it. It simply existed and that was about all.

"We'll go on foot," he said.

"That will be nice," Locey enthused.

They walked cautiously through the side streets, checking a palm computer that now displayed the tracking screen.

"Looks like they're on the far edge of town."

"It must be there."

Locey pointed to the end of the narrow street. A large modern building in red brick, half house and half office block and surrounded by a high wall. A couple of security men stood at the entrance.

Ford grimaced.

"Not easy. We'll be noticed if we watch from the town and I guess that the people here could already be under their control. We can't risk anything that could raise the alarm as they'd just move on somewhere else. We need to get in and observe without being seen."

"Pretend to be guards? Make a delivery? Climb over the wall?"

Locey asked all three at once.

"No, no and maybe. Let's check the wall. I guess the security won't be tight. There can't be a lot of activity around here."

The wall came good. At the rear, they found an unmanned door with a security keypad lock.

"I can open this but we'll wait until night. The general idea is to set bugs then get out again."

"I love bugging," Locey declared with sincerity.

"Problem is we don't know where they'll be meeting. The house part is more likely. I think the office section is probably their admin centre."

Locey shuddered.

"Ford, you're so clever. You know how that gets me excited. How long before we start?"

"A couple of hours."

"Plenty of time. Let's go back to the car now."

"Well, okay then."

124 minutes later, they were through the gate. Ford had placed a mini decoder on the lock and it was open in seconds. Now they were creeping silently towards the house.

Ford looked through each ground floor window. No one in sight and they moved round to the rear. A pool of light spread from double glass doors and Ford crouched near the lower corner to glance inside.

Mariom Wander sat at a round table, almost facing him. One other person. A woman with her back turned. All he could see was that she had bright blonde hair. Ford fixed the bug to the corner of the window.

"Let's go. Fast," he whispered and they crept back towards the gate. They were within four paces when the noise came. A deep, vibrant sound, far too powerful to be a dog.

"Tigers!" hissed Locey, sounding almost pleased.

They hustled through the gate, barely glancing back. Something was coming. Something big, bounding towards them and its eyes were diamond yellow. Ford slammed the door and they ran.

"It looked like a tiger. Except it was bigger, no stripes and yellow eyes," Locey gasped.

"Yes, I think you're right again," he responded.

Ford parked the car on a disused track a mile from Bleeksville but still within transmission range of the bugs. Locey set up a laptop to receive and record the audio. They could hear Mariom Wander's voice, loud and clear.

"We need to proceed quickly with the search. What is your report?"

Then a woman's voice. It had to be the blonde.

"You instructed me to start in Colorado and I have purchased a ranch to act as our headquarters. It's just outside Frankloom, near the centre of the State."

"There are two possibilities. The orb is either in someone's possession or still lies undiscovered somewhere. To check the first, I have called in a team of young people recently recruited to the Trysse."

"How many?" asked the blonde.

"Over three hundred. They will travel through the State as charity collectors. It will give an excuse to visit every house," Wander replied.

"I've got nearly two hundred here or on their way. Forty of them are my military people. They will be split into groups of four to visit every collector and dealer of antiquities, bric-a-brac or collectables. We can rely upon them to get answers quickly. Can you give any guide to a more precise location?"

"The Leader has indicated that the Colorado area is the most likely. That's all we have."

"When do …"

The sentence was cut short by a phone ringing. The blonde answered and there was silence for fifteen seconds before she spoke.

"Go to alert status. Immediately."

There was a click as the call finished and then her voice again.

"That was security. A gate has been opened and there could be intruders."

"Then no further talk. We could be monitored," Mariom responded.

Ford looked at Locey.

"Let's go. Fast," he hissed.

They screeched off the track and aimed for the highway.

"Colorado?" asked Locey.

"Yes, but not direct. They'll be watching the approach roads. We'll go the opposite way now to an airport. Helicopter, I think."

He reduced speed and pushed an arm around Locey, so her head was leaning against his shoulder. They were performing the cruising loving couple when a blue Callibani fizzed past in the opposite direction.

"Four tough guys inside," Locey observed.

"I think we should use disguises again like we did in Spain."

"Oooh, great. I love that. I've got a pretty nurses uniform. It's not very big and I'm sure I could look sort of nursey in it."

"Good plan but I was thinking more of a schoolteacher couple."

"Yes! Fake glasses, tweedy skirt and no knickers. I can do that."

Ford looked puzzled.

"Why no underwear?"

"Inside every drab teacher, there's a lusty woman itching to get out."

"Itchy would be right in a tweed skirt. Well this is just a disguise so you can keep the pants on."

"If you insist. Anyway, I was just thinking about their security. It's very heavy stuff for a place like that."

"It's all got tighter in the last few months and they seem to know everything that's going on."

"Maybe they have a team of robot insects patrolling everywhere and reporting back. Flies, bumblebees, mosquitoes and maybe even ants. There could be thousands of them all made with teeny little electronic bits."

"That's a possibility. It's also feasible they possess some supernormal powers."

"Wow. Like Remote Viewing. I know about that. Remember the time I tried it when we were in bed. I wanted to hover over us and look down but I couldn't quite do it. I think I just need to practice."

"Okay. Here's the plan. First, we stop off and buy disguises. Then we freshen up for a couple of hours at a motel and I'll charter a helicopter. We'll fly to Colorado this evening."

8

England, the grey land of concrete and brick with the odd fragment of manufactured green parkland. Bound tightly by unending chains of vehicles and suffocating in the poisonous fumes of traffic. Eliza nudged along the clogged motorway to Devon.

"I still think we should have telephoned," John remarked.

Eliza shook her head.

"No. Bad idea. If they are still there, then we'd just be warning them we're coming."

Devon in May is a revelation of surging nature, blooming with a sharp sunny smile. But this was November and the county slumbered, sombre and heavy lidded. The villa showed no sign of life as they approached.

"Go past the house and park in the roadside. Then we'll walk back," John instructed.

"You've become very masterful."

"I feel different somehow. Stronger. More like Wincepole."

"Perhaps I helped it come out?"

"I still don't know what you did. Locey told me you were alone with me for an hour but I don't remember a thing."

"I'm not going to tell you. Let's go."

They walked back along the road and behind a tall hedge that led to the side of the villa.

"Back entrance, I think," John said and he moved silently and quickly to the door, opening it with his key. The kitchen. Sue Wormgrasper would normally be there but now it was clean, tidy and unoccupied. As John pulled open the door to the hallway, they could hear the murmur of conversation.

"Lounge," he whispered and they crept along the hallway to stand each side of the door. Eliza pulled out the gun she had acquired in Brazil and waited while John counted down from five. Then he flung the door open.

The Wormgraspers were seated together on the sofa looking up at a figure that dominated the room. A tall, lean woman dressed entirely in dark blue. Her long legs clad in tight trousers, thick shirt and long jacket.

"Don't move," shouted Eliza, aiming the pistol.

The woman gazed at her icily. Her dark hair was tightly pulled back, exposing a narrow, tanned face with sharp grey eyes. Age could have been anywhere between twenty-five and forty.

"Who are you?" asked John.

She didn't reply, just stared at him with polar ferocity. Then she moved. He saw just a flash of blue and almost instantly found Eliza pushed next to him. The woman stood in Eliza's place, holding her gun and no emotion visible in her lean features. Then she spoke.

"You are weak. Improve or they will kill you."

Her voice cut like an icicle through butter. Providing, of course, that the butter had been left in the sun and then been brought in to a subzero environment to have a nasty shock as it was instantly inserted by a point of frozen water.

"Are you on our side?" Eliza enquired.

"I am always alone. Our paths have coincided."

"Do you know about the Trysse?"

"Yes. They have sent the Fuffax and Akur to kill me. Pray you do not cross their path. I leave now before they track me here."

She strode lightly to the door.

"Wait. You didn't tell us your name," called Eliza.

"I am Hagg. Hagg Snowmine."

And she was gone. For a full half-minute, John and Eliza stared at each other in silence.

"Did you want a nice cup of tea?" asked Sue Wormgrasper.

John returned from his state of disbelief.

"No thank you. What happened here?"

"Well, not a lot to say really. Four days ago, I was in the kitchen when the doorbell rang. It was an old lady who said her car had broken down and she hadn't got her phone with her. I invited her in but as soon as she entered, two men rushed past and grabbed me. They tied me up in the kitchen and then did the same to Percy who was out, worming the cabbages. The old woman took off her hat and scarf and it was a young girl of about twenty. I heard her talking to you on the telephone but we couldn't do anything."

"You didn't mention what they said to us," interrupted Percy.

"Oh yes, I nearly forgot. The girl said she was going to kill us by chopping bits off our bodies until we bled to death or something like that. Anyway, we were all in the kitchen today when this Snowmine woman appeared from nowhere.

She killed the first man with a long knife and then she broke the neck of the other. Just grabbed his head and jerked it. The crack made an awful noise."

"They were drinking coffee at the time," added Percy helpfully.

"Yes, that's right. Well, the girl ran away before the woman could get to her."

"What happened to the corpses?" asked Eliza

"Oh, those. Percy buried them near the carrot patch."

"Food for the soil," her husband commented sagely.

"Anyway, the woman asked us to come in here and we told her everything that had happened. Then you two came. Are you sure you don't want some tea?"

John shook his head.

"Not now. Did you search the bodies?"

"The woman did but there was nothing worth talking about. Obviously they had guns, commando knives and that sort of thing. One also had a garrotte."

"You two must be exhausted after all this."

"Oh no, Mr Smith. All in a days work, isn't it Percy?"

"Nothing to get bothered about," he responded.

Two hours later, John and Eliza were back in the car, heading for Herkshire and the country house of Lord Ian Feltspen.

"It's our best lead, I think," John remarked.

Eliza nodded.

"We can't be sure he's involved. It could just have been his wife."

"That's unlikely. Remember the house in Brazil was bought by him."

"Presumably he'll know about his wife's death?"

"Maybe not. The Trysse could have kept it secret," John responded, thoughtfully.

"We'll see. Do we have a plan to get inside?"

"Remember what we found when we checked out Feltspen's interests?"

"His only non-business hobby is cricket. Silly game, that," Eliza stated vehemently.

"Listen, Pongo. No one calls cricket silly. It isn't just an interest with him, it's an infatuation. He's fanatical about the game, the history and memorabilia."

"Sounds as if you're a little bit entranced yourself. Maybe I should wear pads at bedtime?"

"I like the game but not as much as he does. I'm thinking I could offer him a stump."

"A stump?"

"You know. Three of them make up the wicket."

"Who the hell would want a little wooden pole?"

"You'd be surprised. I plan to offer him a stump from the final test, England versus West Indies of seven years ago. One of the most famous matches ever."

"So that's why I've never heard of it.

"Typical woman."

"John, you have changed. That's the bravest thing you've ever said so I won't hit you."

"Don't forget, I'm a sports memorabilia dealer and you're my assistant. We need to arrive in the evening and try to get invited to stay the night."

"Do we use our own names?"

"No, too risky. I'll be Horace Wincepole and you can be Anne Winters.

"I hate Anne. Melanie Smythe, I think. Sounds more in keeping with the upper class."

"Okay, Smythe."

"Right, Wincepole."

It was just after nine in the evening when they sat in the lounge of a huge mansion, Lord Feltspen's modest residence of just fifty-two rooms. It was set in acres of grounds and even had stables at the rear. The maid who answered the door wore a uniform that would have been risqué in a nightclub. A short, dark flouncy dress that attempted to rise up each time she moved, exposing bright pink pants. The top was cut in a low V shape that barely did enough.

Now they waited alone on an ornate sofa in an even ornater lounge, waiting for the Lord to come.

"The maid seemed attractive, Smythe," John remarked to fill the time.

"Stop ogling or I'll make your pole wince, Wincepole."

"Just a comment, that's all."

The door opened and a half unexpected man entered. The expected part was that it was Lord Ian Feltspen. The other half was the jeans and T-shirt on a muscular frame. He was no more than twenty-seven and a picture of healthy vigour. Eliza found herself involuntarily squirming in her seat.

"Mr Wincepole, Ms Smythe. I am Ian Feltspen."

John shook his hand.

"Thank you for receiving us at this late hour, sir."

"Not at all. However, I'm usually in bed by ten thirty. I like to rise early."

He looked steadily at Eliza as he spoke. Dark eyes housed in a rugged face, topped by short black hair. Eliza opened her mouth to speak and found her lips were wet.

"I understand," she breathed.

"You told the maid that you had something of interest for me?"

His voice was assertive and very Eton.

"Yes, sir. A stump."

"Stump? Presumably not of a tree?

"A cricket stump. Final test, England versus West Indies."

Feltspen's eyes brightened.

"Not the box line series?"

"Yes."

"My god, man. Where is it?"

"I have exclusive rights to purchase from, shall we say, an anonymous enthusiast. In these circumstances, my invariable policy is to give first refusal to one who will cherish such a rare item."

"And the price?"

Feltspen asked but didn't appear too interested in the answer. He was hooked.

"Well, sir. This is the only one we know to have survived the turmoil at the end of the match. As you will recollect, it is generally believed that all six stumps were burnt by the crowd. So difficult to place a value on such a unique item."

"Authenticity?

"I'm sure you will recall that each stump was signed by both captains before the match. Their names are clearly legible. There is a slight marking from the flames but barely noticeable. I have independently but confidentially had it appraised by an expert who assures me it is genuine. You are welcome to conduct your own tests."

Eliza saw the perfect grin spread across Feltspen's face.

"Consider the item sold, Mr Wincepole. Would fifty thousand pounds be an acceptable figure?"

"That coincides exactly with my estimate."

"When can I have it?"

"Ms Smythe, my assistant can go tomorrow morning and bring it here. This opportunity only arose earlier today, hence our late arrival."

Eliza admired how the new John was manoeuvring for an invitation to stay. She enhanced it by stifling a yawn.

"Then you must sleep here tonight," Feltspen said emphatically.

Eliza smiled with sincerity.

"That is very kind."

"I hope I can make you comfortable," he murmured meaningfully.

Their rooms were not adjoining. Eliza on the first floor and John on the second. After retiring, he visited her room to discuss plans.

"I'm a bit worried about you. To be honest, I suspect that the Lord may plan to visit you tonight," he said with concern.

"I'm sure I can handle it."

"Yes but he might, you know. Try something."

"Honestly, I can handle it."

"I propose to come back here in an hour. Then we'll take the chance to explore. If anyone sees us, we're just looking for a midnight snack."

"Okay, but you must promise not to interrupt if the Lord is inside when you come."

"Yes, right."

An hour later, the house was silent. It was only just past midnight and everyone apparently adopted Feltspen's desire to get between the sheets as early as possible. John tapped quietly at Eliza's door and she opened it immediately. He was puzzled by the look of disappointment in her face.

"I'll go to the upper floors while you search downstairs. Don't forget, if anyone asks, you're looking for a snack," he whispered.

Eliza nodded and watched him depart. Then she descended the stairs. Start with the kitchen. That was a good place to find notes and information in this sort of house. It was the expected spacious layout. Large, smooth pine table. Solid fuel stove and a walk-in larder that was bigger than most lounges and stocked with a vast selection of food. She found a diary and was just beginning to read when she heard the sound of approaching voices. Only one refuge, the larder. She moved inside, just as the kitchen door opened and the lights were flicked on. The larder door had vertical slots for airflow that gave her a good view of the room.

First she saw the maid who had greeted them when they arrived. Attractive, dark hair and the scanty outfit.

"How may I serve you, sir?" asked the girl.

Feltspen came into view.

"I think I would like a feast on the table," he said casually.

"Yes, sir."

The girl turned two chairs sideways and then sat on the table, legs apart with a high-heeled foot on each chair.

"We won't require these," Feltspen said.

Eliza heard a ripping noise and a tiny bright pink garment was thrown to the floor. She sighed, opened a diary and began to read in the faint light. Six minutes and thirty seven seconds later, the noises abated.

"I hope you were satisfied, sir?" asked the maid.

"Your performance was exemplary."

Eliza looked again through the slots. Feltspen was leaving the kitchen and the girl gathered up the torn pants and threw them in the waste bin. Then she pulled out a mobile phone and Eliza pushed her ear against the slot.

"My report, tutor. He took another pill, twelve minutes ago," the girl said.

A pause.

"No, he's convinced it simply increases his sex drive."

Another pause.

"No, he has made no attempt to contact his wife. As instructed, I told him Lady Feltspen had left a message that she was out of range of her mobile. He is very easy to control now."

Pause again.

"Yes. We have four films and over two hundred photographs of him. My eight weeks here are completed this week and you have assigned me to work for the American financier in London."

She clicked the phone off.

Eliza smiled softly. Questions were being answered. Feltspen was kept under control by some drug in the sex pill. The maids were working for the enemy on a sort of rota. And she had more information. Coinciding with a critical point on the kitchen table, she had found a diary note with a name. Three days ago, someone called Tung Hot had come for dinner. The entry was emphasised with an asterisk.

She returned to her room, flushed and excited. That is, she had these emotions, not the room although it had got quite aroused on occasions. The unforgettable episode of Lady Wettkipper and her two male servants in 1988, for example.

Eliza sat on the bed to wait for John. Two minutes later, there was a quiet knock at the door. She opened it to find a smiling Lord Feltspen. His muscular frame was clothed in a long, loose white robe that fitted him well, except at one point. The pills were certainly effective.

She had told John she could handle it but after witnessing the episode in the kitchen, she didn't want to handle it now.

"I'm so pleased you've come. I've been sick and I was going to see if I could find some aspirins," she said with a grimace. An old trick but there was visual evidence it was working.

"I'm so sorry. I'll tell a maid to bring you some. Nothing too bad, I hope?"

"Oh, no. Just a bit over hectic today. I'll be fine tomorrow."

Eliza 1, sex pills 0, she thought as he walked away.

Five minutes later a maid arrived with a packet of tablets. Ten minutes after that, John came. He was flushed and excited. Just as much as Eliza on her return and certainly more than the room had been in 1988.

"I've been in a maid's wardrobe," he said, significantly.

"Did you find something in pink to fit?"

"No. I was checking the rooms on my floor and found one that had papers and books on a table. I'd started to look through them when I heard someone coming and hid in the wardrobe.

"As a wild guess, was it a maid?"

"Well, yes. Actually, two maids. I couldn't see anything but I could hear perfectly."

"They were talking?"

"Yes. Afterwards."

"After what?"

"Well, you know."

"For goodness sake. Were they having sex?"

"Yes."

"Right. And afterwards they talked?"

"Yes. They had both arrived only a week ago under instruction from someone they called the tutor."

"Any name mentioned?"

"Unfortunately, no. But they did say they had been trained for the job at a big house near Chutney By The Water."

"That's a weird name. I don't know the place."

"I went past it a year ago. It's a tiny village next to the Thames, north of London. Anyway, the maids left after talking for a couple of minutes. Said they had to check on Lord Feltspen."

"I've also been in a cupboard. Larder, actually."

Eliza described the events in the kitchen, deliberately embellishing the table activity to discomfort John. She was pleased to see him squirm slightly.

"Now we know a lot more. Our visit has been a success."

"I haven't mentioned that Lord Ian came here, just before you arrived."

"Came here?"

Eliza was delighted with the disappointment in his voice.

"I made an excuse and he went away. But tonight, I do need looking after."

"You want medicine?"

"Yes and you've got just what I need."

She pulled him to the bed.

Ripples of bleary morning light spread across the bed. Eliza grinned as she looked at John slumbering peacefully. Her mood was good and her body invigorated. She visited the bathroom, dressed and was ready for the day.

"What time is it?" John mumbled when she nudged him.

"Just after seven. Time to get up."

He washed and dressed but still seemed a little weary.

"Did I tire you out?" she asked, perkily.

He managed a sleepy smile.

"It was wonderful."

"First, we have to decide what to do about this stump thing."

"It's a good price. We should sell it to him."

"What? You really have it?"

"Yes, of course. A friend of mine took it during the pitch invasion. Sold it to me for ten pounds."

"Nice profit. As if you need the money."

"The stump is actually in the car. My plan was for you to leave after breakfast, drive around and return in a couple of hours."

"I'm impressed. But it means leaving you alone with these maids. I hope I exhausted you last night."

"To use your words, I can handle it."

"Where in the car did you hide this thing?"

"Under the rear seat."

"So after we eat, I go for two hours and then return waving the stump. When I've handed it over, we need to get away as quickly as we can."

It was quiet at the breakfast table. Lord Feltspen was apparently still in bed but two maids served them attentively. Too attentively, thought Eliza as she munched a croissant. The girls were taking turns to squeeze against or lean over John on the pretext of placing various pots of jam on the table. She recognized one as the kitchen table girl and hoped she wasn't planning to serve him with the sex pill as his next course.

She was.

Eliza saw her drop something into a coffee cup, stir it vigorously and place it in front of John before leaving the room. Grabbing his arm before he could reach for the coffee, Eliza began a conversation with him and placed her own cup next to his. When she had finished her meaningless story, she picked up his cup, as if by mistake. Lord Feltspen arrived and she completed the circle by asking about a painting on the wall behind him and then exchanging cups with him when he twisted round to look.

The maid returned and kept glancing at John with a seductive smile. Meanwhile the Lord consumed his coffee in gulps, seeming to develop a new vitality as he finished. He began to ask Eliza if she had recovered but his eyes were constantly moving to the legs of the maids. Within a minute he made excuses and asked one of the girls to come with him to help sort something out.

Eliza was pleased as a puppeteer. Men were so easy to control. She finished breakfast and departed in the car, driving five miles and parking in a country lane. After listening to a radio debate for seventy minutes, she motored slowly back.

Feltspen greeted her in the hall. He took the stump and handed her a cheque.

"Wonderful. Just wonderful," he murmured, totally entranced by the short wooden pole and before she could speak, he disappeared into one of the rooms. She was about to follow when a blonde maid appeared.

"Mr Wincepole went back to his room for a short rest," she said with an innocent smile.

Alarm bells. Eliza climbed the stairs and found the girl was following her. John was dozing on the bed, naked, as if he had just indulged in an extremely vigorous session with three maids who had found new ways of making him last as long as possible. Eliza was not pleased.

"After you left, he had a second cup of coffee," the girl said with an icy smile.

"I'll just get Mr Wincepole dressed and we'll be on their way."

The girl didn't move.

"You are known to us."

"Sorry?"

"You were warned. Now the Fuffax have been instructed to hunt you. I am truly sorry for this man, he has great potential."

"But not sorry for me?"

"I do not associate closely with women who do not serve the Trysse."

"So what are these Fuffax?"

The blonde laughed.

"They kill. Unfailingly and painfully. It is an agonising death. You should consider suicide before they reach you."

Eliza pulled out a gun and pressed it against the girl's head.

"Tell me the name of your leader and who is this tutor?"

"Don't be silly. I serve with body, mind and my life. If you're not going to kill yourself, I suggest you leave now. Your man was very satisfactory, by the way. Much more so than that pathetic Lord Feltspen."

She laughed again and then left, totally ignoring the gun.

Ten minutes later, Eliza was driving with a still snoozing John slumped in the passenger seat.

9

Colorado lies in the very heart of the USA but its bright crystal pulse resounds from coast to coast. A State of mountains and streams, valleys and green plains. Significantly, the area is not renowned for surfing, beachcombing or English breakfasts.

Ford had already negotiated car hire with an isolated garage, fifty seven miles from Frankloom. He landed the helicopter at the rear and handed over a wad of notes to cover parking of the craft, rent of the car and to cover the cost of silence. After advising the owner they were detectives investigating a bogus charity, he asked for a call to his mobile if any collectors called.

"You're so clever," Locey said as they drove away.

"I've had to learn how to survive."

"How do I look?"

"Exactly right."

Locey wore a sensible jacket, loose dark trousers, a short cut dark wig, no makeup and dark rimmed glasses. Ford was dressed just the same, except he had no hairpiece. He just parted his anonymous brown hair on the other side. He also didn't wear makeup. The grimy, ten-year-old Scuttburn car completed a perfect 'academics on vacation' picture. They were headed for the ranch at Frankloom, where they knew the blonde woman had set up base. The idea was to identify the opposition before starting their own search for the sphere.

The ranch covered a huge area. They were still some distance from the central building as they drove past the boundary fence, watching clumps of horses cantering freely around the grassy fields. As the road curved nearer the house, they saw groups of young people earnestly indulging in mass aerobic exercises. Most wore a chocolate and pink outfit, obviously the uniform of the fake charity. The main entrance was crowded with groups of dark suited women and men, many carrying holstered guns. Parked vehicles occupied a massive area at the side of the house.

"These guys are not playing. There's a small army in there," observed Ford.

Locey looked disapproving.

"Chocolate just doesn't go with pink. It's a horrible mixture. Do you think they're all brainwashed?"

"Yes, in a way. The Trysse use drugs where necessary but the experience with John showed that anyone making contact with a sphere could be converted immediately."

"Well I'm not touching any of their balls. How do we get inside?" asked Locey.

"I've no good ideas. I suppose we could try to impersonate a guard or charity worker."

"I'm not wearing those colours."

"No, right. And the only way we can get the outfit is to knock out a couple of their people. Even if we get away, they'll be found some time and the leaders will know we were there. I really want to get in and out undetected."

"We need an invisibility potion. I'm certain it exists. When I was younger, I'm absolutely sure an invisible man got in my bed almost every night. He was nice, though."

"Unfortunately, we haven't time to discover the formula. I'm thinking we could make a delivery."

"A tiger, maybe?"

"Not exactly."

Ford went through his plan.

It was seven thirty a.m. the next day when a small horsebox entered the main gate of the ranch and the armed dark suits motioned for it to stop.

"What do you want?" asked one, who looked as if he chewed iron railings for relaxation.

"We're delivering the mare," responded the plain woman behind the wheel.

"What?"

The woman sighed.

"The mare. She is to be covered by your stallion. I just need to deliver her to the stables."

"Who's that with you?"

"Obviously, he's the groom."

The thudding of hooves and a whinny from the back.

"Calm down, Priscilla. You'll get what you want soon enough," called the woman.

The railing muncher checked it out. It was a horse all right and no area for anyone to hide. He looked again at the occupants of the cab. Nothing dangerous there. They could have been schoolteachers. He waved them through.

"Priscilla?" Ford enquired as they drove to the stables.

"It's a lovely name for a woman horse."

They had purchased the box and mare from a farm ten miles away. Not cheap but the plan seemed to be working. Locey parked out of sight around the side of a large barn and then led the animal to the stables. They were completely empty.

"I think they just let the horses out to roam around. They've got more important things to bother about," remarked Ford.

"I've never been in the hay with a man," Locey said wistfully, releasing the skittering animal.

"Maybe later. Let's find a way to the house. Are you recording?"

"Yes."

She pointed at a badge on her coat that contained a micro-microphone, connected wirelessly to a memory chip recorder hidden in her bra. It could only be discovered by a detailed search of her chest area.

Ford commenced a casual conversation with her and they strolled unhurriedly towards the house. Both actions were intended to dissuade any interest from the various groups of people they passed on the journey. Eventually, they reached one of the rear doors of the mansion and Ford opened it quietly to reveal a kitchen, where two men were preparing a meal. He waved an official looking document and then continued to chat with Locey as they walked through. The men barely glanced at them.

A hallway. A blonde woman walking towards them. The blonde from the meeting. Ford heard Locey give a little gasp and the reasons were not hard to guess. The woman wore only a minuscule white running kit that could have doubled as a bikini. More than that, her looks were like an ice pick in the eyes. Pale skin, dazzlingly blonde hair and ice grey eyes that could move mountains.

"You two. Bring milk," she ordered.

Locey was still transfixed but Ford nodded obediently and hurried back to the kitchen, returning quickly with a glass of milk. The woman consumed it in three gulps (the milk, not the glass).

"You are good boy. Is she brain-dead?"

Locey remained static, staring at the woman with mouth slightly ajar.

"No, madam. She's been working real hard. Thirty six hours with no sleep."

"She needs fitness. Stiff workout every morning. But you very obedient. I like that."

As she handed the glass back to Ford, her fingers lingered over his hand momentarily. Then she jogged off down the hall.

"She was magnificent. I'd love to be exactly like her," breathed Locey, starry eyed.

"She's one of the enemy. That was the woman with Wander at the meeting."

"Did you see her figure?"

"Tall but not very curvy. Much prefer yours. She called me a good boy," Ford smiled.

"Well I think you're a good boy as well."

"Now I know her name. The guys in the kitchen told me on my milk run. Let's move on."

They entered the main hallway and Ford led the way up the stairs, moving purposefully to avoid suspicion. They passed only one person, a big man in dark uniform who looked at them without interest and didn't speak. The first floor was just a row of doors and they continued up to the next level. An identical row of doors.

"Let's walk along. We may hear something," Ford whispered.

They didn't hear anything and began to return along the corridor.

"What are you doing here?"

A question from behind them. Ford turned. A bald man. He was as square as a human could get. Massive shoulders, thick legs and a very fit body of someone who looked middle-aged. He wore only a bath robe. It was pink and decorated with little cartoon ducks.

"Hello. We've been trying to find someone to sign the receipt papers for the mare. We were told to come up here."

"Mare? I know nothing of this. I'm the manager here."

"All I can tell you is that the Johnson ranch near Denver, asked us to deliver the mare to be covered by your stallion. We've made the delivery and just need someone in authority to sign."

The man's face was as square as his body, his eyes as grey as the blonde woman but now his cheeks were turning as pink as his robe.

"Listen you. Get out now or I'll order you shot. You have five minutes."

He emphasised the point by moving forward and jabbing a square finger into Ford's chest.

"Eeek!" squealed Locey.

The man's robe had come apart at the front. Eeek was definitely the right word. But he made no attempt to cover up.

"Shut up, stupid woman. Guard!"

He shouted the last word with enough volume to wake the dead. Two corpses turned over in the nearby graveyard but only one living person responded. He burst through a door behind the bald figure, pistol in each hand.

"I kill, boss," he screamed, desperately looking for any suitable targets. He was unkempt, unshaven, ungroomed and unfriendly.

"These two leave in five minutes or kill them."

"Yes, boss."

The guard's lank, dark hair bounced around as he rushed towards them and Ford held his palms up.

"No problem. We're going."

He quickly guided Locey away from the scene. The wild-eyed man followed closely, jabbing guns in their backs as they moved.

"Take time. No rush. I rather kill you. Sixty eight hours since I last shot someone. Need fix urgent."

Ford and Locey increased speed until they were running towards the horsebox. They leapt into the vehicle while the gunman hovered alongside, counting down.

"You got forty two seconds, forty one, forty, thirty nine…"

Locey began to drive.

A throng of armed figures around the gate turned to watch the pistol waving man running alongside the vehicle and stood back.

"Fools. Make them wait. Just ten seconds," the man shouted.

He was still yelling as they passed through onto the road and Locey accelerated away.

"Good and bad," muttered Ford.

"She was gorgeous, wasn't she?"

"The blonde woman? Sure, she was okay. The good is that we've identified her. The name is Pheela Lipstrider. Bad news is we created enough ruckus to be remembered forever."

"But we were disguised so they won't know us next time."

"Let's hope. The main concern now is that they're bound to try to follow. I'll try to shake them off."

Ford drove calmly. Negative attention to be attracted.

"I think we lost them now," he remarked.

Locey squealed.

"Look, something moved on that hill. It just might have been a bear. Oh, and we haven't lost them."

"I haven't seen anything. Where are they?"

"Up in those mountains somewhere. In caves and other mysterious places where herds of bears love to go."

Patience had to be Ford's long suit.

"I meant the people chasing us."

"Oh, them. They've been following for ages now. Switched between five different cars to avoid us noticing. And Pheela was in one of them," she beamed.

He grimaced.

"Then they must have attached a tracker to the van somehow. Our problem is this area. Lots of long, narrow roads and no cities to get lost in."

"I need to see her again."

"Pheela? Why?"

"I just can't remember exactly how her hair was cut in the front. So we'll have to stop in that town ahead."

Town was an exaggeration. A small collection of buildings like grimy dice on the unspoilt baize of countryside.

"One-horse town," murmured Ford.

"A horse! Where is it?"

Ford sighed.

"The bar's open," he remarked as they coasted past a saloon right out of a Western movie.

"That's silly. Horses don't drink alcohol. But we need to go in there. Pheela will follow and I can check her hair as well as stopping them chasing us."

Ford pulled up twenty yards past the bar and they walked back to the entrance. He saw another vehicle pull up further down the street.

Inside was a scene of desolate filth that wallowed in a pool of disgusting obscenity. And that was just the customers. It was packed and the smell of stale sweat and liquor assaulted the faculties from all directions. A gloomy menagerie of tables and seated at every one was a group of desperate, grimy men, all wearing holstered guns, western-style. The bar was stained by countless spilt drinks and the walls pitted with dents and bullet holes.

On one side was a tiny stage where a young but excessively flabby girl gyrated in bra and thong.

"No women served here," grunted the barkeeper over the loud babble of conversation. He had narrow eyes and a greasy, unhealthy complexion.

"She can do a strip for us. Make a change from Fat Alice there," a voice shouted.

Ford groaned inwardly. Trouble was on its way and he was surprised to see Locey smiling.

"I agree. Women are hopeless. They just go on about food, babies and illness all the time," she shouted at the crowd.

"You're right, girl. So get your clothes off," came the response.

"Okay. I will if I lose the game."

The noise of conversation abated. They were taking an interest.

"What game is that?"

"The gun game. Look, I'll show you. Someone give me a pistol."

No volunteers but without appearing to move, she suddenly held a gun and the holster of the nearest man was empty. The crowd all lowered their heads as she waved the weapon around while speaking.

"Now this is a really good game. It's called Rabbit. I go first and if I fail, I'll take off all my clothes and parade on that stage for five minutes. If I win, I'll pick one of you to do the same."

"Has she escaped from somewhere?" a man shouted to Ford but he shrugged with the look of someone waiting for the ground to open up.

Locey continued with enthusiasm.

"When you know the rules, you'll all want to play with me, even if you don't already. All you do is throw a dollar coin in the air and I have to hit it. If I miss, then off they all come."

She ran a hand over the dowdy schoolteacher's outfit.

"I'll go with that. I reckon you might be worth a second look without those old lady clothes you're wearing," a voice commented.

"She ain't gonna pick me if she wins, so what can I lose?" added a gnarled old man in the corner.

Ford saw the door open and two thickset men entered, followed by the blonde Pheela Lipstrider. Locey didn't seem to have noticed them.

"Whoooo! Let's do it then," she yelled, spinning round on her heel in a circle while randomly aiming the gun. It appeared to cut a swathe through the audience, men ducking low below table level as it passed. A heavy thump indicated that Fat Alice had taken evasive action and was now flat on the floor.

Ford felt a prod in his back.

"Start walking outside," a voice growled in his ear.

"Who's going to throw the coin?" Locey shouted.

"You ever used a gun before, girl? I ain't risking being anywhere near it," came a response.

"Oh, come on. Look what you could get."

She unbelted her trousers and they fell around her feet. The men appeared surprised to see the tiny pink briefs under the schoolteacher clothing but the sight certainly got their attention. She bent forward and turned in a circle but still no one seemed prepared to risk their lives for more. Locey shrugged, pulling up the trousers.

"Okay then. My friend will do it," she grabbed Ford's arm and pulled him in front of her. The man behind quickly pocketed his gun.

"Got a dollar?" she asked.

He shook his head and she handed him a coin.

"Wait till I get loosened up."

Another spin on her heel, another scattering for cover.

"Ready!" she yelled.

Ford closed his eyes and spun the coin as far away from him as possible. He heard the gun crack three times, so close together that it could have been one shot. With a loud ching, the coin landed on the counter, wobbled and then lay flat. The barkeeper's head appeared.

"Anyone killed?" he bawled.

"We're okay. Ready for the strip show," a shout came back.

Mr Greasy rose to full height and picked up the coin.

"Well I'm damned," he said and held it up.

One shot had bitten deep through the top edge while the other two had taken a small chunk at each side. The result was a piece of metal looking like an animal with two big ears.

"Rabbit!" Locey shouted exultantly in the ensuing silence.

"Jeez, woman. Where the hell did you learn to shoot like that?" asked the nearest onlooker.

"Maybe it was just luck. Anyway, I win and I've got to choose."

She looked round the disreputable gathering to see the men now smiling with admiration. Locey shook her head.

"I don't know. I'll just pick by chance."

She closed her eyes and spun round again, this time pointing a finger. Then she apparently stopped randomly and looked along the line of her arm.

"I choose her!"

The digit was aiming directly at Pheela Lipstrider. Her snow maiden face iced up some more.

"I'm not getting involved in your childish games. Come outside now. Take them, men."

The two heavies took a step forward. Then stopped, as anyone would when faced with an array of guns aimed directly at them.

"She won fair. Get on that stage, woman and take 'em off."

Pheela edged for the door but no chance of escape. She was forced up to the stage but simply stood with hands on hips.

"I'll sort her," yelled Fat Alice with an obvious relish that maybe betrayed a lifetime's hatred of women who were too attractive. She grabbed a knife from one of the men and began to slice off Pheela's clothing. The cuts were deliberately small, to eke out the process as long as possible and it took nearly twelve minutes before the blonde was completely naked.

"She's gorgeous and I've memorised her hair now," Ford heard Locey whisper.

They sidled out of the bar without anyone noticing. The customers had their attention and weapons directed elsewhere.

Ford looked perplexed as they drove away.

"I think I know how you did it. I didn't notice at the time but that coin you gave me must have had notches already in it."

"Then I'd have had to hit it in exactly the same places. That would've been much harder," Locey responded.

A couple of hours later, they sat in a motel room, drinking coffee. Ford had rigged an internet connection and was checking a name.

"Okay, Locey. I've found something on Pheela Lipstrider."

"Feeler with an F?"

He spelt the name.

"That's a shame but it's still a great name. I bet she likes tigers."

"She seems more like an ice woman to me. Polar bears, perhaps. Born in Greenland, Finnish parents, thirty-three now and obviously fit as an iceberg. She used to be a tennis player."

"I wonder how she gets her hair that colour. I want mine like that."

"She's no shrinking violet. Puts the big into big business. Plays the stock market but specialises in currency. Buys and sells dollars, euros and pounds like they were ears of corn."

"Why do corns have ears?"

Ford smiled.

"Interesting. It's actually from an entirely different root to the things on the side of our head. They come from the Latin 'auris' but the corn ear comes from another Latin word, 'acer' which sort of means sharp."

"What about the Old English 'aeher'?"

Ford was silent for a full six seconds.

"Yes, maybe that too."

Locey never failed to surprise him.

"The big square guy, who called himself the manager, is actually a gangster as is his gunman sidekick. I guess they're the ones heading the military team. Anyway, I'll enter all the data in my archives."

Ford's archives were duplicated into chunks of web space with the access passwords only in his memory.

"Polar bears are cuddly," Locey murmured, interestingly.

10

Eliza drove to a country hotel with John asleep beside her. Her patience was stretched by his inactivity and as soon as they arrived in their room, she pushed his head under the shower. He shouted with the shock of cold water.

"Let me rest."

"You need to be awake and I must let out some annoyance."

She began slapping his face. Hard. It was ten seconds before he began to resist the blows.

"Hey, stop. I'm on your side."

"Right. Get your clothes off and go in the shower. I've got coffee coming in ten minutes. I want you washed and back in the room by then."

She slammed the door of the bathroom. Another release.

John emerged eight minutes later, looking sheepish. Two less legs, no woolly coat, not partial to grass and able to converse. In fact, he was nothing like sheepish, more humble mannish.

"Sorry Eliza. I expect you're angry at what happened to me."

"It did not happen to you. It was your willing participation with no less than three oversexed maids, just a day after spending a night in bed with me."

"But they gave me a pill. I couldn't help it."

"You should have tried harder."

"Well, at least we got away and have gained some interesting information."

"Did you hear what the blonde creature said to me when we were leaving?"

"Don't really remember. Something about not liking women?"

"She said that they were sending the Fuffax after us. The same things that Hagg was trying to avoid."

John suddenly became alert.

"What? They're after us? Do you know what they look like?"

"The girl wouldn't tell me. Just said they never failed to kill their target and it was an agonising death."

"Very comforting. So we need to avoid these things but have no idea as to their appearance."

"That's right. So we'll just need to continue and be on our guard. Let's talk about what we discovered at the house. I found a diary. A VIP called Tung Hot. We'll begin with him."

Eliza had already connected a notebook computer to the hotel's wireless internet signal. Tung Hot was a very powerful businessman, based in Hong Kong. Astonishingly, he was now the forty third richest person in the world although no one had heard of him until about nine months ago. He possessed seemingly unlimited wealth and had bought up great chunks of companies throughout the world. Financial journalists had scoured their sources but his history was still a complete mystery. There were a number of photos and he was not as she had imagined. A very tall man of over two metres or six and a half feet with a lean, almost gaunt, hawk-like face and dark, murderous eyes. None of the pictures showed him smiling, that didn't appear to be a regular occurrence. He wasn't married and apparently had no regular partner.

"He must be someone important in the Trysse. Maybe the Leader?" Eliza theorised.

"I'm sure that's right. He could be running the whole thing."

"We've got two choices. Either find this Tung Hot or go to that place by the Thames."

"Yes, Chutney By The Water. That's where the maid said they had their training centre. I vote we go there first."

"I agree. Perhaps the romp with the maids hasn't entirely ruined your brain. We've got to go carefully. These Fuffax could attack any time."

"We'll stay here tonight and start tomorrow," John affirmed.

"But separate beds. That's the rule now until further notice."

No argument from John. He couldn't win that one.

Eliza awoke at 6.08 a.m.

Something. A faint scratching noise near the door. Then silence and she began to doze again. A soft thud. It sounded like the door closing. She grabbed the gun she had placed on the bedside table.

"John, wake up," she hissed, jumping up and moving to the window.

He was out of his bed instantly and standing next to her. She dragged him down into a crouch and then pulled open the curtains behind her. The pale morning light illuminated the room clearly.

Nothing.

"What is it?" asked John.

"I'm sure the door opened," Eliza responded with a puzzled expression.

She took a pace forward and suddenly it was there.

"Hey, that's sweet," she murmured with a motherly smile.

A light brown furry creature, no larger than her head. Lovely big, appealing eyes and a mouth slightly open. The fur looked soft and very cuddlesome. It had six little fluffy legs and squirrelly tail.

"Smashing little chap," exclaimed John, beaming.

"She's so cute. I must hold her."

The creature gave a gentle little cry of pleasure as she lifted it to her chest. Soft arms clung to her and a tiny head rested next to hers as it gently purred with comforting satisfaction.

"Please, let me hold it," John appealed but Eliza didn't want to let go. A little paw lay across her nose and she giggled with delight.

"Look, he's got a friend," called John.

Another, almost identical creature had appeared and he was already cradling it.

"You're a swell little fella," he murmured with fatherly pride.

Eliza felt complete. The cute baby needed her, loved her. Its soft paws brushed over her face and along her mouth. She parted her lips in sheer joy and two furry limbs touched her tongue. And held it. The paw over her nose now clenched tightly.

More legs thrust between her lips. Breathing was hard. She tried to shout but the soft limbs were rigid now, totally blocking her mouth.

Couldn't inhale or exhale. Dizzy. Dizzy and falling.

She screamed again and again but only in her mind.

The brain was suffocating. No oxygen left.

A faint crash and she felt warm liquid on her face. Suddenly the blockage was removed and she gasped desperately for life, for air.

It was two minutes before Eliza's senses began to return and she opened her eyes. She was on the floor, looking at a furry head with yellow slime oozing from it. Then human legs. She followed them upwards to see a lean face, looking down.

"Nasty little things. Need to cut their heads off to stop them."

Hagg Snowmine.

A violent coughing. John was recovering.

Eliza rose unsteadily to see the decapitated creatures in little pools of yellow sludge.

"You were fortunate that I was tracking these two. Another few seconds and you'd have been dead," Hagg observed, dispassionately.

"These were the Fuffax?"

"I warned you about them. They configure themselves exactly to the subject's parental instincts. A very powerful emotion to control. I guess you were thinking protective baby stuff?"

"Yes. Exactly."

"Men see something a little different but basically hitting the same irresistible vein. Smart little murderers, aren't they?"

"But they suddenly appeared out of nowhere."

"That is their best trick. They can deflate their body to almost nothing. At their smallest, they're no bigger than a knitting needle and just line themselves up with anything vertical. Inside, that's usually a piece of furniture or outside, a bush or tree. When ready, they just expand to normal size in an instant."

"Impossible to see in needle size."

"Almost. Good news is that they can't move when deflated. Plus the smell."

"Smell?"

"I've learned to recognize it."

Hagg picked up a headless body and thrust it under her nose. Eliza gulped back the disgust and sniffed obediently. A faint aroma, like crushed strawberries.

"I smell it," she confirmed.

John had staggered to his feet.

"Maybe the best way is to wear a helmet."

Hagg shook her head.

"They have more than one way of killing. Suffocation is preferred but they have retractable claws, like razor blades. It is their second choice as a number of slashes are required to kill. Certainly cut your finger off and it doesn't take very long to slice through the neck or wrist arteries."

Eliza stared at the gaunt woman but saw no emotion.

"I have to thank you."

"Express gratitude by learning to defend yourself. More will come for you. I suggest you wash and move fast."

"Can I ask…," John started but the woman had gone.

Nine minutes later, they were in the car and heading in for the Thames.

Chutney By The Water remained a solidly typical English village. Old ladies gossiped outside the village store. Tweedy men chatted about fishing and cricket. Groups of school kids guzzled alcohol and flashed knives.

The Manor house was a mile outside the community, right next to the Thames. It was surrounded by a wall on three sides with the river on the other. Immaculately manicured green lawns slope down to the water, no more than fifty metres from the building. There didn't appear to be any security. No guards on the wrought iron entrance gates, no obvious sensors or alarms. No one visible at all. It slumbered in tranquillity like a sheep on sedatives.

"Look, swans!" Eliza called, pointing at a group of the elegant birds beside the river.

"In England, swans outside private areas are the property of the King or Queen, originally from laws passed in the fifteenth century. They usually begin to breed at the age of four with eggs laid in April and May. The cygnets hatch after about five weeks," she continued educationally.

"I wonder how many maids are training here," mused John.

"You will not get involved with them. I'll make any contact that may be necessary with those girls. We're not interested in maids, we want to find out who runs this place."

"Yes, sure. How do we do that?"

"We're reporters for the 'Old British Chronicle' magazine and doing an article about the house and the village. Do you think you could manage that?"

"I can handle it."

"You said that before the maid foursome, so I'll be the journalist and you've just joined to learn the trade."

"I'm ready, boss."

They drove slowly through the gates and up a gravel driveway to park in front of the house. Still no sign of anyone.

"Maybe they've closed it down and moved out," said John.

As he spoke, the front door opened and a slim, elegant woman emerged. Sensibly cut dark blonde hair, standard cosmetics, trim and correct clothing. An image of frigid self-assurance.

"Hello. Are you journalists?" she called.

Eliza masked her surprise and answered immediately.

"Yes, that's right. How did you know?"

The woman smiled.

"Oh, we get lots of visits from your profession. We always seem to be appearing in some magazine or other. I'm Sandra Inkell, by the way."

"This is Peter and I'm Angela. We're from the Old British Chronicle."

Eliza had a sudden fear that the same journal might have already visited the house but Sandra looked delighted.

"Oh, excellent. I read that every month and we've never been featured. What would you like to see first?"

Going well, thought Eliza. Too well?

"A tour of the house, if possible. Then maybe the grounds."

"You'll need your camera."

Eliza gratefully remembered that her digital camera was stored in the glove compartment.

"It's in the car. We didn't want to use it without permission."

"How very civil of you. Traditional courtesy is so rare nowadays."

John acquired the camera from the car and then Sandra led them inside.

A magnificent arched hallway, shimmering with marble and mahogany and paintings adorned every wall. Sandra glowed with pride.

"These are originals, of course. That one is by Twickers, 1829 and the next by Forrecull, 1747."

"I recognise that," John said, pointing at a painting of three laughing men, sitting astride a horned animal.

"Yes. Three Men On A Goat by Ponsontry Gumbleton, 1862. It's very famous."

Eliza looked around.

"They must be very valuable. I'm surprised you don't have more alarms and security people."

"The paintings alone are valued at twenty three million pounds. As regards security, try and touch one."

Eliza reached a hand towards the nearest portrait and found her hearing battered by a loud siren. Every painting retracted back into the wall and steel shutters slid down. She pressed fingers in her ears and stepped back. Something cold and metallic on the back of her neck.

"Don't move a muscle," a voice said.

The alarm was cut off and Eliza heard Sandra speak.

"Thank you everybody. This was a test."

92

The cold metal was removed and she turned.

Six people, three women and three men, all in skin-tight black bodysuits and each carrying a pistol. They wore belts containing an array of knives and ammunition.

"That was impressive," she exclaimed.

Sandra laughed.

"We try to be efficient."

She nodded to one of the women who spoke into a transceiver. The wall shutters opened and the paintings returned to view. The six guards disappeared as suddenly as they arrived.

Eliza took a breath.

"Right, let's begin. I'd like to ask about the house while Peter takes photographs."

"Yes, certainly. Ask anything. I have an idea. Let's talk in one of the rooms and leave him to do his job in peace."

Eliza readily assented. More chance to explore. Sandra guided her to a compact room at the rear of the house and they sat together on a leather sofa.

"Now, that's more comfortable isn't it?" the woman asked. Eliza guessed a private school education from the way she spoke. Her appearance was perfect, not a hair out of place and make up exactly right. Her age was hard to estimate. Maybe thirty five, maybe forty five. She exuded a discomfiting withdrawn iciness.

"Yes, it's very nice. Now I'd like to know a bit about the current owners and their predecessors of course."

Sandra didn't seem to hear.

"Peter seems a nice boy but men can be so, well, crude."

"Yes, sometimes. Now, about the current owners?"

"They're so hairy. Legs, chests and it's horrible to see hairy backs. Women are always so nice and smooth, don't you think?"

"I guess it comes with the gender. Do the owners come here often?"

"And men often don't smell nice. It's still unusual to find any that regularly use deodorants. They normally have this nasty old socks and stale sweat aroma. It can really turn your stomach."

Eliza abandoned the owner question for the present and travelled the ingratiating route.

"That's a bit of a generalisation but in some cases I'd agree. You obviously prefer the company of women?"

"Well, naturally. For the reasons I've given and also I find that a conversation with another woman is much more fulfilling. I believe that social intercourse is so important in a relationship."

"Absolutely. Do you want to go to bed with me?" Eliza asked with a stunning smile.

Sandra appeared mildly surprised.

"Oh no. I haven't slept with anyone for six years. I do hope you didn't think I was trying to seduce you?"

"Not at all. I was just making a polite offer. Why six years? You're very attractive and I'm sure you must have had approaches."

"Yes, all the time. Maybe two or three a week but we've never got as far as the bedroom."

"Why's that?"

"Because I killed them, of course."

"Sorry?"

"I killed them with a knife. This one."

She pulled a gleaming stiletto from her jacket.

"Okay. Right. Well, it's been a lovely chat. I think I should be getting back to Peter."

"You mean John? Don't worry, he'll be a little tied up for now. Let's have tea."

"John? He's called Peter."

"Now Eliza, don't be silly. I'll ring for tea."

She pressed a button on the coffee table in front of them, and then rested her hand on Eliza's thigh.

"Don't worry. I don't usually kill women. Just these crude, hairy, smelly men. They deserve it."

Eliza didn't respond. It had been going much too well and now everything was crumbling like a biscuit in tea.

Tea and biscuits arrived, conveyed by a maid. She was dressed in the same, scanty uniform as at Lord Feltspen's house. Presumably one of the trainees. As she placed the tray on the table, she bent towards Eliza, the loose top of her dress exposing plenty.

Sandra waved a finger.

"No, no girl. That's for the men. Women need to be touched, as if by accident. I won't discipline you this time but you must get it right."

The girl's cheeks reddened and she scurried from the room.

"Some of the girls are so slow to learn. However, I pride myself in saying that when I have completed their training, they perform very satisfactorily. Discipline is so important."

"Bend them over the desk, pull their knickers down and give them a good spanking?"

"I've never thought of that. Perhaps I should introduce it."

She poured tea and handed a cup to Eliza.

"You seem a good teacher. Can I leave school now?"

"You really are a delightful girl. I'd love to have you working under me. Unfortunately, I have explicit instructions. Both you and John have to be converted to our path. If I fail to achieve that, you must be killed, of course."

"Well, naturally. Will you tie me up now?"

Sandra considered for a moment.

"We do have certain restraints amongst our training equipment. Leather thongs, furry handcuffs and the like. Perhaps I may wish to see you in them later. For the moment, we'll just wait for the tea to have an effect."

"That was sneaky," said Eliza but the drowsiness had already begun.

"Just lie back and relax. You are a very charming girl, by the way."

Sandra's words became slurred in Eliza's mind. No point in resisting. Her final thought as she went under was a fervent hope that the maids hadn't got their hands on John again.

Just as Eliza had expected, she woke in a bed. However, she had anticipated that Sandra would be lying beside her but was alone. Alone in a tiny cell. Just space for the bunk bed, a toilet and wash basin. A small barred window, well above head height and a solid steel door. The decoration was artistic polar in designer terms or rough whitewash to humans.

"I'm awake," she called, suspecting microphones and cameras. No one came. Eliza began to hum to herself. Things could be worse, they hadn't taken any of her clothes but her pockets had been emptied.

"When do I eat," she shouted. No response again. She rose from the bed and idly checked the door. Just solid metal. No keyhole, no view hole, no means of opening it. Standing on the toilet, she peered through the barred window. A view of a brick wall, just a metre away. No natural light, just illumination from concealed fluorescents. Back to the bed to think. Sandra had said they had to join the Trysse or be killed. How would they do that? Brainwashing? Torture?

Hypnotism? Drugs? Eliza would just have to wait and see. She wondered if John was in the same situation.

What seemed like two hours passed. Pure guesswork as her watch had been taken.

A click and the door swung open. Eliza jumped up but no one entered. Pulling the door fully open, she saw metal shelves backed by another sheet of steel. Food and drink on the shelves. Lunch on cardboard plates with coffee in a paper cup. The inner door closed as she carried it to the bed.

Clever. Double doors with metal shelves fixed to the outer. There was sure to be a safety lock preventing both doors opening together. She ate, dozed, toileted, washed, dozed again. No means of judging time. Another meal, similar to the first. Maybe this was lunch. She guessed the feeding cycle could be every five or six hours and scratched marks on the wall to keep count.

More meals, sleeping and ablutions. Eliza already suspected their technique. Start with isolation for a period, and then take her clothes. When she was screaming for companionship, they'd send a man to have her. Then another and another. Eventually it would result in her mindless subservience. This procedure was in every schoolgirl's 'What a Young Woman Should Know' book.

When she was sleeping after meal number seven, the door opened and three men in dark uniforms entered. Maybe they just missed out the taking her clothes part. She deliberately minimised her reaction, looking at the men with disinterest.

They didn't speak. Two of them grabbed her arms and dragged her from the bed. The third man approached, producing a knife. No conversation but he began to systematically slice off her clothing, leaving just the underwear.

Eliza grinned.

"Do you like pink? It's not my favourite colour but I got this set in the sales."

The man bent towards her, his steely eyes a good match for the blade he pressed against her neck.

With a crash, the door burst open and a figure shot into the cell. It immediately landed a flying kick at the head of the knife holder and Eliza felt the man's body falling away from her. His companions lasted no more than thirty seconds. They had knives but were hammered by a series of kicks and punches. They went down, unconscious. The new arrival wore a black, woolly mask with just slits for eyes and mouth. She could only identify the figure as a man. A man with blood dripping from cuts on his arms and legs.

He beckoned and led her from the cell. A narrow concrete corridor. Empty. She jogged after him, passing a flight of stone steps leading up. Voices overhead. She ran faster. At the end of the corridor was a steel door with an adjacent button that her rescuer hit with his palm. The door opened and he pushed her inside. An elevator. She saw him push the top button of five and they ascended rapidly.

After a few seconds, they stopped. Out into a sunny hallway, lit by skylights overhead. Eliza saw the man push the third button before leaving the elevator and heard it descend. Clever. Any pursuers would believe they were two floors below. He grabbed her arm and she was hustled towards a small door in a corner of the hall. A bedroom, small and obviously unused.

"Thanks for the rescue," she said.

"No problem."

He pulled off the mask. John Smith.

"Have you been taking secret agent pills?" Eliza gasped in amazement.

"I suppose I've changed," he replied with new steel in his voice.

"You're wounded."

"It's nothing. I'll just wash off the blood. I've got things to tell you. Important things."

She helped him remove his clothing and clean the wounds. Nothing serious, just lacerations. A wardrobe next to the bed was productive. A stack of clothing for both sexes. Presumably backup supplies for the trainees in the house. John found a jacket, shirt and trousers and Eliza covered her pink underwear with jeans, top and a waistcoat with pockets.

"So what happened?" she asked as they sat on the bed.

"I was taking photos when someone hit me from behind. I woke in a cell like yours with a double door. When I worked out how the door system worked, I pushed a nail next to the hinge of the inner door so it wouldn't close. I could hear them trying to open the outer door and the safety lock prevented it. Eventually, they overrode the lock and two women with guns came in. I hid at the side of the door, knocked the first woman into the other and grabbed their guns. Then I tied and gagged them with bedclothes and got out."

"Then you rescued me like a hero."

"No. That was a day ago. I could hear plenty of people around and it would have been stupid to get caught immediately. I found the elevator, got up here and hid in this room. There's no one on this floor, I think it's just used for storage. I knew you'd be locked up but each time I went down, there were guards about. So I took time out to see what I could find in the house. Eventually, I went back again to the cells and found you with those men and that's it. Listen Eliza, I've discovered something really important."

"Are you sharing or is the new John a silent, secretive type?"

"I'm definitely stronger and I'm being serious. This is important. I'm now convinced we were wrong to fight the Trysse. We should be helping them."

"What? You need to explain."

"As I said, I had the time to look round. I found a library here and right in the middle was a leather bound book, contained in its own glass case. The Trysse symbol was embossed on the front. So I read it. Eliza, it explains all about them."

"Tell me."

"The book is a record of how and why they began. It's the words of David Codue, the first Guardian or leader of the organisation. The whole thing started in 1833 when he was a brilliant young academic, already teaching in a French university at the age of twenty-two. One day, he woke with an irresistible urge to go to a remote part of central France. It was like a voice inside him, giving him explicit instructions that he had to comply with. He was to leave his work, take transport to Clermont-Ferrand in the middle of France and go on from there by foot. He was to tell nobody about his journey or where he was going."

"So where was he going?"

"Into the mountains. He simply followed the directions of the voice. Eventually, he was following a track in the middle of nowhere. After a few minutes walk, he saw two people, a man and a woman, waiting by the side of the track. The man was a professor of medicine from Spain and the woman a scientist from England. They had also heard the voice. It told them not to exchange names but continue together. By now they were almost in the mountains and then they came across a monastery. It was their destination."

"You're sure this wasn't in Tibet?"

"No, this is serious. They were greeted by six monks, who seemed to expect them. It wasn't a large building and the six were the only inhabitants. They were given refreshments and David was amazed to find that the monks were his superior in all knowledge. They possessed a detailed comprehension of all the sciences, mathematics, medicine and the like. It exceeded anything he had previously known. He couldn't believe that they had gained the awareness while shut away in this remote place. They were completely self-sufficient, growing their own food and making anything they needed. What was obvious was that they were exceedingly old and frail."

"Why do people never find old nuns?"

John ignored the question.

"The next day, the three visitors were led to an underground chamber that contained three boxes. They must have been the same as the one we saw in Brazil. The monk waved a hand and one of the boxes flew open. The sphere appeared and hovered directly in front of them, glowing bright blue. David said it was like being bathed in learning. Then it returned to the box and the lid closed again. The monks then explained the purpose of the orbs, as they called them."

"And what was that?"

"I'll come to it later. The three were told they had been selected to be the guardians of the secret. Each one was to take a box, containing the orb and conceal it. It could be anywhere in the world but it had to be a safe hiding place. They had to meet the monk individually that night and tell him the country or general area where it would be hidden. They obviously couldn't give an exact place until they reached it. When they had completed the job, they were to return and advise the precise location. The next morning, the woman left and the man followed a day later. David departed on the third day."

"So none of them knew where the others were going."

"Absolutely. Also, the monk would have ensured that each of them was going to a different part of the world. Anyway, as you'll appreciate, travel was much slower then and over three months passed before David returned to the monastery. As soon as he reached it, he could see something was wrong. Five of the monks had died and the one that remained was barely clinging to existence. The old man asked him to divulge the hiding place quickly and as soon as David told him, he was offered a cup of water. He took one sip and began to feel ill. The monk tried to make him drink the rest but David fought him off and by accident, the old man's head struck the wall. He was killed instantly."

"Murder at the monastery. Sounds like a novel."

"I'm convinced it's true. David fell into a comatose sleep, obviously caused by sipping the liquid. He woke some two days later as he judged from the growth of his beard. The first thing he noticed was that his memory of the hiding place had gone completely. He couldn't even remember what country it was in. The second shock was that the body of the monk had disintegrated into a pile of dust, covered by his habit. David managed to find scraps of bread and rainwater to sustain him and then began a search of the building. No sign of the corpses of the other monks. Presumably they had also immediately gone to dust. But he did find two bodies. The man and woman who must have returned from their concealing process before him and drunk the full cup of liquid. He looked everywhere but the place was empty of anything except furniture. Then he returned to the room where he had lain and noticed something under the powdery remains of the monk. A small scrap of paper. It simply listed the target locations that the three had given before they left."

"What next?"

"David had to make a decision. He was the only one in the world who knew the secret and the purpose of the orbs. He realised that this knowledge must be retained."

"You haven't told me what it is yet."

"I'm just coming to it. The monks told them that the orbs were the solution to the problems of humanity. The next stage in our development. The world as it was meant to be."

"Unlimited wealth and happiness for all?"

"That's flippant. It's not that directly. The six old men explained everything on the first day in the underground chamber. The orbs represent wisdom and you can include knowledge and understanding under that heading. Just being in the vicinity of one of them would increase the wisdom of any person. But combined together, the three orbs would influence the whole planet with their power."

"That doesn't sound too impressive. So when the great day comes, we'd just get better marks at school?"

"No, no. Much more. Every person in the world will become much more intelligent, gain insight and understanding and clear their brain of bigotry and prejudice. Just think back through the evil acts of history. They were all conducted by people who would never have carried out if they had possessed true wisdom. Even natural disasters can be averted by the development of safeguards that a new breed of intelligent and compassionate scientists could develop."

"That makes sense, in a way."

John was now brimming with enthusiasm.

"I know it's right. The more I think about it, the more certain I am."

"So why didn't this David Codue start things off immediately?"

"That's the critical point. As I said, individually the orbs possess some power but it is very limited, just covering people in the vicinity. It's only when the three are together that they become really effective. They can only be combined by the Joiner. That was the name they used. This was the one the monks were waiting for. They were simply the guardians who were looking after the orbs until the Joiner arrived."

"And who or what is he, she or it?"

"That was never said. The monks only indicated that the arrival was well overdue. They had been doing the guardian job for all their life and knew they couldn't exist much longer. Their plan had been to use the three people to hide the orbs in different locations so they couldn't be found by anyone else. Then they would leave a clue so the Joiner could locate them when he or she finally came."

"I suppose it makes sense in a fantasy way. So where did these spheres originally come from?"

"That is completely unknown. The monks only said that the purpose was to generate the next big step forward for humankind, when the time was right."

"And that would be when this Joiner arrived."

"Yes. So you can now see the situation that David was in. The exact locations of the orbs had been lost but he did have a guide to the general area. He therefore began the Trysse, a group dedicated to locating the spheres and preserving them until the right time."

"So, in the light of recent events, we can assume that the Joiner has finally turned up."

John grinned with a strange fire in his eyes.

"Yes, exactly and we must do everything we can to help. First thing is to hand over the orb that we obtained in Brazil."

Eliza was about to reply when they heard the sound of voices in the hallway outside. She moved to the door and looked through the keyhole. A thickset, armed guard with one of the maids. The girl was talking.

"We can't do it up here. The Tutor will be furious if she finds out," she said with a fearful look around.

"Look, I just can't wait any longer. It's been weeks since we last got together," responded the guard.

"You know the Trysse rules. No sex between employees. I think that's fair as we need to dedicate ourselves to finding the orbs."

"But you understand how I feel about you. I'm being sent away to help with the search and I don't know when we'll see each other again."

"It will be such a wonderful day for the world when the three orbs are joined. We can wait until then."

She kissed him quickly and then they departed.

"The orb, Eliza?" asked John.

"I'll think about it," she replied.

11

Ford completed his log update and he reviewed it before uploading. The text included a summary before the pages of detail. It was succinct as usual.

'USA. Mariom Wander plus assistant Romnia Growmasse arrived at Frankloom ranch, Colorado. Met woman, Pheela Lipstrider. Believe sphere is in this state. 300+ people, purporting to be charity collectors, visiting everywhere. Two ex-gangsters leading armed team targeting antique dealers, memorabilia, dealers etc.'

He looked across at Locey who was sleeping naked on the bed. A body that any man would go through hell to reach. She began to stir.

"Ford, you're ogling me."

She gave a vampish smile and reorganised her limbs into a sultry pose.

"You're a good woman, Locey."

"And you're my own personal tiger. Have you made a plan? Where are we going?"

"The general answer is nowhere. We need to stay in Colorado and locate this sphere before they do."

"That sounds lovely, I'm looking forward to it. When do we start?"

"In 27 minutes and 13 seconds. Just time for you to shower and eat. Then we try to solve the garbled message in the letter we took from Wander in Brazil."

"I love puzzles. What was it? Something about trees smiling?"

"The leader said in the letter that it was a transcription of a telephone message from one of their agents who had located the sphere. But the line kept breaking up and they only got words or fragments of words. They believed that someone was deliberately putting interference on the call. Here's a copy I made."

He handed her a slip of paper with one line of text.

'Trees smiles best. Mike speaking. Down wick. Building. Biker search. Bearing hairs here ripped.'

She scanned it quickly.

"I'll give it my best think."

"Muse about it in the shower. I know how you sometimes get inspired."

Locey wandered back to the room thirteen minutes later and began to munch one of the sandwiches that Ford had ordered.

"Any ideas?" he asked.

She returned slowly from her reverie.

"What about?"

"The message."

"What message? I was thinking about running through the snow with a herd of polar bears. But I'd need to have bright blonde hair, just like that Pheela. Can we stop somewhere so I can get hair colouring?"

"Sure. I just wish I could make something of this text."

He waved the paper.

"Oh, that message. I think the words were mangled by the bad connection. It could say 'three miles west of Pikes Peak in a town called wick'. The three miles could be 23, 33 or whatever and the place could just have wick in its name somewhere. Then I'm guessing the last bit. Maybe something like 'building in birch, daring beer here shipped'."

Ford was speechless for seven seconds.

"Locey, you are a genius," he said finally.

"If I grew it longer it would flow in the air behind me, like the mane of a blonde lion. I would be called Locey the Bearwoman."

"I promise we'll get the hair dye. Maybe you shouldn't use it just yet. It would make you too noticeable.

"Every day I'd have a bear hugging session with each member of my herd."

"Right. I'll check the charts while you finish eating."

Ford began to scan a large-scale map of the state. Pikes Peak, follow it west. Something with 'wick' in the name. Nothing at 3 miles, 23, 33. Got it. Gestwick, about fifty three miles west. He quickly ran an internet search. Gestwick, population 294. One motel on the outskirts. That was it. A tiny place, buried away on the edge of the Rocky Mountains. He showed the location to Locey.

"Bear country," she breathed excitedly.

"So we can check if there's a birch building there and something to do with beer."

"I expect they'll be brown but all shapes and colours will follow the Bearwoman, from little cubs to huge grizzlies."

The highways were smooth, clear and free and it was under two hours when Ford turned off towards Gestwick. Then the route became a lot more difficult. The road narrowed until single lane, no wider than a lorry. They began a tortuous tour of seemingly every gully and crevice in the landscape.

"We needed a four-wheel-drive," Ford muttered tersely.

"Shout if you see a bear," responded Locey, peering earnestly out of the side window.

It took nearly an hour of bumpy driving before they reached the township. A dead-end road, Gestwick was ringed by mountains on the other three sides. Ford expected a run down, dusty, partial ghost town with decaying buildings and a bunch of ageing hardcore residents clinging to their remote existence.

Just about the complete opposite. Gleaming houses, carefully tended lawns and trees, streets that could have been vacuum cleaned two minutes ago. People of all ages in smart designer wear chatted happily in groups. A few turned and waved at them as they drove slowly past.

"Something not right here," Ford remarked.

"Many of the buildings are new or recently refurbished. The clothing they're wearing is expensive. We need to discover the source of their finances," responded Locey, now in smart mode.

"Right and we need to act casual. Mustn't look suspicious. We're on vacation, just touring around and took the turning to this place on an impulse."

"I'll find out. Women are good at that."

Ford followed a sign that read 'Siestra Motel'.

"A lot more than 294 people here," he observed as they coasted down an immaculate street lined with fresh, white houses on each side where groups of children played contentedly in the spacious front gardens.

The Siestra Motel was straight out of a catalogue. A central office surrounded by eight buildings. No drowsy, unshaven man with his feet on the counter but a smart young woman in a perfectly fitted light brown suit and a sunshine smile.

"Hello folks and welcome to Gestwick. May I offer you accommodation?"

"Thank you. We'd love to stay here. My partner and I were just driving around and thought we'd drop in. We are on vacation with nowhere to go in particular," said Ford.

"It's a lovely town with great views. I hope you're not looking for nightclubs and bars. We don't have those here."

"Not at all. We don't drink alcohol. What's the room price?"

The girl told him a figure that would have been cheap for a back street dump in one of the big city slums. After completing the formalities, she handed over a key.

"I'll escort you. Residence number six."

She led them to one of the surrounding buildings and opened the door.

"Jeez," Ford murmured as they entered.

The hallway was modern and beautifully furnished. Two double bedrooms, a lounge and separate kitchen diner. The windows displayed stunning views of the Rockies. Fresh bed linen and towels. It would have been a showpiece in Beverley Hills. The girl left them with a smile and returned to the office. Before Locey could speak, Ford hustled her into a bedroom.

"We need to get cleaned up. I must make a reminder. Promised to send a postcard to mother," he said loudly, pulling out a pocketbook and scribbling.

He handed the book to Locey who read his note. 'I think we're under observation. Careful.'

She gave a sweet smile and began to strip off her clothes, slowly and performingly.

"I need a shower," she said in a breathy voice.

Thirty minutes later they were cleaned and changed. Locey was now nearly bursting out of a low-cut pink top and knee length skirt.

"I'll go ask the lady where we can eat and see you later," she said.

Ford nodded. She would get more from the reception girl alone.

He left her at the office and ambled away. The motel was adjacent to the dwellings at the edge of town and he walked past a row of houses. Three young kids playing on the front lawn, an old man smoking a pipe on the veranda, two workmen repainting a garage, a naked woman waving at him from her kitchen, an old lady tending her rose bushes, a teen who was test driving her father's car. He smiled amiably at them all, ignored the come inside pose of the naked woman and continued to the centre of town.

The main street wasn't overburdened with establishments. A general store and a combined coffee house and diner. No bars, as the receptionist had said. He wandered into the general store, past a row of buckets and brooms arranged outside. Just an ordinary looking storefront but inside was very different.

To his left was a vast array of top line designer clothing for women and men. A food mini market on the right. Further back, he could see furniture and hardware. An escalator leading down displayed a list of departments on floors -1 and -2. Two levels underground. This was one very special general store, comparable with the best in New York.

"Good day. Can I assist you in any way, sir?"

A suited, smart young man approached with a welcoming expression.

"Hello. We're just passing through and I was looking for a few bottles of mineral water to take for our journey."

"In the far corner of the food store, sir. If you'd like to browse for other provisions, we will deliver them to the motel."

"That's great. Thank you."

Ford grabbed a trolley and mingled with the shoppers in the food hall. The checkout total was half the price expected and his purchases were already being wrapped and taken to the delivery van as he waited for his receipt. He carefully showed no surprise at anything, continuing to smile amiably and inconspicuously. As he left the store, he nearly collided with a passing woman, carrying a dog.

"I am so sorry," she said softly. Maybe mid thirties, auburn shoulder length hair, slim and beautiful.

"No, my fault."

She held up the tiny dog and it gave him a baleful stare.

"Not at all. I was talking to Poggle here and not looking where I was going. You must be a visitor here?"

"Yes, it's a beautiful town and everyone is so kind. So much rudeness in this country these days," he replied, not finding it difficult to say the right words.

Her eyes gleamed and she smiled very directly at him.

"Oh yes, you're so right. It's a great pleasure to meet such a nice man. My name is Belle."

"Peter. I was just getting mineral water. Drink it all the time. Occasional tea or coffee but never touch alcohol."

He thoughtfully embellished the favourable impression.

"Then I must get you coffee to compensate for my foolishness. Let's go this way."

A chance to find out about the town. He accompanied her to the coffee house but she passed it, turned a corner and walked towards a luxurious mansion in the next street.

"I'm afraid the house is very untidy but we'll use the upstairs lounge."

A housekeeper opened the door and nearly curtsied. She received a coffee request with a smile and Belle led him upstairs.

"Does your husband work in the town?" Ford asked casually.

"I'm not married, never have been. We don't do a lot of that here," Belle responded.

Ford was still thinking how to follow up the question without appearing over inquisitive when she opened the door and led him inside. A large bedroom.

"Lounge?" he enquired.

"We don't have an upstairs lounge. The housekeeper will serve coffee when we come downstairs."

She folded an arm around his neck and kissed him, wet and deep while her body squeezed impressively against him. Ford hoped she wouldn't notice the sound of his brain working like a hive of bees. He was not skilled in bedding women for a purpose. However, it appeared to come naturally and Belle was very hard to resist. Her fingers were now tracking to all parts of his body and her lips seemed happy to follow. Then she stepped back and pulled off her dress with her other garments following soon afterwards.

"Take off those clothes and join me," she whispered, kneeling on the bed.

He obeyed but retained his boxer shorts. Ford relied on instinct, plus some things he had learned from Locey. He now put some of them into practice. Thirty minutes later, she laid back, pink cheeked and glistening.

"You're such a nice man," she murmured contentedly.

"How can a lovely woman like you not be married?"

Now he was looking for answers.

"Oh, lots of competition in this town. Sixty nine percent female here."

"I think it's good to have independent women, not relying on their husbands for income."

"Yes, the Dividend stops all that. We don't have any stupid girls selling themselves to a rich husband. That's disgusting."

"So how does this Dividend work?"

She opened her eyes and giggled.

"We're not allowed to tell outsiders."

"Then how do I become an insider?" he asked with a cheeky grin.

"Well, I'm not sure I can say."

Ford pulled off the boxer shorts. Seventeen minutes later, her cheeks now glowing bright crimson and body shining with sweat, Belle sighed.

"I wish you lived here. I'd keep you occupied all day," she breathed.

"Maybe I should stay? Would I get this Dividend if I did?"

"Okay, I'll tell you. Everyone's income goes into one town fund. Then we each get a monthly dividend based on the years we've been here."

"But you all seem so wealthy?"

"The income is bigger than you could imagine. We have some very rich residents."

"A load of oil tycoons from the look of the place," Ford said with a deliberate laugh.

"Just two of those. Most are into finance, computer software and internet. The software people sell their work under licence. The core of computer processing firmware, web search engines and the like. The licenses are worth billions every year."

"You mean millions?"

"No, billions. Honestly."

"Like a Silicon Valley, all in one town?"

"Richer than that."

"And you must be a fashion model."

She smiled gratefully.

"No, I write software, firmware and hardware manuals. At least one every week in sixteen languages. It only takes me a few hours so I have plenty of leisure time."

"A manual in an hour? In all the languages?"

"If you stay here longer, you'd gain the ability. It begins to show after a week or two."

"Something in the water makes you smarter?"

"It's not the water. You just need to live here. I was high school educated and came to this place with my partner twelve years ago. He was killed in an accident but I stayed. After a couple of weeks I began to develop skills and knowledge that had been completely beyond me. Every day here I get more and more intelligent."

"How come the place isn't overrun with visitors?"

"Because everything I've said is a secret. No one is allowed to invite outsiders here, even for business. All dealings are done electronically or by telephone. Of course many residents regularly travel out of town on business visits. We're so out of the way that hardly anyone drives through. Food, clothing and anything else we need is conveyed here by our own fleet of vehicles and helicopters. Even the mail and carrier shipments come that way. No outsiders."

"Well, I'm glad I came. I guess you try to encourage any tourists to leave after a day or so?"

"It depends on what they discover here. Anyone who finds out too much is killed."

Ford felt the chill but maintained his grin.

"That seems a bit drastic."

"It's necessary. We allow them to leave and then send the hit team after them."

Chillier now.

"You have a hit team?"

"The best in the country. We pay the highest."

"Isn't anyone ever allowed to stay?" Ford asked, avoiding the obvious question about his own welfare.

"Yes but only if a resident recommends them. The person then goes before the Visionary. Only about one in fifty are accepted."

"Visionary?"

"I can't tell you more."

Ford didn't pursue.

"I assume the hit team get the other forty nine."

"Yes, that's how it works."

"So now you've told me all this, does that mean my death warrant is signed?"

Belle gave a whimsical look.

"It will be such a shame to kill someone with such interesting bedroom abilities. Of course, I'd also be executed for telling you."

"Just our secret then. I can guarantee I won't be telling the authorities, if that helps."

It was the truth.

"I'd like you to come here again," she said meaningfully.

"Is tomorrow too soon?"

He didn't plan to return but said the right words again.

"I'll be ready. That's another thing about living here. It makes you, well, you know, viagric."

"You're a lovely lady, Belle."

"Let's get coffee. You'll need to start building up for tomorrow. Set aside at least two hours."

Ford ambled back to the motel, tired but buzzing. He was trying to work out a way to tell Locey what he had learnt. Not for her benefit but she did have an ability to come up with answers. He couldn't communicate by speech. Even outside they could have tracker microphones and it would be suspicious if they saw him writing it all down on paper. Then he thought of a way but had to hope he could now manage it. He stopped off at the general store and found just what he needed.

Locey was waiting when he arrived back at the motel.

"You've been ages. I've got something important to tell you."

Ford gave her a warning look but she continued.

"Bears. There are bears here. Isn't that great?"

"Brilliant. I love them," responded Ford with relief.

"There's a place just nearby where they're often seen. We can go there."

Ford briefly considered a change of plan but it was too risky. They would be followed to the bear place with directional microphones.

"Let's do that. But first, I've really missed you.

"That's nice."

"I mean really missed you. I want to show you how much."

"Okay, show me."

"Well, not here. Maybe in bed?"

"Ford, you want sex. Why didn't you say so?"

Locey grabbed his hand and led him to the bedroom. Within seconds, she was lying naked on the sheets.

Ford smiled at her.

"I had an idea while I was out. You remember that stuff we tried in California. The body stuff?"

She obviously didn't know but bluffed perfectly.

"Oh yes. We should try again."

He produced two tubes of edible body paint, one chocolate and one strawberry that he had purchased in the store. Locey's eyes lit up.

"Wow. We'll try that," she said with excitement.

They had never used body paint before but the scheme was going well.

"Remember how we did it. Like kids under the bedclothes with a torch and we sort of reversed positions," Ford said with enthusiasm.

"Chocolate and strawberry, my two favourites. Hurry, I want to start now."

She crawled under the top sheet and held it up like a tent. Ford stripped, grabbed the torch he had taken from the car and climbed inside, his legs opposite her face. Then he began to write on her stomach in chocolate. When Locey saw what he was doing, she dutifully began to giggle and squeak while reading carefully. She took the strawberry tube and began to write questions on Ford's torso. The paint was nearly all gone when they finished.

"I want to lick first," cried Locey.

Another thirty minutes passed, lickingly. Ford had even surprised himself but was now definitely exhausted while Locey appeared invigorated.

"That was terrific. We'll be doing it again lots of times. Now let's go see bears."

The excursion proved almost fruitless. Locey closed her eyes and extended her arms, mouthing a silent invitation to all passing bears. One appeared at last, just visible next to a craggy outcrop, way above them. Locey jumped ecstatically.

"See, they come. They know that the Bearwoman is their leader."

The animal soon disappeared and they returned to the motel. Ford cooked a couple of packet meals and then bed. To sleep.

Next day, they walked into the town. Ford knew he was in a time box. He also noticed they were being tailed by a relay of people from old couples to young girls and wondered how long they had before the hit team moved in. One thing seemed certain. The sphere was here and he had to find it.

Locey's analysis had suggested a birch building but she had strawberried him that the receptionist had told her there was nothing like that here. They continued past the store and diner, and then turned off. The next street had a school with the kids lining up outside. All ages up to college. He assumed they were sent from here to the State University for final education.

Beyond the school was a church, or at least it looked like one. Traditional spire on typical slanted roof. But no markings at all, not even a notice board outside. He took Locey's hand and strolled casually towards the entrance, a solid wood door.

"I love to visit churches," he said loudly.

"Me too," added Locey.

Ford turned the iron handle and opened the door. A completely bare stone chamber with an arched entrance to the main hall at the end. Then he saw it. Cut into the stone above the arch. The Trysse symbol.

"I regret that we are not open to visitors."

Emerging from the archway was a tall man with white hair brushed tightly back and wearing a navy blue suit.

"Sorry, we just wandered in. We can't resist looking round churches," Ford responded amiably.

"I understand. However, I must ask you to leave."

A young couple entered behind them and stood expectantly, holding the outer door open.

"Yes, many apologies. We'll be going now," said Ford, obsequiously.

"I can see a bear," Locey cried, pointing past the grey-haired man.

He moved to block her line of sight and his eyes hardened.

"Go immediately."

"There's a bear inside and I want to see him," Locey said, more than stubbornly.

The young couple moved towards her and the woman grabbed her arm. A mistake to come between her and a bear. Locey hit her with a short Ki-Ting punch on the side of the jaw and she fell, unconscious. Ford stood back as the other two men moved in. The male half of the couple lasted four seconds before going down from two chops to his neck and the tall man found his height was not an advantage as it only made delicate areas more accessible to Locey's heel. He squealed with pain and doubled up, just in time to receive her other foot in his face. All three down and out.

"Maybe that wasn't the best way to make new friends," observed Ford but Locey was already racing inside the main hall of the church. He followed her and then took a deep breath.

This was not a church. An auditorium and a strange one. Rows of sumptuous, padded leather seats faced a raised stage area at the end. At the rear of the stage was the Trysse symbol, etched deeply on a massive stone slab, over four metres or about twelve foot high.

"Weird," Ford muttered and turned to see Locey hugging a bear. A dead, stuffed bear. There were three of them on each side of the hall. He walked to the nearest and read the engraved plaque.

'Norman. The second Visionary. 1874-1895'

He moved quickly round the others. Jack, Tom, Bill, Pete, Doug plus Norman. Visionaries one through six. Doug was the latest, expiring just eight years ago. The first was Tom, 1857-1874.

It made no sense. A mix of the Trysse and some sort of bear cult. Ford saw Locey was now clasping Pete as she worked her way through the six, hugwise.

"I'll just finish looking then we'd better get out of here before the hit team comes," he called to her.

Two large doors, each side of the stage. Need to check out. The one on the left was labelled 'Crypt' and the other 'Visionary'. He reached the one on the right just as it opened and a huge brown bear emerged.

Ford staggered back.

"What the hell?" he shouted.

"Hi, I'm Ted," said the bear.

Silence for a second.

"Wheeeeeee!" screamed Locey and rushed towards the massive furry creature, curving arms round it and pressing her head against its stomach.

"You wish to be called Locey the Bearwoman," Ted remarked. Its voice was low and guttural but very clear.

She raised her face in delight.

"Yes, yes. That's me. I love you, Ted."

"You have an attractive bosom," the bear observed.

"Really? I'm so pleased you like it."

Ford regained the power of speech but couldn't believe what he said next.

"Listen bear, that's my lady you're talking to. Back off on the personal comments, if you don't mind."

"No problem, just being honest."

"Don't be so jealous, Ford. Ted was only being nice to me. Do you realise what this means? I can understand their language. I just knew I had it inside me, I must have been born with it."

Ford exchanged a look with Ted.

"I guess some of your magic has rubbed off on me. He seems to be talking English. Ask him how his words are recognisable to me."

"Yes, okay. How does Ford understand you?" She spoke slowly, in syllables.

Ted made an effort to sigh, although that didn't come easy to a bear.

"Bears who have been born in the immediate vicinity of Gestwick since the mid-19th-century, possess enhanced abilities. The first was Tom. Our history relates that he began to remember and interpret words used by people he overheard. After a couple of years he understood a wide vocabulary. Speech was more difficult, the bear's vocal chords were initially very limited. However, after five years, Tom could reproduce a large number of words and by the time he became the first Visionary, he could converse very well. Subsequent generations have further perfected our ability."

Locey looked downcast.

"So it's not just me who can understand?"

"Truthfully, no but I can discern a unique, innate talent in you. There is no doubt that you are exceptional."

Locey beamed and hugged the huge beast again.

"So what does Visionary mean?"

"Every generation, one bear is born in this vicinity with certain powers. Beyond anything possessed by humans."

"What powers?"

"You would represent them as intellectual superiority. I am more intelligent than anyone around here, bear or human."

"Can you predict the future?"

"No, of course not. That question indicates you are far below the mental level of my people here in Grestwick."

"So do you live in this place?" enquired Ford.

"This building was constructed specially for the Visionary, the spiritual leader of this community."

"What is it about this area that has such an effect on the residents?"

"The answer to that is no one knows. Hello, looks like we have company."

The bear gestured towards the door. A dozen figures, wearing body protectors and badges, poured into the hall. Each was carrying an automatic weapon.

"Raise your arms vertically and legs apart," shouted the commander.

"Help us, Ted," Locey cried, arms still clinging to the bear.

Ted grabbed the back of her pink top and dragged her away from him. She staggered backwards and fell. As claws are not perfectly designed for holding garments, the action ripped the top from her, leaving just a tiny white uplift bra as cover.

"Not bad. Not bad at all," remarked Ted, staring at the twin mounds.

Within seconds, the armed team had them pinned and handcuffed. Locey was quivering with fury.

"Ted, you're an evil creature. I understand now. You're a renegade, you're not one of our clan. We call you poo bear."

"For gods sake, shut her up," the bear said and a woman obediently stuck a strip of tape across Locey's mouth.

"We'll take them to the reform centre, if the Visionary approves," the commander announced.

Ted nodded.

"Sure, that's fine. Kill the man but I'll have the girl if you can find a way to mute her."

Ford and Locey were hustled from the building, down a couple of streets and into an ordinary looking house. The exterior was a facade with the real structure inside. Guardrooms, cells and many other unlabelled rooms. They were pushed into a cell and the handcuffs removed. Without speaking, the guards walked out and slammed the door shut.

Ford understood the strategy. The cell would be riddled with cameras and microphones and any scrap of information they divulged would be recorded. He hoped Locey would realise the situation.

"That renegade bear was a disgrace. Wait till I tell the others in the clan," she said emphatically.

"Maybe he's just been led astray by the people around him."

"When we put him on trial, he'll get his chance to explain."

Ford shrugged.

"We just seem to be unlucky. Two people having a nice tour of the country and we end up here. I've got no intention of talking about anything to an outsider but this town seems a bit paranoid about keeping their secrets. It's just an ordinary place that happens to have an unusual animal."

"A horrible bear."

"Even if we told anyone about it, they wouldn't believe us. All I want to do is get back in the car and tour round for a few more days."

Locey nodded.

"Yes, it's silly to keep us here when we haven't done anything."

"Keep smiling. We'll play some word games while we wait."

Ford was satisfied that the conversation gave exactly the image he wished to convey. He tried to anticipate the next move of their captors, when they found that nothing was to be gained from observation. Probably split them apart and try the 'your friend has told us all' trick.

"Listen Locey. I saw a film about two innocent people being captured. They split them in different cells. The plan was to tell each of the pair that the other had revealed everything."

"But we've got nothing to reveal."

"I know but they must think we do. I only mention it in case you were puzzled if they told you I'd disclosed something."

Ford grinned inside. Going well and Locey was on his wavelength. Then, out of nothing, it came to him. He knew where the sphere was.

The last part of the garbled message had been given as 'Building. Biker search. Bearing hairs here ripped.' Locey had proposed the equally puzzling 'building in birch, daring beer here shipped'. But now we knew it, knew it exactly.

'A building like a church. Bear in there. Sphere in the crypt.'

The crypt. The door on the stage opposite the bear's living area.

12

The Joiner was relatively satisfied. One orb found and closing in on another. Now it just needed to manoeuvre these human puppets to succeed in finding the third. Easy to kill and replace them if they failed.

Eliza and John were in hiding on the top floor of the large house by the Thames. It appeared that this level was rarely visited by the occupants of the house but Eliza knew they couldn't remain here. She moved closer to John and spoke carefully.

"Let me see if I understand. From what you told me of this book you read, the situation has reversed."

"Yes, completely."

"Your new idea is that the Trysse are good guys, trying to bring peace and prosperity to the world. You were telling me that David Codue was the man who started it."

"Yes. The situation was that he didn't have the precise location of the orbs but knew the general area they were in. One in Brazil, one in central USA and the other somewhere in England. That information had to be kept safe, ready for the arrival of the Joiner, the only one who had the ability to merge them together and give universal wisdom to the world. So David started the Trysse in 1851. He selected two others he could trust with the secret and they have passed it down until the present day."

"So the current head of the organisation is the one they call the Leader?"

"Yes, that must be right but I don't know his or her name. The important thing is that the Joiner has now arrived and we have got to help. As I said, the first thing to do is to hand over the orb from Brazil that you hid somewhere."

"I'm not doing that yet. One sphere is no use to them anyway. But I will help to find the other two, starting with the one here in England."

"I still think we should give them the first orb as a gesture of goodwill."

"No. I'm still not totally convinced. For a group on an altruistic mission, they are pretty underhand and violent."

"They've just been resisting our attacks. I think they believe we're enemies, trying to sabotage the merging of the orbs. Don't forget that we've initiated burglaries, assaults and deceptions against them."

"The answer is still no and we need to get moving. If you suddenly approached them and said you're on their side, they wouldn't believe you anyway."

John looked somewhat crestfallen but gave a wry smile.

"Okay Eliza. We'll find the English orb. I'm sure they'll believe us when we hand over two of them."

"I think I know where to look for it."

John almost jumped.

"What? You know? Why didn't you tell me before?"

"I said I think I know. To identify the place, I need to talk to Sandra. I've got to be honest, John. Ever since she welcomed us to the house, I felt a real attraction to her. You understand."

"Oh, right. Well, now we know she's a friend. What information do you need from her?"

"I'll have to talk to her about that."

John ruffled his hair.

"Maybe we can try to get to her tonight."

Eliza smiled mysteriously.

"Yes, let's wait for a while."

39 minutes later, they heard voices. Two people had emerged from the elevator. Sandra, accompanied by a young maid.

"Leave me alone for an hour, girl. I just need to check these rooms as possible new accommodation for the trainees."

The maid nodded and departed in the elevator, leaving Sandra in the centre of the hall. She began to walk towards the room where they were hiding.

"It's our chance," whispered John.

They hid behind the door and pounced as she entered. Eliza found a small revolver in Sandra's pocket and pressed it against her head.

"No sound or I'll kill you."

The woman nodded obediently and Eliza turned to John.

"You have to leave us. I need to be alone with her."

She whispered in Sandra's ear and the woman began to remove her clothing.

John looked uncomfortable.

"Okay, I think I understand. I'll go to the lower floors and try to get more information."

He left quickly without looking back.

Eliza waited until the door was closed.

"Lie on the bed," she instructed and Sandra complied, posing in her underwear.

Eliza moved to the door and locked it. Then she slid on to the bed alongside her, propping herself on one elbow with the pistol in her other hand.

"Put that gun down and I'll give you an experience you'll never forget," Sandra offered invitationally.

"I'd rather make love with a chainsaw, you scumbag witch."

That changed the atmosphere and the woman's expression moved from 'anything goes' to 'where's everything gone'.

"What are you saying?"

"You told me when we spoke before that you'd try and find a way to get us to join the Trysse. John has just told me about the book he found in your library."

"The Book of Codue? Everything in it is true."

"Stop it, Sandra. It's not just the book. I'm sure that was planted for him to read. You know he possesses the least resistance of any of us and you've got into his brain somehow. You've also been listening into our conversation. We had the choreographed couple arriving and then you conveniently appeared as soon as I mentioned your name."

Sandra's eyes sparked like diamonds but not with fear. They held only fervent belief.

"Eliza, I don't care if you believe this or not. I tell you again that the book is absolutely genuine. There are other records to prove it. Secondly, you surely can't doubt the power of the orbs. You saw one in Brazil, surely that convinced you? I do admit to a little deception. It's true that I let John escape and then release you. I also influenced him to come to this room where we have hidden microphones. The people you saw earlier and my visit were arranged as a result of your conversation. The Trysse would much prefer to be a peaceful organisation but we have had to defend ourselves against a number of enemies."

"Like Hagg Snowmine?"

"She is not normal. Got it into her mind that we had killed her lover. Now she roams around the world, attacking and sabotaging our efforts. She's just a solo lunatic, not like your Ford Rampon."

"Why is he different?"

Sandra paused before replying.

"You know the true history of the orbs. My personal belief is that they have been on earth since its creation to provide humanity with a great step forward when the time was right. That moment was when the Joiner arrived. But there have always been two forces at work on this planet. Good and evil, fighting a perpetual battle for domination. The agents of evil are our enemies and I'm certain that Ford is one of them."

"He doesn't look like a demon."

"They never do. He is only the latest in a series that goes back in history. Even the original monks had to guard the orbs with their lives."

Eliza put the gun on the bedside table.

"This may come as a surprise but I believe you are sincere."

Sandra smiled and then kissed Eliza gently on the cheek.

"I'm pleased. I knew you were not another like Ford."

"The main mystery now for me is the identity of the Joiner."

"I simply don't know that."

"Then how do you know it's the real thing?"

"Two reasons. One is that our Leader told us that the arrival had been announced in a sort of vision. Now I know that sounds silly but let me explain. Eleven months ago, the Leader was sleeping one night and saw three blue lights hovering in a triangle above the bed. It was impossible to tell if it was dream or reality. A voice came, announcing that the Joiner was presenting a gift to the heads of the Trysse and would be with us in exactly twenty eight days. Then the lights disappeared."

"You're right. It doesn't sound too convincing."

"But there's something else. The vision was so clear that it was unlike any fantasy but the Leader fell unconscious immediately afterwards. On waking in broad daylight the next day, three tiny pyramids had appeared on the bed. The Leader retained one and gave the others to the two senior members of the Trysse, Mariom Wander and myself."

An unpleasant expression crossed Sandra's face as she mentioned Mariom.

"This still seems like a fairy story."

"The Leader then was capable of deceit but when you have experienced the influence of the pyramid, you know it is genuine."

"So did this Joiner actually arrive, a month later?"

"I'm sure of that. Exactly twenty eight days after the pyramids manifested, the Leader, Wander and myself were told to wait together and to place our pyramids on the table in front of us. At the very moment predicted, they turned a brilliant white, so bright it was impossible to look at them. Then we all heard a voice. It just said three words. 'I am here'. We all believed then."

"But you didn't see this Joiner?"

"No. The Joiner has never been seen by anyone."

"What? So not even the three heads of the Trysse know what he, she or it looks like?"

"We don't need to. We're aware of the presence, guiding us to fulfil the cause. That is all we need to know."

"You implied earlier that you changed Leaders?"

"Yes. Soon after the arrival, we thankfully deposed the corrupt person who headed the Trysse. The Joiner exposed their crooked activities in direct contact with Wander and myself and we took action. Subsequently, the replacement was personally selected by the Joiner. We were told to be at a certain location where the chosen one would present themselves. They were to be given the pyramid that we had taken from their predecessor. Since the change, everything has been so much better."

"I would have thought that you or Mariom would have wanted the job. Weren't you upset?"

"I can't answer for Wander but I never sought to head the Trysse."

There was meaning in her response.

Eliza shrugged

"Spheres and pyramids. Sounds like a geometric heaven. Without sounding cynical, your Leader could just have got them in a shop and put on a light show for you."

Sandra smiled and shook her head.

"You need to see one."

She reached for the spherical gold pendant she was wearing and unscrewed the lower half. Eliza saw something glinting inside that Sandra tipped into her palm. A tiny pyramid. As soon as it made contact with her flesh, it began to glow like a beacon. A dazzling blue light. Sandra gazed as if it were her newborn baby.

"It shines blue when touching one who follows the Trysse. The more you believe, the stronger the light. For those who don't understand, it remains transparent but when it makes contact with an agent of evil, the colour is bright red."

"You use it to determine the loyalty of people?"

"John has touched it. It turned blue."

"Now you would like to test me?"

"It's your choice," Sandra challenged but with a smile.

She watched as Eliza reached out her hand and then placed the pyramid in the centre of her palm. Nothing for a second and then it began to glow, stronger and stronger. A brilliant blue.

"I knew it. I was sure your spirit was with us," Sandra cried with delight as she carefully replaced the pyramid in the pendant.

"So you're not going to lock me up now?"

"The answer is behind you."

Eliza knew before she turned. John stood handcuffed between two men who were pressing guns against his head. She displayed no emotion.

"That's nice. I've just been given the blue light by your pyramid and you're now trying to kill us. Haven't we proved we are on your side?"

Sandra rose from the bed and dressed quickly.

"I have just one question. You told John you knew the location of the orb. Was that just a bluff to get me up here?"

"I must admit it was."

"I thought so. I know your spirits are with us but you can only hinder rather than help. The leader's real instructions were to test both of you but ensure you were incarcerated. All our efforts must be directed to locating the orb and you are just a distraction."

"Back to prison, then," said Eliza with apparent unconcern.

"I'm sorry."

John looked disappointed as they were led to the cells.

"They caught me. I told them we were here to help but they wouldn't listen."

"That's life."

This time they were both placed in the same cell, an upmarket version of the previous ones. It even possessed a separate shower room with toilet.

"What do we do now?" John asked as they rested on the separate beds each side of the chamber.

"In the absence of one of Locey's herds of lions, I don't know. It's a shame as I really think we could have helped them find the orb."

"Do you have some ideas then?"

"Better not to discuss it. They could be listening into this conversation."

"Okay. We'll just have to hope they let us out then."

A meal came through the double doors as before. Time passed. Another meal. Thirty minutes later the outer door opened again. Then the inner door. A single guard entered, tall and lean.

"You will come with me," said Hagg Snowmine.

John started to speak but Eliza slapped his arm. They followed the tall figure into the corridor and along to the elevator, this time stopping on the ground floor. Hagg raised her gun and prodded them forward into the large hallway. Keeping to the perimeter, they moved round to a door at the rear. Then through an entrance chamber and out of the back of the house.

"The red car," Hagg muttered in her icy voice.

A pair of armed guards moved to block their path.

"What are you doing?" asked one.

"Special instructions. Prisoner relocation."

"Three people are required to supervise the movement of two prisoners."

"I said special instructions. From the top. You are risking your life by interfering."

The man was disconcerted but pulled out a communicator.

"I'll just check."

He didn't make the call. A pistol butt cracked into his the side of his head and she repeated the procedure on his companion.

"Move. Fast," Hagg shouted and ran for the assembly of cars parked in a separate tarmac area. She travelled like an Olympic sprinter with her long strides and it was a couple of seconds before the others joined her at the red car.

"In the back. Get low and hide under a blanket," the woman instructed.

Eliza pushed John inside and scrambled on top of him. She dragged a tartan blanket from the back seat to cover them as the car moved forward. After a minute, they stopped and she heard voices. Must be the security at the outer gate.

"Where are you going?"

"A special mission."

"We haven't been notified."

"Emergency."

"You will remain here while we check."

Eliza knew what was coming. Three-two-one and the vehicle shuddered as Hagg hit the accelerator. No stopping now. Tyres screaming. Engine revving. The car rocketed forward. It spun right and then left. Another twenty seconds and right again. The journey continued for another fourteen minutes with the two bodies in the back rolling like grains in a sugar shaker. Suddenly they came squealing to a halt and Hagg called to them.

"Get out fast."

Eliza clambered from the vehicle then helped John who was rubbing a bruise on his forehead. They were in a small lane surrounded by thick trees. A small white delivery van was parked a few strides away.

"In the back," instructed Hagg.

They obeyed and the journey began again. More space now and they travelled at normal speed. It was another twenty minutes before they stopped. The rear doors were opened and Eliza and John emerged at the side of a typical suburban house. Entering through the back door, they walked through to a comfortable lounge.

"Don't forget that Sandra told us this woman's completely mad," John whispered.

"I don't care. She got us out of the cell."

Hagg looked across at them.

"My hearing is very acute," she remarked sharply.

Even the new John appeared a little uncomfortable with that.

"I'm just repeating what they said to me."

"They told you I was a dangerous lunatic?"

"Well, sort of."

Hagg shrugged, unconcerned.

"They have ways of influencing your mind."

Eliza smiled at her.

"I want to thank you for saving us again. We'll try to avoid calling on you next time."

"I was watching the building. I knew you were being held inside."

"We did discover some information there. The history of the Trysse. Do you know it?"

"Yes."

"They said your lover had died. Is that why you're fighting them?"

"Not a lover, a companion. He was killed by Mariom Wander."

"Really?" Eliza prodded for details.

"Wander did the killing and Sandra Inkell helped her."

"I don't believe you," announced John in a voice that shimmered with anger.

"Your judgemental abilities are impaired."

Eliza remained calm.

"How come you were involved with them?" she asked.

"I was the Leader."

An astonished silence.

"What?" John almost shouted.

"I was the previous Leader of the Trysse. I had a personal secretary and we were very close. Wander and Inkell were the senior members, jealous of his status. They killed him."

"You led them and now you fight them?"

"Yes. After I left, the two murderers became joint senior officials and subsequently, the present Leader took over."

"What exactly happened to your secretary?"

"He was killed in a supposed car accident in England. The vehicle was sabotaged. Went off a cliff road. I suspected Wander but found she had already influenced the other members against me. They tried to assassinate me twice. So I left. Combating them ever since."

"You know the present Leader?"

"No, I don't think it's anyone I knew in the organisation. I believe it is an outsider who joined the Trysse soon after I left."

"And I guess you've never seen the Joiner?"

"No. I was there at the arrival but only heard a voice."

John interrupted.

"I think you're doing the wrong thing. The merging of the spheres is vital to the future of humanity. Even if your story is correct, it's just one or two bad eggs in the group. The true purpose must not be delayed."

"Perhaps you're right," Hagg said unexpectedly.

"So you also want these spheres to be merged?" enquired Eliza.

"I have never seen one of the orbs. But I believe you located one in Brazil. The Book of Codue tells us that the merging will result in a universal enhancement of wisdom. That would be good. I am also aware of the power of the three pyramids that were bestowed by the Joiner. I possessed one for a short period before it was taken from me and I know that they give almost hypnotic powers over others."

"I thought they were just for a loyalty test?"

"The pyramids have other capabilities."

"I still don't really understand why you are attacking the Trysse," said John.

"I can't explain exactly. I just know that the orbs must not fall into the hands of the present Leader and those two witches."

"That seems a bit vague," John responded with a cynical expression.

"I headed the organisation partly because of my powers and sensitivity. I have certain abilities you should not underestimate."

Eliza broke up the increasingly frigid conversation.

"Our reasons are unimportant. We all have one objective, to locate the missing ball in England."

Hagg nodded.

"I know you have already secreted the one from Brazil. That suits me at the moment. We do have the same objective but I will not allow you to hand over any of the orbs to the Trysse. Remember that."

Without further comment, Hagg turned and left the room. They heard the sound of a vehicle and saw a small blue car driving away from the house.

"Strange woman. I think Sandra was right," remarked John.

"I'm happier to be free than stuck in a cell. We need to decide what to do. I think that we'd increase our chances if we split up."

He looked surprised.

"What? No, it's much better to be together. We're a team."

"It could get dangerous and I really don't want you hurt."

"Not long ago, that would have convinced me. Now I feel stronger and more confident than ever before. I've found my mother and share her desire to achieve a breakthrough for the world. Nothing frightens me now."

In a wooded area behind the house, the Akur waited patiently. Nightfall would be here soon. It enjoyed killing in the darkness.

13

Ford sat on the bed of the cell and composed plans. He was imprisoned with Locey in Grestwick, the town apparently under the spiritual leadership of Ted, the talking bear. He now knew the location of the missing orb. It was in the crypt of the pseudo-church that also housed Ted but he couldn't get that information to Locey at the moment as they were sure to be monitored.

"You're thinking," Locey observed with unerring accuracy.

"Yes."

"I've already thunk. The Bearwoman cannot be held here like a common criminal. I'm wondering if I should summon a posse of bears to get us out."

"I expect our jailers are listening into this conversation."

"I don't care. I know where the sphere is and I'm not telling them," Locey almost shouted.

Smart, thought Ford.

"Quiet, Locey. They'll hear you."

It was just two minutes before the door opened. Two tall men with the officer who had captured them earlier. Each was armed with a pistol.

"We've come for the girl," he announced tersely.

Locey looked at him with scorn.

"I go where I wish. All of this land belongs to the Bearwoman."

Ford noticed that she was edging back to the far end of the cell and the guards would have to break formation to reach her. She didn't need to explain what to do. The officer aimed the gun at him while motioning to the others to get Locey.

She began.

"Look, I'll prove I'm the leader of the animal kingdom."

She gave an imperious look while unbuttoning her shirt. That got the attention of the two men. She pushed her chest forward to display the crude lion's head pendant but the men's eyes were looking somewhere nearby. Ford hadn't seen her next manoeuvre before. Both fists rose simultaneously, striking the upper throats of the two men. They gasped for breath while her arms continued in an arc, descending, with fingers now extended, on the back of their necks. An impeccable Zet Kittu movement.

The officer couldn't help being distracted. Contraction followed distraction as Ford levered a foot directly into his groin. He squealed, kneeled and then keeled after a heel struck him directly in the face.

"They won't be allowed in my clan," stated Locey, buttoning up.

"You're sensational. Let's move," replied Ford, leading her through the doorway.

He knew the house was full of guards but guessed that prisoners were not a frequent occurrence and security could be lax. He was right. They had entered an empty corridor and now moved in the opposite direction to the way they had entered, hoping to find a back exit. There it was, just off the end of the passageway. A simple fire door. Eight minutes later they were on the edge of town, concealed in a thicket of bushes.

"I'm calling the bears now," Locey announced with a grim expression.

"Maybe we should also consider alternative plans?"

"I've decided."

She closed her eyes and pressed fingers against both temples, mouthing unidentifiable words. Meanwhile, Ford was preparing a plan to get to the crypt. The orb was there and he had to have it. He had allowed Eliza to take the first one but knew he would be able to get it from her when he needed to. Then just one more to find. The one in England.

He worked out the details of his plan. Wait until night and then find a side entrance to the pseudo-church. The bear could be taken out by simply locking or blocking the door to his quarters. They would have to overcome any other resistance quietly as they would need to get out again when they had the sphere. He turned to repeat his plan to Locey who was still in a monk like concentration.

Then the bears came.

A crashing through the undergrowth nearby and a huge brown animal emerged. Others were already in the streets. Locey rose like a goddess and strode purposefully towards the centre of town.

"Follow me," she shouted. The message was for the bears but Ford also complied. He knew where she was heading. The guard building where the main opposition was housed. He found himself amongst a mass of hairy bodies trundling to the place where they had recently been imprisoned.

When Locey was about twenty metres away, a man emerged from the house. Impossible to imagine what went through his mind when he saw the massive bear throng heading towards him. It took him three seconds to reach for his gun. Too long. Locey hammered him to the ground and the heaving multitude of furry creatures charged inside.

Ford ran round to the fire door at the back to intercept any escapees. He waited. And waited. Noises from the interior but no one came out. He returned to the front door, just as Locey emerged. She was smiling like Venus and her eyes shone brilliantly. Barely glancing at Ford, she turned to her followers.

"Now we'll get the renegade."

They were away again. Ford couldn't count the number of bears following her. More seemed to be joining all the time. They charged across the town like a herd of unstoppable buffalo, but meaner. He sprinted to get ahead of them and saw various residents, some with guns, attempt to halt the stampede. They were brushed aside without a shot fired.

The lumbering mob cleared everything in their path. Lampposts, bins, bushes, bikes and even cars were scattered as if by a snow plough gone feral.

Eventually, they reached the pseudo-church. No one in sight. Ford got to the outer door first and glanced back. It was a sight to make a block of granite tremble. Locey ran just ahead of the fearsome horde, a strange radiance bursting from her. The bears looked mean and purposeful and Ford was thankful he was on their side.

Three people stood in the entrance hall. The tall, white-haired man they had met and two more guards. They didn't look as if they were enjoying their job of protecting of the building.

"Run, you idiots. They'll tear your throat out," yelled Ford.

He hoped that was a lie but it had the necessary effect. The three abandoned their weapons and ran outside in blind panic. They veered away from the approaching throng and bolted for the forest.

Ford continued into the main chamber and climbed up on the raised stage area. He was just reaching for the door of the crypt when he heard the bear.

"How the hell did you escape?" asked Ted.

"I wouldn't want to be in your paws," responded Ford.

Astonishment is not often seen in a bear's face but Ted revealed all of that when Locey rushed in, followed by the hairy horde.

"Get him," she cried and Ted was quickly surrounded by a growling, hirsute throng.

Then the gang paused, heads turned to Locey. She raised an arm.

"Now take him away. I leave him in your custody. It is not for me to judge and he must be tried by his peers. I have one farewell message to you, my faithful followers. I love you all."

She shouted the last four words and blew kisses to the heaving mass of creatures. The response was amazing. All the bears rose on their back legs and growled loudly. A cry of unity and loyalty. Then they left, shuffling the whining Ted in their midst.

Ford was speechless and immobile. His eyes were fixed on Locey as she gazed at the departing mob. It was maybe twenty seconds before she turned to him and he saw that the magical light was no longer in her eyes.

"Damn. I forgot to take my clothes off. I should have led them naked."

"Locey, you always amaze me. You really are the best."

She gave him an enticing look.

"A girl likes to impress her man sometimes."

He kissed her. A long kiss. Eventually Ford stepped back.

"I know where the orb is. In the crypt."

He opened the door to reveal a flight of stone steps leading down into darkness. He found a row of switches just inside the door and flicked them all. Lights came on but they showed only steps stretching far below. He began to descend with Locey close behind.

"Watch out for killer bats," she called.

"And vampires," she added.

"Okay, thank you. This goes down a helluva way."

The steps finally ended in a flat area but the only exit was a second flight leading further down. Then a third. The shaft they were descending was clearly lit with modern fluorescents embedded in the walls. The main difference was that the air had become warmer and strangely dry as they went deeper. More steps. Like going down to Hades. Now it was really hot and perspiration glistened on Ford's face.

"How much lower?" he muttered.

"I think I see a door," Locey observed perkily.

Ford guessed they were well over a hundred metres below the surface now and at the top of another long flight of steps. Thankfully, they finished this time in a flat area that appeared to be the end of the shaft and he could see a single unprepossessing oak door against the far wall.

By the time they reached it, the temperature had risen again. Like standing next to an open furnace. Ford was now bathed in sweat, his clothing sticking uncomfortably. Locey looked as if she had just been in a shower and her upper garments were just about invisible. He attempted to ignore the distraction and approached the door, expecting an antiquated lock. No lock at all. The door opened smoothly and he stepped back four hundred years. A medieval stone room about thirty metres square. Blazing torches hung on the walls but how they were kept burning was a mystery. Three simple tombs, oblong blocks of stone. Otherwise bare.

"Got to be in one of these," he remarked.

"Maybe the inscriptions will help," Locey responded and walked to the furthest tomb.

"It just says 'Shine on Tinto'. Weird."

Ford checked another.

'Shine on Paddite'. Very informative.

They looked together at the third.

'Shine on Birto'.

"They like to shine on people. Tinto, Paddite, Birto. Who would they be?" Locey enquired.

"Okay. Let's assume someone was trying to conceal an orb here. I guess they'd hide it in one of these tombs then maybe put something else in the others that wouldn't be nice. Maybe lethal. That way, if anyone picked the wrong one, they wouldn't be alive to get the orb."

"It's going to be sheer luck with the odds two to one against us."

"If it's pure chance, I'd pick Paddite. Birto and Tinto sound similar so I'd take the odd one."

"Let's open it then," Locey cried and began to push at the heavy stone slab covering the tomb.

Ford still had an uneasy feeling but added his muscle to the operation. It took a couple of minutes to move the slab just a short distance, revealing a dark recess beneath. Then Locey spoke again.

"They're anagrams and this is the wrong one," she said with a pained smile.

"What?"

"The first, 'Shine on Tinto' means 'not in this one'. 'Shine on Birto' is 'orb in this one'. We should have chosen it."

"So what does 'Shine on Paddite' on this one mean?"

"Open this one and die."

"Hell."

Ford started to push the heavy stone back but it was too late. Maybe hell was the right word. Something was inside the tomb and it was now trying to get out. Something pale and mucous appearing in the crack they had opened. Not pleasant. Not pleasant at all.

"Don't touch it," Ford yelled and Locey stepped back to the wall.

"What is it?"

He didn't answer. The glistening white matter had now fully emerged and hovered above the stone tomb. Then it reformed. Very pleasant. Very pleasant indeed. A shimmering angel in purest white with a large pair of wings folded behind its back. Fair hair flowed to its shoulders and the face was a vision of benevolent serenity.

"You seek the orb."

Not a question. The voice was melodious but powerful.

"Yes. We have come to take it," Ford responded, screening his eyes against the radiance.

"You may not be worthy."

"Then how would you judge us?"

"I do not judge. Merit is within you. I simply read your soul."

"And if we are unworthy?"

"Then I must end your earthly existence. The orb has higher import than a single human."

"Two humans," said Locey, stepping forward with a smile.

"Are you really an angel? What's your name?" she continued.

It turned to her.

"Our existence reflects your spirit. We cannot be denoted by simple words."

"Then check my soul first. Can you do it through my clothes or should I undress?"

A momentary hesitation before it responded.

"Do not remove your garments. I will study you."

Locey held up a hand.

"Wait. Before you start, how is it that an angel can be confined in a stone box? I thought you could pass through anything?"

Another hesitation. Longer.

"This is not for discussion. My assessment begins now."

"Assessment means judgement. You said you wouldn't do that."

"Cease these spurious words. Your life is in my hands."

To emphasise the point, it produced a short sword that shimmered with pulsating radiance.

"Then it's simply not fair. You're saying you'll check my soul and if you don't like it, you'll kill me. Where's the justice in that?"

By now, Locey's hand had moved to her hip. Ford cringed and even the angel seemed uncomfortable.

"I have examined your spirit and decided you must die. Do not dispute the verdict of we higher ones."

"That confirms it. You're as bad as that bear. If you're an angel at all, you must be another renegade. You've got no right to kill me."

"The decision is made."

The entity raised the sword over its head but it didn't descend. Instead, the angel began to emit a screeching whistle that jarred the hearing. Ford fell to his knees, hands clamped over his ears but he saw Locey still standing.

"So that's how you do it. The sword is just for show then. Right."

She took a deep breath and screamed directly at the glowing figure. A piercing, sibilant scream but Ford found the pain was lessening. Locey's voice was overcoming the killing sound of the entity. But how long before her breath ran out? Five seconds, ten seconds. The two sounds continued, reverberating round the chamber. Fifteen, twenty seconds. Locey's eyes shone with determination but she was weakening. Her scream was not so strong now as she struggled for reserves of oxygen. Her face had turned crimson. Ford knew she couldn't last. He saw her swaying on her feet and reaching the end.

A sudden crack and the angel exploded. It simply fell to pieces like a pricked balloon of white jelly and the fragments just disappeared into the air. Nothing left except merciful silence.

"Locey," Ford shouted and ran to her.

She was on her knees now, wheezing for air in great wheezing gulps. But he saw her smiling. Smiling in triumph.

"Now you're taking on the angels," he said with a smile.

"That was no angel," she gasped.

Her breath was coming easier now and her face reverting to normal colour.

"I'd agree there. It was trying to kill us sonically. Fry the brain eventually. You're the hero again," he remarked.

"Not me. Any girl would have done the same."

"Want to try the other tomb?"

"Yes. We deserve to get the ball after that."

Moving to the Birto tomb, they began to push the top again. Ford saw it as soon as a small gap appeared and they continued their efforts until it was a quarter open. Enough. He reached down and picked up the carved wooden box then handed it to Locey.

"You did all the work," he said.

She held it carefully in both hands with a beaming smile.

"We did it together."

"Maybe we should go now."

Locey looked quizzical.

"That pretend angel. Where did it come from?" she asked.

He knew the answer but embellished his response.

"I've been thinking about that. I can't believe that any residents of the town set it up and it certainly wasn't the bear. My best guess is that it was a manifestation created by the orb. A sort of defence mechanism. We know these things have strange powers."

"Well we've got it now. What happens to the town when it's gone?"

"I'd have to guess again. The orb has obviously imparted wisdom and intellect to the locals. I wouldn't think that those that have it will now lose it but future generations will grow up like normal people. In some years it'll be the same as any other small town in central USA."

"And the renegade bears?"

"I assume Ted will be the last of them."

"Good. My followers will be fair and just with him."

"So let's get out of Grestwick now."

Locey checked her sodden garments.

"We both need a shower first."

Back in town, Locey was the centre of attention. Everyone moved well back out of her way, whispering together and gesturing in her direction. The ability to lead a huge mob of bears may well have been the reason for the new respect. Walking directly to the motel, they reached their luxurious apartment. While Locey showered, Ford looked for a way to conceal his precious possession. He settled on a brown paper grocery bag, placing the box in the bottom and piling a selection of vegetables and fruit on top. Just temporary. He would need to find something better.

Locey returned, naked and glowing. Ford took his own shower with brain working overtime. Their next move was obvious. Go to England to help Eliza and John find the third and final orb. Then at last, all three would be in his possession. He dried and dressed quickly. No time to waste.

The doorbell rang as he returned to the lounge.

"Perhaps it's a bear?" offered Locey.

"Don't think so. Take the bag and keep out of sight in the bedroom."

Ford opened the door as soon as she was out of sight. Two bright blonde girls with gleaming smiles. They wore chocolate and pink outfits. The fake charity collectors.

"Hello sir. We're just asking folks if they'd like to help a good cause. You look like a very intelligent man and we'd love to share the details with you. No commitment, of course."

Both girls cracked into a seductive pose and Ford idly wondered what technique they used for old ladies.

"I'm just passing through the town. Actually, I was just about to leave."

"We'll only be as long as you want us," one blonde suggested with meaning.

"Sorry, I need to rush. Got a flight booked."

Then he saw it. A micro camera, disguised as a badge and pinned to her jacket. He mentally cursed. They'd recognize him. Just a question of when they reviewed the transmitted pictures.

"Well, goodbye girls and good luck to you," he said with a smile and closed the door quickly.

Moving to the corner of the window, he watched them walk down the path. Eight paces and he heard a phone ringing. One of the girls answered and nodded vigorously, looking back at the building.

"Hell," Ford muttered and called to Locey.

"We need to get out. Fast. The Trysse are here."

She was still holding the paper bag and stuffed a few possessions into her pockets.

"No back door but there is a window," she said.

Ford took another quick look at the scene in front. The two blondes had planted themselves at the end of the path and he could see a number of other chocolate and pink figures running towards them.

"We'll use it," he called and followed her to a small window at the back of the house. A tight fit but they both squeezed through. Now he could hear voices at the front, telephones ringing and vehicles screeching in their direction. Car or run?

"You men round the back. Shoot to stop them but no killing," a voice shouted.

That's decided it. The Trysse hit team must be here. No chance of getting away in the car now.

"Go for the trees," he whispered to Locey.

They kept low and ran. A chest high wall at the back of the motel. Ford levered Locey across it then dragged himself over. They crouched down, listening. Running footsteps and someone shouting.

"Cover the back. We're going in."

It wouldn't take long to discover the place was empty and just a simple deduction that there was only one way they could have gone.

"They'll come after us quickly. We need to fool them," he muttered.

"I can't ask the bears again today."

"Let's move round. Forget the trees now."

They edged along behind a wall then Ford glanced over it. Motel car park with at least five new cars already there. Another drew up and two men jumped out, followed by Pheela Lipstrider.

"Chance. They left the keys in the ignition," Ford hissed.

Unfortunately the trio didn't leave the area. Pheela drew a gun and stood beside the vehicle, obviously waiting for an update. Just twenty metres from their hiding place. Ford was still composing plans when Locey decided the issue by jumping over the wall.

"Help me, Pheela!" she screamed.

The blonde woman looked astonished at the site of Locey sprinting directly towards her, waving her arms above her head.

"Help! Help! It's behind me," Locey screamed again

She had nearly reached them now and turned sideways as she ran pointing at the wall. They just couldn't help looking. There's something in the human psyche about a scream for help and a pointing finger that demands total attention. The three weren't looking for long. Locey hit the first man with her heel, the second with her fist and then turned to Pheela.

"Crazy slut you," the blonde yelled and raised the gun.

"Yippeee," shouted Locey, diving under the weapon and grabbing the pair of long legs. The impact threw Pheela forward and she was unable to prevent her head cracking into the surface of the parking lot.

"You might be gorgeous but I fooled you," Locey chanted at the unconscious woman.

Ford ran across to her.

"I'll drive," she announced, leaping into the car. He wasn't going to argue.

Locey had already started the engine and she pulled open the passenger door. Ford jumped in and they were away.

She didn't rush, that would have drawn attention. A smooth drive towards the motel exit. Bad news. The way was blocked. A car parked sideways across the road with three men standing behind it. Ford pulled a sheet of paper from his pocket and pressed it against the windscreen. Two reasons. First, it would partially mask their faces and second, it would cause hesitation. They might even think it was official and wave them through.

No waving through. One man held up a hand and all three raised their guns. Ford glanced across at Locey and then somehow wished he hadn't. Her face was like a statue. A bust of Genghis Khan. He knew what was coming.

His body was rammed back in the seat as the car shot forward. A loud bang as it hit the parked vehicle, followed by a teeth grinding scraping noise. Another bang. More scrapes. A third bang and they shot forward.

The impacts had shaken Ford's mind into pieces. Like a jigsaw puzzle. He began to put them together while vaguely hearing Locey saying something about no one stopping the Bearwoman.

When Ford had driven to Grestwick, the twisting journey had been slow and difficult. Locey didn't seem to find it a problem. She arrowed round sharp turns like a missile with sensors. But the price was paid by the suspension of both car and humans. Ford felt the jigsaw breaking up again as he was thrown in all directions. He would have to endure it as there was no way he would dare stop Locey, or even speak to her.

A car, coming towards them. Probably the Trysse. They were in a canyon with steep sides the road was single track. This was a time when you just had to trust the driver. Trust their skills, intelligence and calm decision-making.

"Wheeeeee!" screamed Locey and rammed her foot even further on the accelerator.

Adrenalin forced Ford's eyes wide open. It was like binocular vision. He clearly saw the faces of two women in the front of the oncoming car. Open mouthed fear, horror and panic. The driver desperately dragged the wheel sideways and the car slewed up a bank at about forty five degrees. Locey barely glanced as they shot past. She began to sing 'Sunshine Days Over The Rockies'. Loudly and badly. Ford sighed with relief and joined in.

The next day, they were in a tourist class cabin on a flight to Birmingham, England. Locey had placed the box inside the outer carton of an electric toaster and it was in her hand luggage.

"We'll soon be meeting up with John and Eliza again. Have you ever been to England?" asked Ford.

"No, but I know they have squirrels there," Locey replied cryptically.

14

The Akur stirred and sniffed the air. Past sunset and now was the time. It stretched its four back legs that each finished in flexible pads. They were the ones that gave the speed and agility. The two forelegs were different. Like arms with two fingers, except the fingers were hard bone points, smooth and conical. Designed for killing. The creature had no head. Its eyes were embedded near the front, each side of the thin, stick like body. A smelling orifice between the front legs. No mouth. No vocal chords. No digestion. It recharged itself from the sun's rays. Animate, but not in earthly terms.

This killing should be simple. It had received instructions and knew its target. The talons were a perfect weapon. Humans had liquid inside, red liquid that spurted out when the outer covering was pierced. Deeper within, they contained a variety of squishy objects supported by a hard but brittle white framework. So very easy to destroy.

The creature moved carefully towards the building.

Inside, Eliza was speaking.

"I still think it would be better if we separated. One of us should find Tung Hot. He could be the leader. The other should continue to keep close to Sandra and her people to continue the search for the sphere."

John shook his head.

"Well, I'm sure we must keep together. I believe we should both try to find this mystery man. I'm also certain we should be helping the Trysse and I can't understand why you're resisting that."

"For starters, they kept us prisoners."

"Sandra explained that. They didn't want freelancers interfering with their search. In their position, I'd have done the same. These are good people and my mother is one of them."

"So it would make sense to split. You can help the Trysse while I go my own way."

He was about to respond when the lights went out. Total darkness except for the mildest glimmer of moonlight.

Eliza moved. Anywhere away from her seat on the sofa. She heard a door crash open and something brushed past her. Hard and powerful. Working from memory, she dashed to the door and tripped over it. It was no longer vertical but lying flat on the floor. A ripping, shredding noise from inside the room. Probably the sofa being murdered. She was up and running again.

Out of the back door. The sound of feet behind her. The rhythm of a horse but a slapping sound rather than clopping hooves.

The street. Visibility still bad. All the street lights were off and no illumination from the other houses. Power cut to the whole area. As she ran, she could just distinguish the shape of a pale coloured car parked outside one of the houses. Impossible to reach it before she was caught. Her pursuer was close now, feet slapping at an increasing tempo. A sharp pain as something ripped through her trousers and down her thigh. She dodged to one side and felt grass under her feet. A front garden. Try to get inside the house. Eliza reached the wall and knocked something over. Instinctively, she knelt to grasp it. The handle of some tool. Swinging it immediately in an arc around her, she felt it strike with an impact that jarred her hands. Another swing, another hit. The far end of the handle felt heavy. Garden spade or fork. She continued the barrage of blows then felt another sudden, searing pain as a sharp point sliced across her stomach. One more mighty swing that hit hard and she ran again.

The car, her only hope. She reached it and swung the tool at a point where she judged the front side window should be. A loud crash and she felt shards of glass in her face. The car alarm began to screech. Another sharp pain, this time on her calf. Eliza jumped through the broken window, hoping that the remaining glass wouldn't slice an artery on the way. Her legs were scraped but she was inside. Need to connect some wires to start the car. She bent low under the steering wheel just as a sharp point slashed where her neck had been. It caught her arm. Painfully.

She fumbled in the darkness. Seen it in movies. Connect two wires and ignition. Pure guesswork and luck was needed here. Then she felt it. A key, taped under the glove compartment.

Thanking the stupidity of car owners, she jammed the key in the ignition, flicking on all the other switches with her other hand. Light. Sweet light.

Duck again. Now she could see a long, gnarled arm with two gleaming white points. They were stained with her blood. She released the brake, rammed a car into gear and it tried to squeal forward. Something holding it. Twisting in the seat, she saw one clawed arm was gripping the edge of the window while the other continued to slash at her. She rolled back in the seat, pressed her hand on the accelerator and kicked both feet into the arm that gripped the car. Again and again she hammered her heels into it. The grip loosened. Just a fraction but enough. The vehicle began to move forward and Eliza gave a final kick with all the force of her legs.

Away. Free. She swung back into the seat, just in time to spin the wheel. The car scraped a lamppost and was back on the street, racing from the town.

She hadn't really seen it, just knew it had claws and several spindly legs. No sense of malevolence. It had just been doing a job it was good at. First the Fuffax, now this one.

Eliza wasn't going back for John. He would have had plenty of time to escape while the creature was attacking her. He hadn't wanted them to split but now circumstances had made the decision. He'd know she would be looking for Tung Hot and could do the same or go back to the Trysse.

Mariom Wander was not content with life. She had failed to retain the orb that had taken so long to find in Brazil. Then she had allowed that saboteur, Ford Rampon and his stupid girl to get to the Colorado one first. Two failures and she knew the Trysse was not a forgiving organisation.

She had arrived in England, summoned by a brief instruction from the Leader and was waiting for him in the penthouse suite at one of the best known hotels in London.

"You remember exactly what to do?" she asked Romnia, an extra sharpness in her voice.

The red haired girl nodded, eyes wide.

"Yes, Ms Wander."

Mariom hoped that was the case. She had spent two hours instructing the girl and it was an important part of her strategy. She checked Romnia's dress again. Turquoise with delicate floral embellishments just under the bosom. She had deliberately selected a size too small and Romnia's voluptuous body filled it tightly. She appeared to have complied with the instruction that nothing must be worn underneath. The design and colour were intended to symbolise an oriental style, targeted at the leader's origins. Minimal lipstick but considerable work on the eyes to give a slightly almond shape.

It was not at all suited to a sitting posture and Mariom stood alongside her as they waited.

The door opened. The Leader's interpreter, Perl followed by the towering man himself. He wore a long, dark blue robe that made him look even taller. His eyes shot towards Romnia who was smiling up shyly from a slightly down turned face, just as instructed.

Mariom stood back as the pair crossed the room. Tung Hot sank into the sofa while Perl pulled up a low stool and knelt beside him, producing a sheet of paper from her coat.

"The Leader has instructed me to read his words. He states that interruptions will not be tolerated. You may have an opportunity to speak later."

Mariom bowed her head, glancing across at Romnia. The girl was doing well, frequently changing her posture to stretch the tight dress over different parts of her anatomy. No expression on Tung Hot's face but his eyes were fixed on Romnia's body. Perl began to read.

"You have disappointed me. I had placed great confidence in your abilities but you have betrayed my trust on two occasions. In Brazil, you actually had the orb in your possession and then the four amateurs took it from you. Your security was inadequate for something infinitely more precious than any other on this earth. Subsequently, you have an opportunity to capture the thieves but instead of mounting a full scale military attack on their house, you merely sent Smith's mother to talk to them."

Perl looked up directly at Mariom before continuing.

"The Trysse then had the opportunity to locate the second sphere. You had infinite resources to search everywhere in Colorado but two of the amateurs were able to find and remove the orb before you. Again, your incompetence allowed them to escape. I have executed many others for similar failures but you are given one final opportunity. You will now work under the direction of Sandra Inkell. Report to her in the London office at ten, tomorrow morning. However, there will be a punishment as you will later discover and you are also now required to give a clear demonstration of your continued and complete loyalty."

Mariom felt a chill run through her body. This was worse than she'd hoped. She saw Perl lean across to Tung Hot to receive his whispered instructions and then rise to her feet.

"You will remove your garments and comply unquestioningly with his demands."

She spoke without emotion, like a machine.

Mariom's plans were shredded away. She saw Perl grasp Romnia's arm and lead her from the room, closing the door firmly and began to remove her clothing. She looked for a change in the man's expression. Nothing. No desire. No joy. Simply expressionless as always.

Mariom had very little in common with Sandra, sharing perhaps just two things. A mutual hatred of each other and an abhorrence of any sexual activity with a man. She was naked now, an exceptional figure for a woman of 48 but the repulsion was building rapidly inside her. The tall man rose to his feet, dominating the room. Then he motioned for her to lie on the deep carpeted floor.

She barely suppressed a gasp as he unfastened his robe and it fell to his feet. Bile was rising from her stomach and filling the back of her throat.

"I will serve you, Leader. Serve you with my soul and my body," she said hoarsely, forcing her lips to bend into a smile.

68 minutes later, Mariom emerged from the shower and dressed quickly. Her whole body ached after the exertions of the last hour and she had been violently sick as soon as he left. He had appeared insatiable, always demanding more from her. And she had complied with all, continually fighting the nausea generated by entwining herself with a man's body. She had forced herself to utter the required murmurs and moans but not one word had been spoken. She was only grateful that he had not lingered afterwards, simply picking up his robe and leaving the room.

The shower had refreshed, cleansed her flesh of the sickening stench of a male body. Mariom began to consider if her participation had been more than an act to confirm her obedience, her subservience. The leader was well aware of her undisguised feelings towards sex with a male. Perhaps it had been the punishment.

She left the building and walked to the car, expecting Romnia to be there. She was. In the passenger seat and looking as sensuous as ever, even in death. She had been killed by a knife to the heart and her tight dress displayed the slit amid a circle of blood that stained the garment.

Mariom made a telephone call before driving off, arranging to transfer to another car further down the road. Her people would dispose of the body. It was useless to her now. Romnia had served a purpose but she wouldn't miss her.

Sixty three hours after her encounter with the Akur, Eliza was settled comfortably in a deep leather chair. No cheap seating in the lounge of the hotel, just over twenty miles south of Birmingham. The rich and famous were frequent visitors here, preferring the unique country setting to the concrete and grime of city hotels. The nearby motorway linked to all the major destinations and London could be reached in under two hours.

Now she was waiting for Tung Hot to arrive. His movements were secretive, explained by members of his entourage as simple security precautions. It had taken nearly five hours of telephone calls to a number of her contacts to get his possible location. Even now, she was more hopeful than certain he would arrive. Tung Hot was supposedly coming here after staying at a secret residence in London. The purpose was a business meeting with the head of a pharmaceutical multinational.

Eliza had booked a room and now could only wait. All she knew was that the man could be coming here in the next few days so it could be a long vigil. She needed a pretext to be in the hotel foyer lounge for so long and had purchased a laptop computer. The hotel register showed her name as Anna Swinntering, novelist.

She still bore the scars from the attack of the creature. A quick stop off at a hospital to clean up the wounds. The arm, calf and thigh were relatively minor and she had removed the bandages after twenty four hours, covering the marks with body make up. The laceration on her stomach was deeper and the plaster remained. She was wearing the most likely novelist clothing she could imagine. Sensible and unambitious long skirt, top and jacket.

No one appeared the first day and at just after eleven the next morning, she was beginning to wonder if remaining close to Sandra would have been more productive. Now the structure of the Trysse was clear. Sandra and Mariom Wander were obviously the driving force under the direction of a Leader, probably Tung Hot. The other unknown was the Joiner, woman, man or thing. Maybe it was also the Leader or at least accompanied that person. That was Eliza's main reason for seeking Tung Hot. If he was the Leader, then the Joiner may not be far away. She needed to know.

Thirty six minutes later, he came. Couldn't be missed. Tung Hot was a full two metres tall or six and a half feet. Slim body with a grim, square face framed by longish black hair. Age perhaps about forty but impossible to be sure. He entered the hotel in the centre of a tight group of four people. A tough character on each side, looking around sharply. Obviously bodyguards. A small man behind, carrying two briefcases. Secretary. In front was a woman, thirtyish and dressed in a smart turquoise suit. She was untouchably stunning.

"Mr Hot wishes to go to his rooms immediately. I will complete the formalities," the woman announced as she approached reception. A demand, not a request.

The keys were handed over and the woman remained while the other four moved on. Suddenly, Hot's head turned and he stared directly at Eliza. It felt like her brain was being quarried. He turned away after a second and disappeared into the elevator but the effect of his gaze remained. She waited until the woman had finished registering, and then intercepted her.

"Hello. I'm Anna Swinntering. A bit of a novelist. Am I wrong or was that the famous Mr Tung Hot?"

She expected a brush off but the woman smiled. About thirtyish with dark hair and intelligent eyes.

"I'm a fanatical reader of novels. We must get together. Perhaps coffee or a meal?"

Unexpected.

"That would be wonderful. I'm sorry, I don't know your name."

"Perl Fortran. Please call me Perl. Perhaps a private dinner tonight in my suite? I never eat in restaurants."

"Yes, I'd be delighted, Perl. Will Mr Hot be there?"

"No. He prefers to dine alone. Security, you understand."

Eliza nodded dutifully.

"Of course. It must be fascinating to work with such a powerful man," she said with enthusiasm.

"You must excuse me. I'm sure we can share many things later. Eight tonight. Room 269."

Perl walked away but there was a backward glance and smile as she entered the elevator.

Far better than anticipated, thought Eliza. But she also sensed an uncertain feeling. Intangible. Sixty four minutes until dinner and she began to prepare a strategy. That would need to include a reason for her stomach wound, just in case they ended up in bed together.

Perl opened the door in person.

"Hello Anna. I'm so pleased you came."

Eliza was stunned. Her own garment was a cover all deep blue dress that stretched below her knees. A simple gold pendant and a slight layer of lipstick. Her host was not so conservative. Not at all. A stunning white silk number that finished around her thighs and started well below the neck, clinging tightly in between. There were indications that no underwear was present.

"I'm so grateful you were kind enough to invite me," Eliza responded eventually.

Perl clasped her hand and led the way to the sofa. Eliza knew that the suite was one of the six most luxurious in a luxury hotel. Tung Hot had booked four of them. Spacious lounge with a dining area set out near to the large sliding windows.

The sofa was a three seater but two thirds seemed unnecessary as Perl pressed up close. In the sitting position, the hem of her dress was hovering around a critical level.

"I'd really like to know more about Mr Hot. He seems a very mysterious man," Eliza enquired, attempting to ignore the close proximity.

"Yes, he's unique. You may know from the newspapers that he speaks only an obscure dialect of the Jin language of northern China. I am fortunate to be fluent in many, including Jin and I accompany him everywhere to translate. It's a great honour for me to be with such a great man."

"Isn't he married?"

Perl laughed beautifully.

"No. He is entirely focused on his work. His business acumen is quite amazing. I don't believe there is a single major financier in the world that he hasn't outmanoeuvred."

"No hobbies?"

"Business is his only interest."

"Don't you get bored sometimes?"

"I have many other interests. And passions."

Eliza felt a hand on her shoulder and found herself drawn to the woman's eyes. Hypnotic, dark ovals that glittered before her. So comforting to descend deep into them. Falling, like a droplet into a pool of serenity.

It was an effort to pull out and speak.

"I'm the same. I enjoy writing but gardening is one of my favourites."

A slight frown wafted across Perl's face but disappeared in a second.

"Let's eat. We'll talk more over coffee."

Dinner was as expected. Exquisite. Three hotel staff dedicated themselves to cater for the smallest requirement. After completing the final course, Perl gave each of them a thick role of banknotes.

"We will not require you again," she announced to the delighted trio.

They quickly cleared the residue of the meal and left a tray of coffee on the table in front of the sofa. 28 seconds after their departure, there was a knock at the door.

"Entertainment is here," Perl announced with a smile.

"I wasn't expecting that."

"I thought it would be a nice surprise for you," said Perl. She opened the door and the perfect man stepped into the room. Early twenties. Tall, tanned with medium length dark hair. Interesting brown eyes above a scintillating Hollywood smile.

He wasn't carrying any external instruments, just a large CD player. Not a musician, then. Two possibilities, one of which was a singer. Perl rejoined Eliza on the sofa, nestling close again. She seemed excited now, her eyes sparkling. The man didn't sing. It was the other possibility.

He placed the player on the floor, clicked on the music and began. It would have been an understatement to say he was good at what he did. Eliza felt herself increasingly immersed and quickly calculated the correct reaction for her novelist character.

"I saw male dancers in America a couple of years ago but this one is so much better," she said without turning to Perl.

"I've had him here before. The performance has a wonderful climax."

Eliza felt the woman's hand on her thigh but couldn't take her eyes away from the supple, muscular, tanned figure in front of her.

Perl whispered in her ear.

"He's beautiful but mute. He can't say a word."

The show continued and Eliza began to react with escalating intensity. She saw it after he removed his final item of clothing. The Trysse symbol, tattooed a little below stomach level. Perl stripped off her dress and joined the man on the floor. She beckoned to Eliza. Irresistible and she didn't resist. The plaster on her stomach wasn't questioned. No questions at all. Just complete carnality.

Over seventy three minutes later, Eliza emerged from the shower room, feeling refreshed and full of vitality. The other two still lay on the floor. The perfect man looked understandably exhausted while Perl had a lingering smile on her lips although her eyes were closed. She opened them as Eliza finished dressing.

"I hope you enjoyed my little show."

"It was great. I'd love to come again," Eliza responded truthfully.

"Me too. Tomorrow, same time?"

"I'll look forward to it."

Back in her own room, Eliza felt a little less content. She had enjoyed herself but hadn't discovered anything new about Tung Hot. The night had only revealed that the performer had the Trysse symbol in a personal area. She would have to do better than that tomorrow night.

Morning. 7.14 a.m. A faint knock at the door. Eliza was just out of the shower and quickly tied a towel around her body. The perfect man from the previous night stood outside. No smiles now, just a hidden sadness in his eyes. He pressed a piece of paper into her hand then disappeared down the corridor.

Just a few words.

'Careful. Dangerous people. They cut my vocal chords.'

The next evening, Eliza stood outside the door to Perl's suite with a firm plan in mind. Two targets. First she would try to stay the night and use the extra time to search for any documents. The second target was to meet Tung Hot, or at least get an invitation to do that. Tonight, Eliza was a little less conservative in her clothing. A new dress, knee length and just exposing the first bit of cleavage. She pressed the bell at the side of the door. This time it was opened by the small man. Tung Hot's secretary.

"Welcome, Ms Swinntering. I am Kin Tuk."

He greeted her with an oriental accent, bowing low from the waist. Then he stood back and she entered an empty room.

"Regret Ms Fortran delayed. Here soon. Can I offer drink?"

"Oh, just orange juice please," Eliza replied, wondering whether to ask him questions.

He brought her drink and stood while she sat on the sofa.

"You have interest in Tung Hot. I can give information," he said.

Good start.

"Well, I'm a novelist and find him so intriguing. I'd like to include a similar character in my next book. On the good side, of course."

"That is very gracious gesture. Tung Hot is not a withdrawn man, despite his reputation. The media say he appeared from nowhere, nine months ago but it's no mystery. He had spent all his life in a remote part of northern China. His parents were both teachers but he grew up in what you would term, relative hardship. A brilliant academic career and then he began to take an interest in the realms of finance. As you would say, he has natural talent for it. Ms Fortran has been with him ever since he came into limelight about nine months ago and I have had honour of being employed by him for nearly six months."

"So what is it that makes him so good at commerce?"

"Ah, like journalists you look for simple answer. There is none. Not one thing but millions. Genius cannot be simplified."

"Ms Fortran told me he had no other interests."

"That is true. I am ready for his call at any time, day or night. I consider myself privileged."

"Then you can't be married," Eliza remarked with a smile.

"No, perhaps later. Too much enjoyment now. He provides me with as many women as I want, wherever we are in the world. I believe you call that job perk."

This man wasn't a master of discretion, thought Eliza.

"I'd love to meet him."

Kin Tuk simply nodded courteously, making no attempt to reply. Eliza hesitated two seconds before her senses screamed and she turned quickly. Tung Hot with Perl alongside. He was a giant, taller than he looked in the hotel reception. She moved her height estimate to well over two metres, probably seven feet. What hadn't changed was the stony, unsmiling expression that gave nothing away.

"Mr Hot. You startled me."

Her surprise was only partly fabricated.

"He decided to inspect the famous novelist," Perl said, looking insignificant in his presence. She was in working mode and unsmiling.

The tall man leant down and whispered in her ear.

"He wishes to know about your books and your personal life. Please sit at the table."

Rather more than an invitation.

They moved to the large dining table, Eliza facing the other two. The secretary had disappeared. Then she saw it. Around Tung Hot's neck. A spherical gold pendant, identical to the one worn by Sandra that contained the pyramid. She had said that only two other people possessed one, Mariom Wander and the Leader.

"Would you be prepared to answer his questions?" asked Perl.

"Of course. It would be a pleasure."

She felt the man's gaze again. Even in a seated position, he still dominated and his eyes burrowed into her. Then the examination began. Each time, he whispered in Perl's ear and she asked the question, Eliza answered and her reply was translated back to him. He enquired about the plots of her books, the practical side of getting words on paper plus a series of personal questions. Her likes and dislikes, family residence, men friends and more. Eliza was grateful she had prepared thoroughly.

They continued for thirty seven minutes and then Tung Hot abruptly stood up. After a final lingering look directly into Eliza's eyes, he walked to the door. It opened as he approached and Kin Tuk stood outside in obsequious pose. The tall man passed him and the door was closed.

"I hope I didn't upset Mr Hot," Eliza said, with emphasised concern.

Perl laughed for the first time that evening.

"You don't know him. I believe he likes you very much."

"Oh, thank goodness. Perhaps he might allow me to ask some questions, if we meet again."

"It would be almost unknown to him to allow an interview. However, if you please him, it may be possible."

Perl emphasised the please word and a mental shudder went through Eliza. She could never bring herself to go to bed with this grim man. The head of the Trysse was not someone she could ever be comfortable with. Her brain clattered through an analysis. Tung Hot, the leader with Mariom and Sandra assisting. Perl probably in the higher echelons and the secretary a bit lower down the scale. Eliza considered the possibility that the Joiner might be with the tall man, maybe in his suite at that very moment. Another thought. Tung Hot could not be limited to the Jin language. He must be very capable in English to have sent the messages and conversed with his minions on the telephone. She doubted whether he would trust Perl to do that part. Her job was probably limited to fronting the operation and providing him with personal services, when required.

Dinner was a replica of the previous night and the hotel staff disappeared, again clutching wads of cash. As Perl closed the door, her eyes sparkled again.

"I have another surprise for you. Something different to yesterday."

"I love surprises," Eliza replied.

"The events of last night lead me to believe you are a woman with extreme desires."

"Well, I don't know if I'd admit to that."

"Extreme desires need extreme measures to satisfy them."

Eliza felt Perl's hand caress her cheek and then curl round her head to pull her into a kiss. As their lips touched, there was a tiny prick on her neck. Darkness came.

She woke talking. Words were coming from her mouth without any instructions from the brain. Eliza listened in to her own torrent of speech.

"And when I was fourteen, I had my first boyfriend. I don't mean had in any sexual way. A lovely boy called Tom. He was three days eighteen hours and twenty nine minutes older than me. I remember reminding him of that all the time. Once, when we were walking back after school..."

The meaningless babble continued, apparently outside her control. She lifted her eyelids a fraction. Tung Hot was leaning over her with Perl and the secretary alongside.

"She knows nothing. This is a waste of time. We are already certain that Ford has the two spheres. We will render her unconscious again," Perl remarked.

Her other face was on show now. A cold ruthlessness that reflected the never changing expression of the tall man. Tung Hot nodded imperiously and Eliza saw Kin Tuk moving closer. She felt another little prick.

She woke again to the sound of music. The rhythm of a guitar and a soft, deep voice that she recognised. Open eyes and look. It was really him. Maybe the top male vocalist in the world, three metres away from her. He was singing 'Loving Pink Syrup', sitting in a chair facing the bed. Perl was lying prone on a mattress, chin supported by her hands and her eyes fixed on the man. Eliza was surprised to see that the woman was still wearing her pink dress and even more amazed when she realised her own clothing was untouched.

She joined Perl, adopting an identical posture and they listened in silence as the singer moved through a repertoire of his worldwide hits. He didn't appear to be concerned that his audience numbered just two, a few tens of thousands less than usual. Eliza wondered at the power and wealth of Tung Hot to be able to call on one of the top celebrities on the planet for a private show to his employees.

After completing the series of hits, the man stood up, smiling directly at the two women. Then he bowed low.

"Shall I continue?" he asked.

Perl looked questioningly at Eliza.

"It's your decision. I can summon him at any time."

"Could I ask him if he would sing a couple of my favourites?" Eliza enquired, mentioning two song titles.

Perl didn't reply. The man did.

"I'll sing anything you want. Anything at all," he said and gave Eliza a look that raised quivers in various parts of her body.

She saw it as he turned to sit again. The Trysse symbol on the back of his neck. Her adulation began to deteriorate. Was there any limit to the powers of this organisation?

The two requests completed, the singer bowed again. He left the room with Eliza accompanying Perl in loud applause.

"That was a fantastic surprise," she said, after he'd gone.

"As I said before, you have demanding tastes and Mr Hot is in a position to satisfy them," Perl responded, rolling over to lie flat on the bed.

Eliza calculated quickly. The episode when she had been drugged was not going to be mentioned. It was important to retain her novelist character and pretend ignorance.

"I had a strange sort of daydream while we were listening to him. Like something out of a film," she remarked with a rueful smile.

"Really? The music tends to make me drift away. What did you dream about?"

"I really don't remember it well. Just a hazy idea I was talking to some people standing nearby. I don't know who they were or what I was saying. It was weird."

"I must tell you about my fantasies, sometime," Perl said with a smile.

"Am I old enough?"

"I hope so. Now for the next show. I forgot to ask if you'd like alcohol or drugs before we begin."

"That's very kind but nothing for me, thank you."

"I don't use either of them. Let's see the show then."

Without any instruction from her, the bedroom door opened and five people entered. Two girls and three men. Eliza cut herself off from the expected performance that followed a carefully pretended enthusiasm. Meanwhile, her companion's interest was very evidently escalating. It was an hour before the five exited.

"I'm ready for bed," Perl said but didn't look at all tired.

Now Eliza had to make the play.

"I'm so comfortable here but I'll go if you want."

"Don't be silly. I expected you would stay the night. Tung Hot has taken four suites and one is vacant. I'll use that one, so you can stay here. Now you just have to pick a partner for the night."

Again the door opened on an unspoken cue. Ten people this time, five men and five women. All young and attractive. The men looked like residents of a Kentucky stud farm for humans and the women could have tied for first in any beauty show.

"Take two or three if you like," Perl offered dismissively.

Eliza smiled but churned with annoyance. She couldn't refuse but this would interfere with her planned night time activity.

"I'll just have him."

She pointed at a blond beach type, his muscles bulging from added steroids. Perl rose in the bed.

"You three."

She gestured at a man and two girls and the remainder left quickly.

"I'll be in the next suite. Have a nice time. See you in the morning."

Eliza smiled and clasped the hand of the blond man as the woman left. She had already noticed the Trysse symbol on his inside forearm.

Thinking time again. Why had she been drugged and questioned by Tung Hot? If they knew her real identity, she was sure that they would never have freed her. Her best assumption was that the questions were a security check, to ensure she wasn't a danger to Hot's plans. She recalled how Perl had tried to hypnotise her on the sofa the previous night. That could be it. They wanted to know why she hadn't succumbed. Anyway, the gibberish she had uttered seemed to have convinced them. The plan now was to incapacitate the blond man, allowing her to explore the rooms and it needed to be done without raising suspicion.

He was waiting obediently beside the bed.

"I think you should lie down and relax. Undress first, of course," she said with a pout.

He obeyed and her hands went to work. Four minutes later, just as he reached a critical moment, she moved her fingers to caress his neck. It wasn't a caress. She jabbed in three critical places and his head rolled sideways on the pillow. Unconscious, with a look of fulfilled ecstasy on his face.

"Damn, he's fallen asleep," she said loudly enough to be picked up by any microphones. Just a precaution as she was doubtful if Tung Hot was listening in.

Eliza walked to the bathroom, continuing to mutter about the hopelessness of men but ensuring she turned off all the light switches as she moved. She entered and closed the door then carefully splashed water in the basin for a time. Then she turned off the bathroom light and edged the door open. Almost complete darkness and it was necessary to rely on her memory of furniture locations.

Her target was a bureau in the lounge. If it contained nothing of importance, she'd try another suite. Carefully negotiating a passage through chairs and tables, she reached the bureau and slid back the top cover. Using a keyring torch, she checked the compartments. All empty. The drawers were the same.

So try another suite. She had an excuse prepared. If it was occupied by Tung Hot or his secretary, she would say she was looking for Perl. If the woman was there, she'd complain about the shortcomings of the man on the bed. The four suites were all in a separate corridor, two each side. She tried the door opposite and it opened silently. Semidarkness again but she could see another bureau, identical to the one in Perl's room and crept towards it.

Strawberry. An interesting choice of room scent.

She remembered just as they appeared. Fuffax, four of them. They couldn't have been waiting for her. Most likely they were guarding the place.

The fluffy creatures didn't attempt maternal appeal, no doubt aware that their colleagues had already tried that. The first sprang to her neck, swinging a little arm that seemed to have a razor blade at the end. The speed of its jump surprised her and it nearly succeeded, the claw slicing through the top of her dress and just scraping her chest. She punched directly into its furry stomach and heard a tiny gurgle. There seemed to be more creatures now but impossible to tell how many as they kept disappearing and reappearing. It was all she could do to defend her upper body and the slashes to her legs would have to be suffered. The Fuffax were trying to get between her and the door. They wanted to keep her in the room and kill her there. She knew she couldn't beat them in this fight and had to get out somehow.

Another leapt up and clung to her chest, gazing at her with appealing eyes while trying to slash her neck. Eliza beat it down with her forearm then made for the door, kicking at the crawling mob of cutie faced assassins. The journey was just a few metres but seemed to last a lifetime. Hacking, clawing, fluffy Fuffax attacked from all directions. Edging forwards, she could feel innumerable cuts to her legs but eventually her hand reached the door handle. At that moment, a movement caught her eye. Tung Hot had emerged from the bedroom. He wore a long bath robe and even in the half light, Eliza could see an emotion on his face for the first time. Maybe a grimace, maybe a smile.

She pulled open the door, kicked away a Fuffax clinging to her leg and dashed back to her room. Inside, she leant back against the wall. Her clothes were shredded and blood was seeping from a hundred lacerations. Think. What would a novelist do? Obviously tell someone. Find Perl and say she was attacked while looking for her.

Back out to the corridor. Eliza ran to the next door. Locked. So was the third one. She hammered on it with her fist.

"Perl, help!"

No response. Back to Tung Hot's room. It was now locked. Think again. She saw a night waiter crossing the end of the corridor and ran to him. His eyes bulged when he saw her appearance.

"Can you help me? I need to get into one of Mr Hot's suites."

He looked open mouthed at the fresh blood oozing out over her clothing.

"You been attacked?"

"No, just an accident. I'm trying to find the woman with Mr Hot."

"Sorry, gone."

"What?"

"Gone. They've all checked out. Left hotel."

The Joiner felt its fingers clicking carefully at the keyboard. Unfortunate that the human body it had created to reside in had little manual dexterity. The inadequate performance of the leaders of the Trysse should have induced frustration and anger but it was incapable of such feelings. A chill ruthlessness dominated, with none of the restrictive moral standards imposed by humanity. It finished typing and sat back in the chair. This incompetent group of humans were failing and its own explorations had proved far more productive. One of the three leaders was now definitely expendable. The Joiner concentrated its mind and gave mental instructions to the third Akur. Instructions to kill.

15

The flight arrived right on schedule at Birmingham, in the centre of England and the car that Ford had booked was waiting. Locey looked meditative as he steered them on to the motorway and then posed multiple questions.

"Where are we going? How do we find our friends? Do we know where the Trysse are?"

"A place I've rented, don't know and no. You know we deliberately didn't set up direct communication with Eliza and John. That way, if one of us was captured, it would be impossible for them to reveal the location of the others. But remember, we did have an arrangement to leave messages on the internet."

"And they've left a note on it?"

Ford grinned.

"No. There's been nothing there since we split up in America. I've posted a few messages for them, the latest one saying that we're travelling to England. I also told them where we'll be staying."

"But anyone could read that."

"One chance in a billion. First, we are using a blog site with half a million users and second, the messages are coded. You read every fourth word of a specific paragraph amongst loads of pages of standard blog waffle."

His response seemed to pass over Locey's head.

"They're nearly all grey, you know," she said earnestly.

"Okay, right. Clouds, buildings or old people?"

"Squirrels, of course. The grey ones came from America late in the nineteenth century. They're more aggressive than the red and grab all the food. They also carry a virus that's certain death to the red."

"We might see some grey ones where we're going."

Her face lit up.

"A tree house?" she asked with excitement.

"Not quite. I rented a little cottage just outside a village not far from here."

"Old oak beams and stuff?"

"No, sorry. Only built four years ago. Externally, it's traditional design but ultramodern inside."

"So the plan is to go to this place and wait for Eliza and John to come or leave a message on the bloggy thing."

"Exactly right as usual, Locey."

The cottage was just as Ford had described. Standard wooden beams and whitewash on the outside, just like a picture in a history book. Pure modern luxury when you entered. There was even a separate office room, laden with electronics. Two computers with large screens were arranged side-by-side and Ford clicked them both on.

"These didn't come with the property. Got them installed specially."

Locey looked out of the window as he sat down.

"I'll go check outside for tigers while you're blogging," she said and left him clicking on the keyboard.

The cottage was surrounded by an extensive fenced area. A large clump of trees behind with green lawns surrounding flowerbeds in front. Locey headed unerringly for the trees and began hugging them. She was embracing number twenty three when Ford arrived.

"Nothing on the blog. I guess we'll just have to wait," he announced with a little disappointment in his voice.

She turned to him. Her blue silk top had suffered more than a little from repeated bark contact.

"I love trees. When you hug them, it's like being with the sexiest man in the world."

"But maybe his shirt buttons are a bit scratchy?"

She looked down at the tattered and discoloured top.

"Oh, that's nothing. They don't feel rough and you have to rub against them. They like that."

"Okay, right. Did you hide the orb away safely?"

"Yes, it's in a secret place."

"You'll tell me later. I'm thinking of going out for a couple of hours. Need to get extra provisions, we could be here for a while. Want to come?"

Locey ruminated. Lots of trees needed hugging and a visit to the supermarket was a feeble alternative.

"I'll stay. As a trade-off, I'll cook dinner when you get back."

She kissed him and started towards number twenty four but as soon as he'd gone, she pulled out her phone to make a call.

Ford was relaxed as he drove away. Too switched off to notice that the man mowing the lawn of the next property was talking in a headset. By the time he turned a blind corner, it was too late. He hit the lorry parked across the road and six of them were dragging him from the car before he could react. He was carried into the back of a van that drove off immediately. The lorry also departed and the remainder of the team gathered at the side of the road. Eight in total.

"Shall we go to the cottage now?" asked an officer.

The commander nodded.

"Yes. Take four people and search the property. You know what you're looking for. It is unlikely to be there as he's probably hidden it already but we need to confirm. Also get the girl. She's not important but we don't want loose ends. We can grab her easily."

Little did he know.

Two cars drove slowly past the cottage. A reconnaissance. Locey was in clear view, entwining with trunks in a huggers paradise. She had now discarded the shredded blue top, leaving only a skimpy bra but amazingly, her chest was unmarked. The first car stopped and two women emerged, quickly joined by three men from the second vehicle.

"Five of us to take that one?" asked one man with a smile.

"I wouldn't mind getting my hands on her. Hell, look at the size of them," remarked his companion.

The woman officer pulled out a pistol.

"That talk is banned. If I hear it again, I shoot you. You know we don't have trials in this organisation. You will stay with the cars, the other three come with me."

Locey was lovingly caressing an oak when she saw the man.

"Hello man. I expect you've come to hug trees," she remarked.

"You're a bloody lunatic," he responded and strolled towards her, reaching for her arms.

"Sorry, I'm busy," she said.

"Don't make trouble, girlie. We've already got your friend. Just leave the stupid trees and let me put these handcuffs on."

Locey's expression hardened.

"Trees are not stupid. They're our equal partners. We can do lots of things when we work together."

Just to emphasise the point, she picked up a fallen branch and cracked it across his skull. The blow took him off his feet and he didn't get up.

The other three came at a run. Two women and one man. The first woman got branched in the stomach, making her eyes bulge. Then they closed as a second blow hit her forehead. The man was not so lucky. A wooden uppercut right between the legs. He screamed in agony until Locey's heel hit him in the face. Silence again.

"I didn't want to kill you, kid," the officer said, pulling out her gun. She shot for the legs. Mistake one, she missed as Locey jumped to one side. Mistake two, the bullet hit a tree. A big mistake.

"You've hurt it," Locey screamed, her eyes like fireballs.

"Shut up, you stupid bitch," the woman replied, raising the pistol again.

No second shot was fired. The gun was kicked out of her hand and she felt the wrath of a lover whose hugging partner had been injured.

"Tree killer!" Locey yelled as she rained blows. The officer was lucky. Unconscious after the first attack but instead of continuing, her opponent ran back to the tree, tears in her eyes. She grabbed a knife from one of the fallen and carefully prised out the bullet. Then, returning to the officer she sliced off most of her clothing and used it to bandage round the trunk.

"I think you'll be okay," she whispered, scanning the area for other possible attackers.

The man had been leaning against one of the cars, smoking. As the battle unfolded, the cigarette was dropped and by the time the tree was receiving first aid, he was standing open mouthed. He should have reacted quicker. Within a few seconds he was watching the woman charge towards him, breasts swinging in her bra. A look of grim determination on her face and a branch of destruction in her hand.

He opened the car door and scrabbled in his pockets for the keys. Not there. Scrabble again. Why does that always happen when you're in a hurry? Eventually he remembered that they had been left in the ignition. He was about to climb in when hit by the branch tornado. Literally. Man against wood or more accurately, the opposite. Wood won easily.

Locey returned to the trees, kissed the branch and lay it on the ground.

A couple of hours later, a car drew up outside the cottage and she welcomed the new arrival. It was first light the next morning when the visitor left. Locey didn't emerge until an hour later, carrying a shopping bag. Key in the ignition and she started the engine just as another car drew up alongside and the window was rolled down.

"Need a lift?" offered Eliza.

A motel room. Anywhere else would have been too public. Eliza and Locey sat on the beds, munching sandwiches and drinking coffee. They had already spent some time exchanging accounts of the events in the USA and England and were now deciding what to do next.

"You came because I asked the trees to call you," Locey remarked.

"I did read the blog as well."

"I've thought of a great plan to rescue Ford but it doesn't work unless we can find a gorilla."

"Okay but we have no idea where he's being held. I'm sure they wouldn't have taken him to the place by the Thames. They're well aware we know all about it," Eliza said thoughtfully.

"Well, we've got two of their balls. Maybe we could trade one for him?"

"No, that we shouldn't do. At the moment, they believe that Ford has hidden their precious orbs somewhere. If we're captured, we'll be used to put pressure on him by threatening us with torture, death or whatever."

"Maybe we need to find this Tung Hot man again. He sounds weird. Just the sort to be the leader of the Trysse," Locey observed vaguely.

"I've been trying to work out what he'll do. By now, he will know that you and Ford are in England. That makes me think he'll tell Mariom Wander to come over here to team up with Sandra. The three of them will then try to get the two spheres from us and find the third."

"What about this Joiner? It must be a thing from outer space that brought all those creatures with it."

"You could be right. Or it may have always been here, lying dormant," responded Eliza.

Locey brightened.

"Yes, that's right. It could be from the alternative earth that exists way underground. It's where all the vampires go because there's no sunlight," she said with conviction.

"Right, that's a possibility but it's more likely that this Joiner is working with Tung Hot to direct the members of the Trysse in their search. You need to watch out for the little pyramid that each of the three leaders possess. It somehow gives them power to hypnotise people or certainly influence them. I know from experience that it's very difficult to resist."

Locey meditated.

"My family aren't here to help."

"Family?"

"My bears, of course. I'm planning to start a special airline for them sometime in the future. They'll be able to travel all over the world then."

"Don't forget extra large seats."

"I've planned that and also great big meals in flight. So what should we do, Eliza?"

"I've a suggestion but only if you're willing. In summary, I propose that we hide your sphere and then allow ourselves to be captured. You'll be putting your life at risk if you agree."

"The Bearwoman fears nothing, even vampires."

"If they get us, I'm fairly sure that we'll be taken to the same place as Ford and also that Tung Hot will be there. He'd want to question us personally."

"I suppose the downside is that they'll probably kill us," Locey remarked without concern.

"I said it was dangerous. My idea is that we'd find a way to escape, preferably while we're in transit to their prison."

"I like that plan. Maybe I can get the squirrels to help. They're good at lots of things."

Eliza didn't appear to require details and asked another question.

"If you trust me, will you give me the sphere? I'll hide it and not tell you where it is. That way you don't need to worry about revealing anything."

"You'll have two of them then."

"It's up to you."

"I trust you, Eliza."

"Okay. Then here's what I suggest we do."

They remained in the motel room for another two hours.

Mariom Wander was uneasy. She had already forgotten Romnia but her body still ached from the variety of postures she had adopted to accommodate Tung Hot. He had instructed her to work under the direction of Sandra Inkell, who she disliked immensely. Another unpleasant instruction she had to comply with. Right on time, Mariom stood outside Sandra's office at the plush London base of the Trysse.

She entered and was greeted with a patronising smile.

"How very nice to see you again, Mariom. I just want you to know that your recent failures are forgotten, at least by me. However, I hope the Leader has made it clear who gives the instructions here."

"He was very explicit," Wander responded frostily.

"We need to cover two areas. One priority is to find the orb in England and in view of your inability to locate or retain the other two, I will control that aspect. The other task is to discover where Ford Rampon has hidden the first two. We must then kill him, together with the other evil people who are attempting to sabotage our efforts. Three women, Eliza Clustbour, Locey Sherron and Hagg Snowmine."

"I am sure that Ford is in England somewhere. We must find him and also the other man, John Smith."

"The first half of the solution is that I have just captured Ford. Very simple. I really can't understand why you had a problem. He is currently being taken to one of my secure locations. Your first job is to question him. We must know where he has hidden the two orbs. Use whatever means you need but do not fail again. I have a driver ready to take you to the place."

Mariom gritted teeth and simply nodded.

"Now for the second half of the answer," Sandra continued, pressing a button on her desk. A few seconds later, John Smith entered confidently.

"Yes, Ms Inkell?" he enquired in a strong, steady voice.

Sandra looked at Mariom.

"See how self-assured he is? He was an innocent little boy when we first met."

"I saw him in Brazil and could sense the inner strength that just needed releasing."

"Ah, yes, that was when you allowed the orb to be taken. It is a pity that you are unable to achieve control over people as I can," Sandra said with a superior smile. She turned to John.

"You know this woman. She would like you to kiss her feet."

John grinned.

"I can do that. It's an honour to serve the Trysse."

He knelt in front of Mariom, removed her shoes and began to apply lips to insteps and soles. His subject watched in silence, thinking only that she had to kill the woman opposite her. Just needed to wait for the opportunity.

Ford woke slowly and cursed himself for failing to anticipate the ambush. He knew the Trysse had members everywhere. Maybe the airline, the property agents or even the company who had installed computers in the cottage. Maybe all of them.

Now he was in a chamber, similar to a hospital operating theatre. Reinforced chains pinned his arms and legs to a white, plastic covered, padded table. Not physically uncomfortable but obviously intended to torment the mind with the thought of agonies to come. Rows of sharp steel instruments lining the walls only served to add to the menace. The Trysse were thorough but limited. They were also merciless and certainly wouldn't be concerned about torturing or killing him. He would be questioned about the location of the Colorado sphere and also what had happened to the one from Brazil. Ford began to refine his answers. He knew he had time. They'd leave him here for at least an hour to build up his apprehension.

Sixty nine minutes later, the door opened and a tall man entered. Northern China origins from the configuration of his face. He also recognized him. Tung Hot, big financier. The man didn't speak but simply walked to the end of the table at his feet, gazing at Ford with a granite expression.

A woman joined him. Mariom Wander. She'd never seemed the jolly type and this was the least cheerful he'd ever seen her. Her voice was like a chainsaw cutting an iceberg.

"I don't plan to kill you, Rampon. You simply have to provide me with information to avoid irrecoverable injury. Alternatively, I will progressively incapacitate every part of your body, finishing with the sexual organs and then your brain. You would be clinically alive but just a useless shell with no shred of humanity left in you. Do you understand me?"

"It's very clear. I'm not going to fight any more," replied Ford in resignation.

"I don't trust you but I'll try the easy way first."

Wander unscrewed the pendant round her neck and produced the tiny, glowing pyramid. It shone bright blue as soon as her hand touched it. She moved forward and held it against Ford's forehead. When it made contact, the colour changed to a vivid crimson. Ford saw Tung Hot bend forward, eyes fixed on the red glow.

"I see. You are very definitely a bad boy," announced Mariom.

She watched as his face contorted, knowing that he would be trying to fight it. The power of the pyramids, ever persuasive, always demanding that his willpower must accept the righteous cause, to serve the Trysse. She laughed quietly as he cried out in anguish, head rolling to one side.

Mariom removed the pyramid and glanced towards Tung Hot.

"I have seen this before, Leader. It's like a coma. We'll soon know if it has been effective. I will question him again in one hour. You can depend upon me to obtain answers."

The tall man didn't acknowledge her, didn't look at her. He turned and left the room, expression unchanged as always.

Locey was bored. She had handed over the box and Eliza had taken it somewhere to hide. That was four days ago and she had spent the time researching and memorising all the information she could find on the animal kingdom, starting with aardvarks. Now she'd finished and ennui had set in.

A car horn outside and Locey ran to the window.

"Wow," she gasped.

Eliza had returned in an azure metallic Connovedo, one of the most expensive cars on earth.

Thirty minutes later they were cruising on the motorway towards the English Midlands. Locey had demanded a turn of the wheel and was enjoying the experience.

"Super car," she said with a delighted smile.

"We want to be noticed and there's no reason not to enjoy ourselves before they get us."

"While you were away, I was having a good think about this Trysse. I'm sure I understand most of it but maybe you should check if I've got it right."

"It's complicated and there are still lots of things I don't know about them. Here's my summary. In about 1850, three people felt the urge to go to a tiny monastery in France. Six old monks there. They gave each of the three a sphere in a box and told them to conceal it somewhere on earth. The people gave a general idea of the area where they were going to find a hiding place and would give the exact location when they returned to the monastery."

"And when they got back, the monks were dead."

"Five of them were. The last one to return was a man called David Codue and he found just one monk alive. David told him the location but then the monk tried to kill him. There was a fight and by accident, the monk died. David recovered but had lost his memory of where he had concealed the sphere. When he searched the place, he could only find a scrap of paper that had the three general areas advised by the people before they left."

"And he wrote it all down then started the Trysse."

"Yes. The monks had told him that the three spheres were to be brought together by someone or something called the Joiner, when the time was right. This merging would result in humanity receiving a great leap forward in wisdom. The Trysse continued to exist like a small secret society, trying to find the spheres but without success."

"Until the pyramids came?"

"That's right. About eleven months ago, Hagg Snowmine was the leader of the Trysse. In a sort of vision, she was given three pyramids, one each for her and her two assistants, Mariom and Sandra. A month later, the Joiner arrived and soon after that, something happened that made the two women want to get rid of Hagg. They took her pyramid and tried to kill her but she escaped. Then this Joiner told them a new leader had been selected."

"That was Tung Hot."

"He presented himself and they gave him Hagg's pyramid. Since that time, about nine months ago, the influence and power of the Trysse has increased enormously. They're even trying to control governments now. But they still haven't got their hands on the orbs and that's the only thing stopping them taking over completely."

"Why should we prevent them from giving wisdom to everyone?"

"That was John's viewpoint. Only your inner self can answer that question, Locey."

"All I know is that just one of these balls created that horrible renegade bear, so I'm with you."

Sandra was satisfied with the procedures she had put in motion. There was no clue at all as to where the sphere was in England and her only guide was the strange influence of the one in Colorado. When she had visited Grestwick, she had observed the massive boost in intellect given to residents in the immediate area. In a country as crowded as England, it was very probable that people would be living in the vicinity of the hiding place. One part of the plan was therefore to look for a super intelligent community. She had allocated a team to research the performance of schoolchildren all over the country and also check for clustered addresses of those with a high IQ.

Helped by the influence of the pyramids, there were nearly ten thousand English citizens in the Trysse. Additionally, Wander had brought nearly five hundred of her best people from America. All had been briefed to dedicate themselves to the search. Sandra sighed and looked again at the map of England. It was still a large country to find something so small. There was just one other faint possibility. John Smith. She had already questioned him and he had told her that Ford had taken and concealed the two orbs. But there was another avenue to explore. Wander had told her of the significant effect on John when he had been touched by the sphere. It was just conceivable that he now carried some latent affinity that could help in the search. Latent now but she had a plan to bring it to the surface.

John entered her office, his new-found confidence making him seem almost jaunty. Sandra smiled, satisfied that he was totally under her control.

"Yes Ms Inkell?"

"Come with me."

She led him to one of the bedrooms on the floor above her office.

"John, I want you to relax completely. Remove all of your clothes and lie on the bed."

He complied eagerly, desperately eager to please her. She bent over him and placed her pyramid on his chest. It immediately turned vivid blue, the glow suffusing his whole body. His eyes closed and an expression of contentment fixed in his face. After a few minutes, Sandra removed the pyramid and walked to the door. She opened it and beckoned to the two girls waiting outside.

"You know what to do. I want him completely emptied of any animal urges that could disrupt his concentration," she instructed sharply.

The girls shed their clothes and joined John on the bed. It was 23 minutes before they left, leaving him thoroughly satiated. Sandra knew he was ready now. She left him, walking quickly to the adjacent room then sitting in front of a bank of video and sound monitors. Clamping on headphones, she watched the screen as a woman entered and moved to John's side. She put her hand on his shoulder and looked down with a gentle smile. He opened his eyes.

"Mother?" he asked.

"Yes, John. It's me. I've just come to say sorry for pretending to be dead. I never planned to deceive you."

"Is father still alive?"

"I'm afraid not. He was killed by river bandits just as the report said and I wasn't with him at the time. You've probably guessed that we were both members of the Trysse and you can imagine how we felt when we received the photo from Brazil with the symbol displayed on the wall. It was our overwhelming ambition to locate at least one of the orbs during our lifetime. Your father was killed soon after we got to the area of the structure. I had already met Mariom Wander and contacted her for advice. She arranged everything."

"Why pretend that you died as well?"

"It was essential to the Trysse in finding the orb. The wall in the photo was actually on the side of a huge mound and everything else was buried deeply. With my background, I was the only one who could supervise the excavation. If I had been found alive, the authorities would have questioned me for weeks and it would certainly have been seen as inappropriate to continue the dig. So Mariom arranged for the body of a woman of similar build to be left near your father. John, you know he would have wanted me to go on, to fulfil our quest."

"I understand, mother. The cause of the Trysse is far greater than any single life."

"You arrived in the area just as we had finally exposed the chambers. There had been so many delays due to heavy rains and flooding but finally we succeeded."

John's eyes brightened.

"I touched it. Touched the orb."

"I know and believe you understand how vital it is that we recover it from the criminals who stole it. They're bad people, John and I'm sorry you got involved with them."

"Yes, me too."

"Now I'd like you to close your eyes and relax. Think about the time you felt contact with the orb and imagine it immersing your body in pure blue light. Go back, John. Back to that wonderful experience in Brazil."

His eyes closed and a beautiful smile crossed his face.

"It's perfection, mother. I can't explain the feeling. For the first time, I feel part of the world with a million people inside me."

"Yes, you're one with the orb, part of it. And you can sense you need your two companions to be complete."

"That's right. The three orbs need to be together. I can hear them calling to me. One is far to the north, deep down. A cellar. No, a tomb"

"And the other?"

"More distant. Way to the North East but I hear it."

"You can be together again. Just ask where it is."

"Rocks. Dark rocks and the rhythm of water."

"Yes, what else?"

John opened his eyes.

"Nothing. Nothing else."

"Don't hide anything from me, John."

"No, mother. That's all and it's gone now."

She lightly kissed his forehead.

"You've been a good boy. Your mother loves you very much," she whispered and left the room.

Sandra was waiting in the corridor.

"Will he give us more if we try again?"

The woman shook her head, eyes like diamonds.

"I'm certain he won't. He's always been a stubborn little wretch ever since he was born but he told me everything. He is as weak as his father was."

"I know you killed your husband although I still don't believe that served our purpose. Remember that John is not to be hurt."

"The Trysse didn't need pathetic creatures like my late husband. I don't know why you're protecting his son. He'll just cause us more trouble in the future. We need strength and decisiveness in this organisation. Why not kill him now?"

Sandra was too smart to be demonstrative and her expression remained unchanged. But her voice was like the edge of a knife.

"I am in total control of all activity in this country. Do not question my authority or I will show my decisiveness in ordering your execution."

The woman pursed her lips and nodded.

Fifteen minutes later, Sandra returned to her office. A marginal success. Rocks and rhythmic water. The sea. Somewhere on the shoreline. A cave, perhaps? Need to concentrate the search on the coast. So far, there had been no success in the search for a super intelligent community. Therefore, an isolated place by the sea. Probably cliffs. Scotland and Wales had many places like that but the original message had specified England. John's subconscious had helped but it was still a massive task.

16

Mariom Wander was absolutely determined to extract the information from Ford. He must know where the spheres were hidden and she'd find out, using any means necessary. She was confident that the contact with the pyramid had reduced his resistance. He stirred as she returned to her seat at the side of the table where he was chained down.

"Who's that?" he murmured groggily.

Mariom leant closer and whispered.

"A friend. Someone you can trust. I think people are close to finding the two orbs you hid. We have to get them and find another hiding place. I'll do that and then you don't need to worry about revealing the location."

"Good. Good plan," he mumbled.

"I've forgotten where it is now. I think you said in London, didn't you?"

The speech was still shaky.

"No, not there. That's too obvious. I told Locey to hide them in another crypt."

"Ah, yes, you'd told me that already. I can't remember the church, though."

He gave a woozy chuckle.

"That's because I didn't tell you and I can't tell you because I don't know. All she said was that the place was under thirty miles from the cottage where we were staying. A church in some town or village but she wouldn't tell me the name of the place. Said it was a big secret."

"Can't you tell me more? I need to move it quickly."

Ford's eyes flickered open.

"No, that's all. Hey, you're a gorgeous woman."

Mariom smiled but not with her eyes. She kissed him on the cheek then whispered again.

"Remember you can always trust me, Ford. I'll be back as soon as I can."

She left rapidly wiping the taste of his cheek from her lips and walked to the office allocated to her by Sandra. Two hours later, the walls were covered with large-scale maps of the area surrounding the cottage and she had four teams checking the churches in every settlement within thirty miles. Her first appraisal supplied the bad news. There were a huge number of towns and villages in the search area. However difficult, the Colorado sphere must be found. She well knew that Tung Hot would not forgive again. Her life depended on the result.

"Slow down Locey," called Eliza as they cruised along the outside lane of the motorway.

"But it drives like a dream."

"Remember we want to be caught. Two cars have been following us for the last eight miles. Turn off on a side road and we'll give them a chance to take us."

Unlike Ford, Eliza had noticed the man with the headset in the garden next to the cottage. She had also recognised the pursuing vehicles, each carrying two people. Locey swung off on a side road, then turned again into a twisting lane that meandered through a series of villages.

"So do we just allow ourselves to get captured?" she asked.

"The plan now is to fight them, find out the location of their headquarters and go there in one of their cars."

"But they'll raise the alarm as soon as they wake up and get free. Unless you're planning to kill them all?"

Eliza shook her head.

"No killing. There's just four of them in total. If we knock them out and tie them up, we should have a good few hours before there is any chance of them reporting in. The easiest way is to pretend to break down."

"No. Let's crash!" Locey cried, a wild look in her eyes.

Eliza was squeezed back in her seat as the car accelerated. Trees whizzed past the window as if strobe lit. Locey edged the wheel left and Eliza saw the target. A metal and concrete mailbox at the side of the road. They rocketed towards it until suddenly she was jerked forward as Locey hit the brakes. The car squealed at the sudden change of instructions but forward velocity reduced and they hit the mailbox at under 3 miles per hour.

Without speaking, Locey arranged herself in a post-crash position, body leaning towards the door.

"Queen of squirrels," Eliza murmured, seeing Locey smile in response. She then stretched back in the seat, allowing her head to roll sideways and down. From that position, her eyes were partially hidden and she could look through near closed eyelids.

Sooner than expected, she heard the door on Locey's side open and an elderly woman's voice.

"Oh dear, are you all right?"

"Yes, thank you. We're filming a TV show," Locey replied.

"I see. I'm terribly sorry, it looked so real. I'd better go then."

"Bye bye," Locey responded in a whisper.

Eliza heard two cars screech to a halt. People shouting. A few seconds later a man's voice.

"Who are you?"

"I'm afraid I'm in the way. Can I have autographs later?" the old woman enquired.

"What?"

"Oh, very well. Where are the cameras?"

The man responded with a torrent of abuse.

"Well, I didn't expect that sort of language from a thespian. Goodbye."

Eliza heard her footsteps clacking away down the road. Then the door on her side was opened and she allowed her limp body to be dragged from the vehicle.

"Lay them on the ground and tie them up." A deep voiced man.

"This one's not much but look at the figure on the driver," another commented.

Eliza opened her eyes.

"There's nothing wrong with my body. You men are all the same, you just like big chests. Don't you think my legs are nice?"

She kicked the man in front of her in a tender place, rolled to one side and got to her feet.

"Get her," the one with the deep voice shouted. Obviously the one in charge. Heavy and unshaven, like an ex-wrestler on hard times.

The man she had kicked was still rolling in pain but the other three moved towards her.

"Stop," Locey shouted. She had risen from the ground and was standing with hands on hips.

The volume of her voice made them hesitate but then the ex-wrestler continued to advance while the other two switched to Locey. Eliza vaguely saw them start to attack her but the big man was already aiming a punch. He obviously didn't intend to capture her without violence but hadn't reached for a weapon. She crouched under the blow, moved behind him and kicked the back of his knee. A grunt but it was like kicking a brick wall.

"Sandra Inkell likes you," she shouted.

He turned quickly, looking puzzled.

"What?"

"She likes you best of all. Said you were her favourite man."

Mess with his mind. No way she could overcome him physically. A thin smile spread across his square face.

"I've changed my mind, girl. Maybe your body is worth a try. Tie you up first. You'd like that, wouldn't you?"

"I've always liked men with muscle," Eliza shouted as she dodged his thick arm again.

Then he feinted with his left hand and grabbed her with his right. She felt the power of his upper body forcing her to the ground. Kneeling astride her, he used one hand to pin her arms above her head while the other reached to tear off her shirt. The cloth was no match for his muscles and he ripped it open. The bra went soon after, pulled apart with one tug. Eliza squirmed, trying to lever a knee into his groin but he was too strong for her. His free hand slid down to her trousers.

"Do you like bears?" Locey asked.

She stood behind him, one hand on hip and he twisted his head to look. The two men were flat on the ground, as was the one kicked by Eliza. Locey had obviously relieved his agony with unconsciousness.

"They said you were a crazy bitch," said the ex-wrestler, rising quickly and reaching for his gun.

"If you like them, then maybe I could join you on the ground. Do you like bears?"

This time, the question was more insistent. What could he lose?

"Sure I like them. I was going to have you anyway but better if you're willing."

He motioned with the pistol for her to join Eliza who had regained her feet and was pulling the torn shirt together to cover herself.

"And squirrels?" asked Locey.

"Yeah. I like them in a pie with plenty of sauce."

Locey looked thoughtful for a moment and then shook her head.

"No. You have to like both of them."

She didn't seem to do very much. Before he could even think of using the gun, her hand had shot out and apparently touched him gently on the neck. The effect was like the last cut of a lumberjack. His eyes rolled back and he fell, insensible.

"You do like men, don't you?" enquired Eliza, scanning the scattered bodies.

"Of course I do. When they're good."

"I'll have to get one of them conscious to find out where they were going to take us. Then we'll go there."

"That one should wake up in a minute or two," Locey remarked, pointing at a prone body.

"I'll question him while you get ready to go."

Locey saw Eliza kneeling next to the other three unconscious figures for a few seconds before returning to the one she had indicated, crouching beside him for a minute. Meanwhile Locey checked the first vehicle. Maps scattered in the back, spare weapons under the front seat and keys in the ignition.

Eliza returned, pulling on a new top she had taken from their own car.

"Pelham Jenny," she said distinctly.

"I don't know her."

"It's a place. Tiny village west of here, not far from the border with Wales. They apparently have a big set up there, disguised as a warehouse."

"You haven't got a bra."

Eliza shrugged.

"I'll go without."

"How long will it take?"

"Under two hours in the car."

"I don't like them."

"Bras?" Eliza asked, struggling to keep in tune with Locey's circuitous thought patterns

"Guns. We don't have them in my animal kingdom."

After 72 minutes driving, they were 69.7325% of the way to their destination.

"Badgers!" Locey suddenly cried.

"Yes?"

"A big gang of badgers could take this warehouse place."

"No horses?"

"Badgers can't ride. They haven't got hands to hold the reins."

"Right. Why not dogs instead of badgers?"

"Mmmm. That's a possibility but dogs are more independent. They always want a big discussion before doing anything together."

"Maybe we should keep them all in reserve. I've got a plan, although your idea could be better," Eliza observed.

"Tell me."

"We stop somewhere near this place and have a good look round. I'd like to know who's in charge. If Tung Hot, Mariom or Sandra is in the building, we can try to capture them and offer a trade for Ford. I also want to know their latest information on the location of the orb."

"While we're looking round, I'll check for antelopes and otters."

A typical fabricated warehouse in the middle of green fields and woods. An unnaturally straight row of trees, required by the planning authority, attempted unsuccessfully to mask this ugly blemish on the land. No fence but alarm signs everywhere with two pairs of guards continuously patrolling around the structure.

"This will be harder than I'd hoped," Eliza remarked.

"Yes. No antelopes and no otters," Locey agreed.

"They have sets of floodlights all round the building. It'll be brighter at night than in the day. I can't think of a sure way to get inside without being seen."

"I could just arrive there and say I'm the Joiner. They've never seen the thing, so how could they think I'm not?"

"Too risky. Your face and I think, particularly your body is well known to them. It's also possible that the real Joiner is already in there. There's just one thing I noticed but it is dangerous. We'll take another look," Eliza said, leading Locey around to the side of the building. They were hidden from the warehouse by a tall hedgerow.

"Look at the third tree."

Locey looked. Unlike the others, it was leaning towards the wall of the structure and its branches were nearly touching a row of half open windows on the upper floor.

"Let's do it. I love climbing trees," Locey announced.

"I'm not sure if that branch will take our weight and we could easily be seen up there."

"We'll try. Come on."

Locey began to crawl on her stomach towards the tree. Eliza gave a sigh and followed her. A slow journey as they stopped regularly to allow the guards to pass. Eventually, they crouched behind the trunk.

"I can climb it, easy. Best if I go first and give you a hand if you need," Locey announced, bright eyed.

"Trees aren't my speciality."

Locey climbed with ease, regularly reaching down and pulling Eliza up by the armpits. Soon they reached an area enclosed by a mass of branches. From this position, they could just see the row of windows through the leaves. Bedrooms. All empty and most of the windows were half open.

"I'll test the branch," Locey said firmly and began to amble along it. Eliza was astonished at her balance. She simply strolled forward as if on a pavement despite the branch bending down significantly as she neared the window. At that moment, two guards appeared around the corner below her. She stopped, absolutely still while the two men passed a few metres beneath her. They chatted as they marched and didn't look up. As soon as they turned out of sight, Locey grinned at Eliza and then jumped the last metre. Her feet landed gently on the window ledge and she was quickly inside, beckoning.

Eliza exhaled. Her legs were already wobbly and she felt totally insecure. She crawled forward, hands firmly gripping the thick branch, until she reached the point where her companion had jumped. Locey pushed the window wide and leant forward, extending both arms. Now or never. Eliza closed her eyes and jumped.

She missed the window ledge, her feet slipping down the wall but then felt her forearms gripped tightly.

"Uppeee!" Locey hissed and Eliza felt herself catapulted up and forwards. Locey had braced her feet against the inner wall and literally pulled Eliza over her head. Flying through the window, she landed softly on the bed.

"Thanks. Really," she gasped.

"This is fun. What do we do next?"

"When I get my breath, we'll explore the place."

Locey took the time to look round the room. No sign of anyone using it. No clothes in the wardrobe. On the table was the Book of Codue along with some pamphlets, the first labelled 'Wisdom and Peace - Our Future.' Search completed, she looked across at Eliza.

"If you have head lice, then the average number is about twenty. Think of all those little creatures being carried around in your hair," she said educationally.

"Do you have head lice?"

"No." Locey replied.

"Nor me. I'm ready now. Shall we go?" proposed Eliza.

She edged the door open. A short, empty corridor.

"We need to look as if we belong here. Act casual," she whispered as they walked to the left. A fire door and through the toughened glass panel, they could see someone approaching. A woman in guard uniform.

"We need to grab her," Eliza whispered but Locey had drifted away again.

"Rabbits are fascinating, don't you think?"

Eliza squeezed behind the door as it opened. The guard stopped, eyes widening.

"Hello. Do you know the difference between a rabbit and a hare?" asked Locey.

"Are you mad?"

The woman pulled out a pistol, holding it in both hands and crouching slightly.

"You only had to say no and I'd have told you," Locey said sweetly, kicking the weapon away and slicing a hand across the woman's neck.

Eliza grabbed the gun and they carried the body back to the bedroom.

"You know, don't you Eliza?"

"Hares have longer back legs and the babies are born with eyes open but rabbits start life blind."

"I knew you'd know."

They dropped the body on the bed and Eliza lightly slapped the woman's cheeks. A few seconds before she was conscious.

"Do not shout. I will ask questions and won't kill you if I get the answers."

Eliza's statement was reinforced with a wave of the pistol.

"I understand," the woman replied.

"Who is the boss of this place?"

"We have a commander but the Leader has arrived with one of his two assistants. They are running the operation at the moment."

"Who is with the Leader?"

"He's alone this time. Usually comes with his bodyguard, translator and secretary. I've never seen him without them before."

"Where is he now?"

"There's an office always reserved for him. I cannot tell you where."

"Try."

"No. I will be tortured and killed when they find out. Please don't ask me."

Eliza paused.

"I think I heard something, Locey. Can you check the corridor? Take a look through the fire door again."

Locey edged the door open. Empty passageway and she walked cautiously to the fire door. Through the small glass panel, she could see another corridor and the slightest movement at the far end caught her eye. Then nothing. She returned to the room to see Eliza rising to her feet.

"She lost consciousness again. Still, we do know that Tung Hot is here."

"I must find Ford."

"We'd never be able to escape with him. Remember the plan was to get the Leader and trade him for Ford."

"So where do we go?"

"We'll just have to trust to luck. I've had another idea."

Eliza stripped off the guard's uniform and changed into it, pulling the cap down over her eyes.

"If we're are seen, I can say you're my prisoner and I'm escorting you."

Locey brightened.

"A jailbird. That's great. I'll look as evil as possible."

"Right. First we need to tie and gag our friend here."

A few minutes later, Eliza led the way again and this time turned right. They arrived at a T-junction as another passageway crossed. Then right again into a compact hallway with red carpeted stairs leading up.

Two casually dressed men there, talking about computers. They both stared at the new arrivals but made no attempt to stop them. Eliza had now pulled out a pistol and shepherded Locey towards the stairs.

"Taking her to the boss?" one man enquired.

"Not your business," Eliza replied frostily, without stopping.

"I gave them my evilest look," Locey whispered when they were out of earshot.

"Keep going. From what they said, it looks like we've hit lucky and found the Leader's office."

"Yes, lucky," Locey remarked distantly.

Just one door at the top.

"We'll just go in and bluff," Eliza instructed.

She knocked once and opened the door.

Deep carpet, panelled walls and big desk. Tung Hot, seated and looking directly at them with his usual lack of expression. And strawberries. The aroma was strong. Two strides into the room, they appeared. Eight Fuffax popped into view.

"Oooh, they're gorgeous," cried Locey, reaching to the nearest one.

"I told you, they kill," shouted Eliza but it was too late. All eight of the furry bodies had leapt on her companion. They clung to her arms and shoulders, attempting to squirm into her grasp.

Locey looked ecstatic.

"You're the sweetest little babies. Now don't try to kill me. If any of you starts the suffocating thing or shows their claws, I'll be very unhappy."

The Fuffax whined in unison, then competed for the best position around her bosom. Eliza took a pace forward.

"They do that before getting nasty."

"Don't worry, they won't be naughty. They know I'm the Bearwoman."

Eliza waited, gun ready but the mass of furry bodies made no attempt to attack. She turned the gun to Tung Hot who had risen from his desk, an emotion finally in his eyes. Surprise.

"I know you understand English, so I will tell you what we intend to do. Ford is to be released and brought here. Then you will tell us the latest information about the search for the orb. After that, we'll go and leave you alive. If you're lucky."

The tall man walked across, towering above her. His hypnotic eyes were like drills, burrowing into her brain. The scene froze for ten seconds. Locey, inundated with loving Fuffax. The icy gaze of Tung Hot and Eliza, craning her neck to look up at him. Finally he broke the silence.

"I love your outfit. Smart girls are my favourites."

Another freeze but now Locey was grinning happily and Eliza's jaw had dropped. She dragged it upwards to speak.

"It's that damn Perl woman, isn't it?"

"Yes, I'm afraid so. She's the Leader, not me."

"But you must know something," Locey said chattily.

"Not a lot unless you include basketball. That's what I did before she found me. Play basketball."

His accent was unmistakably West Oklahoma.

Eliza held a hand to her forehead.

"Let me think. Perl is the real leader. She wanted a front man to allow her to work out of the limelight. You're effectively a prisoner, always surrounded by a bunch of Fuffax."

"Pack. They're fussy about that," Locey interrupted.

"Sorry, pack of Fuffax. All you have to do is travel around looking grim."

Tung Hot nodded.

"It doesn't sound too attractive when you say it like that. I suppose I'm a prisoner but I travel the world, stay in the best hotels and Perl supplies me with all the women I can handle. Not really suffering, is it?"

"Don't your old friends recognise you from your basketball days?" asked Locey.

"No. I wasn't real famous, even locally and the first thing Perl did was to arrange plastic surgery. I'm American but my ancestors are from northern China. They changed my face and I guess I look more Chinese now. Anyway, no one would associate an international financier with a guy from backwoods Oklahoma. The only real thing about the act is that I do speak Jin. I learnt it with respect to my heritage."

"So who knows your real identity?"

"Only Perl. Even Sandra and Mariom believe I'm the Leader."

Locey began to divest herself of Fuffax.

"Now be good, babies and hide away again. Mummy needs to talk to this nice man."

The creatures reluctantly abandoned her ample chest and she walked towards the tall man, then reached up and kissed him.

"Why did you do that?"Tung Hot asked, looking surprised but pleased.

"Basketball players are cute. I had one as a boyfriend but he wasn't your size."

"That's nice of you."

Eliza held her hands up.

"Wait. Before you two go any further, can we get back to the point of our visit? We risked our lives to get in here and I'm not leaving without Ford. So, Mr Hot, tell us what you do know about the sphere hunt?"

"Actually, I can help a bit there. I overheard a message from Sandra to Perl. John, your old companion, had revealed something under hypnosis. Apparently, the orb is in rocks near to rhythmic water. Obviously, somewhere near the sea and Sandra's message said she was redirecting all her people to the English coastline."

"Not very helpful. That's thousands of miles to search."

"Sorry, I don't know anything else."

"Okay, now for Ford. You must have some way of communicating with the people here."

"To an extent. All my regular needs are prearranged. Meals, coffee and women are sent to me automatically. This suite has every modern facility including separate bedroom and bathroom. If I do want anything unusual, I message to Perl on the computer and she sends instructions to the people here."

"Do you know how?"

"She just telephones. Simple really."

"Right. Then I just need to impersonate her on the phone."

"Can you do that?" Locey asked with excitement.

Eliza paused before speaking.

"Instruction from the Leader. Bring Ford to his office immediately."

It wasn't perfect but a good imitation of Perl's voice.

"Wow, I don't know what this woman sounds like but I'm sure that's just like her," Locey gasped.

"I know the voice and you should get away with it on the telephone," added Tung Hot.

Eliza pulled out her mobile phone and asked him for the number. Then she repeated the practised phrase to the man who answered, clicking off as soon as she'd finished to avoid subsequent questioning.

"When they come, you'll need to send the guards away by gestures," she remarked.

He smiled.

"Has it occurred to you that I may be the real Leader and my story was a bluff?"

"Yes, I thought of that but I've got to take the chance."

"Then you two need to wait in the bedroom and hope your gamble comes good."

Tung Hot returned to his chair behind the desk while Locey accompanied Eliza through a door at the back. An extra size bed, long enough to accommodate the tall man. Locey bounced on it.

"I love springy mattresses."

Then she joined Eliza at the nearly closed door and peered through the crack. They saw three men dragging Ford into the room. His hands and feet were manacled together and he seemed to be drugged. He was pushed to the floor and lay very still. The men looked enquiringly at Tung Hot and he gestured with his arm for them to leave.

"Are you sure, boss? He's out now but could wake up," one of them said.

The tall man rose from his seat and Locey could see fear in the man's eyes.

"Sorry, boss."

The three departed swiftly and Locey rushed to the inert body. For nine seconds, she covered his face with kisses. Then he opened his eyes.

"Hi Locey, how have you been?"

"You were pretending!" she exclaimed.

"Sure I was. Best trick to use when you're captured. Hello Eliza and you must be Tung Hot."

The man nodded.

"I am. To save you asking, I am not the Leader, just an ex-basketball player. Perl is the boss of the Trysse. You're very fortunate to have two associates like these."

Ford didn't seem astonished by the revelations.

"They're the best. Does anyone have a key for these manacles? If not, give me a paper clip. Only simple locks."

"I always carry one for repairs to my underwear," Locey remarked, handing him the piece of wire.

"I don't understand that. What repairs could you do with it?" Tung Hot enquired.

"That's a girl's secret," Lucy said complacently.

Eliza looked puzzled.

"You'll have to tell me, Locey. I didn't understand it either. I usually carry spare pants with me, just in case."

"Different colours?"

"Well, I don't bother much. Just wear the first thing I find in the undies drawer."

"That's no fun. You need yellow ones and light blue and pink, obviously. I love the plain colours, don't like frilly."

"I was the same until I found some great designs in that UndyFundy shop."

The conversation drizzled on as Ford finally unlocked the last manacle and stood up.

"Still keep in touch with the sport?" he asked Tung Hot.

"Sure. I watch every game on TV, even college."

"Who's the form side? I've lost touch recently."

"Hey, you missed something. Three teams fighting it out at the top."

For a further six minutes, the room was filled with talk of lacy trims, full court presses, thongs and dunks. Just at the critical moment when Locey was about to reveal the paper clip secret, Eliza held her hands up again.

"Stop, everybody. We've got a job to do. I'd just like to ask a couple more questions and then we need to go. First, what about that spherical pendant you're wearing?"

Tung Hot held it up.

"I was instructed to wear it but it's empty. I know Sandra and Mariom keep little pyramids hidden in theirs but Perl doesn't. She has special bras made with a small compartment built in to the design."

"Frilly or plain?" asked Locey.

"Both. She has hundreds of them."

Eliza gave Locey a look before continuing.

"Another question. Do you have any idea who the Joiner is?"

"None at all and I don't think Perl has, either. It's the only thing that makes her uncomfortable. You know, the thought that there's someone more powerful in the background."

"Last question. We were told that one of your assistants was here. Which one?"

"Mariom Wander. She's not in a good mood after all the problems you caused her. She doesn't like men much does she?"

"No, that's for sure. Why do you mention it?"

"It's not important but always remember that I can be influenced by the pyramids like everyone else," he said cryptically.

"She was grumpy when I met her," added Locey.

Tung Hot shrugged.

"I think Perl regards her as a failure and would like to get rid of her. I suppose she'll want to kill me too, when she finds out what's happened here."

"I thought of that and it's also a way out for us as I'm certainly not jumping trees again. The general idea is to take you with us as a hostage. Is that okay?" Eliza enquired.

"I thought you'd never ask."

"We'll give you money and an air ticket to anywhere in the world. I don't think the Trysse will spend much time chasing after you while they're looking for the orb," Ford remarked.

Tung Hot grinned.

"Fly me to Beijing and I'll go north, among my people. No way I'd ever be found there unless the Trysse wants a world war."

Eliza returned the smile.

"Good. You just need to look a bit scared and stop any rescue attempts. Let's move."

"I'll need to talk to my babies before we go," announced Locey.

She knelt on the floor and called to the Fuffax who appeared instantly, assembling in a huddle with her arms curled around the circle. Locey whispered for a few seconds and then the creatures deflated again.

"Ready now," she said, rising to her feet.

The four walked tight together. Ford in front, followed by Tung Hot with Eliza and Locey behind him, both holding guns. Ignoring the elevators, they began to descend. The first group of people stood back, a couple of them talking into communicators. That situation was repeated until they reached the entrance hall at ground level. Mariom stood in front of the outer door with six armed guards behind her. A film of sweat glistened on her face as she spoke.

"I cannot allow you to go."

Her voice had somehow lost its certainty and Eliza felt mildly sorry for her.

"Then your Leader will die. Let him decide," she said firmly, nudging the gun into his back.

He didn't react immediately. She knew she couldn't kill him if he changed his mind and began to consider options. Then he raised an arm and waved the group to one side. Six guards obeyed immediately but Mariom remained, her face contorted with hatred.

"My people will find you three wherever you go. I promise I will kill each of you, very slowly."

Silence for a few seconds and then she edged back reluctantly. They were through the door. Ford checked the cars parked outside. A couple were brand new with keys still in the ignition. He took the wheel with Locey beside him and the others in the back. Within an hour they were on the motorway, heading for a motel near Birmingham.

Mariom returned to her office, face now pink with anger and frustration. She would have to report another failure to Sandra and she was dreading it.

The day got worse.

The Akur emerged from beneath her desk, its yellow eyes bright and confident. There was no hurry, this one couldn't escape now. It heard the human utter a scream and shout some words. That was good. No pleasure in the ones paralysed with fear. The first slash of its foreleg raked across the woman's chest and the next ripped her leg open. Then it aimed for the neck, the weakest part.

The Akur left eight minutes later. Pools of blood covered the desk and large areas of the carpet were soaked crimson. Pieces of flesh scattered around the room. Nothing recognisable as a body remained, just pieces of cracked bone, shredded organs and human tissue.

Mariom had been removed from her position with something a bit more final than a golden handshake.

17

Perl Fortran stretched herself on the bed as chunks of morning sun nestled comfortably on her naked flesh. She was surprisingly satisfied. Mariom had been exterminated. That was good. Tung Hot had escaped. Also good. Perl had become increasingly frustrated by the continued pretence of his overall control. Now she would be recognized by all as the true Leader.

The Joiner had first contacted her in Hong Kong, where she was the unseen head of a very lucrative organisation. An organisation that killed people on contract. Very lucrative. But the offer to take control of the Trysse had been too good to refuse. Although all communications were electronic, she was irresistibly attracted by the Joiner's guarantee that she would become the most powerful person on the planet.

As part of the arrangement, the Joiner had instructed her to employ a puppet leader to keep her identity secret but she had never been satisfied with the idea. Now the members of the Trysse would look up to her with respect. And fear. Yes, that was good. She now possessed two of the pyramids and already sensed that her powers over others had increased. No one now seemed able to resist her commands. Very, very satisfactory.

There was a downside to the current situation. The despised lunatic, Hagg Snowmine was still out there somewhere and now the three irritating amateurs were all free again. Ford Rampon, competent but limited. Eliza Clustbour, earnest but average. Locey Sherron, as crazy as they come. Not a trio to be feared but by sheer good fortune, they now possessed two of the orbs.

Perl thought back to the time when she had met Eliza at the hotel when the girl was pretending to be a novelist. After giving her a drug, Perl had questioned her and discovered absolutely nothing. Eliza seemed to be just a streetwise, ordinary woman. Perl was still sure that Ford was the one in possession of the spheres and was annoyed that the stupid Mariom had believed his fairy story about the hiding place being in a crypt.

A bright light and Perl's eyes flicked open. A message from the Joiner. The two tiny pyramids at the side of her bed were glittering brightly. She held one to her chest and heard the unspoken words.

'My patience is now limited. Wander has been removed for her incompetence. Eliza has concealed the two orbs. Find her, take them and kill her. Inform Sandra Inkell that she has four days to locate the orb in England. If she fails, she will die on the fifth day. You are also not immune to my powers. I selected you and in twenty eight days, I will judge you. One month to live or a future of virtually unlimited wealth and power. It depends on your performance. I am ready to take full control of the Trysse if you also fail me.'

Perl was not so content now. The Joiner had never threatened her before. Another emotion flooded her. Anger. She was the leader of the Trysse, in total control of a massive number of people worldwide. Threats were unacceptable and a plan began to form in her mind. She was sure she knew the identity of the Joiner. In its human form, it was within her powers to control it, make it plead for mercy, beg for the chance to obey her. A clear vision in her mind of its body, strapped to a table and she was standing over it, bloody scalpel in hand.

She smiled. There was no rush. She would begin by complying with the message. Inform Sandra of her four day deadline. A very dead line. It was unimportant to Perl if she lived or died. A woman of some intelligence but certainly not essential.

The following morning, Sandra Inkell was still in her office. She had been there through the night, feverishly communicating with all her agents. They had to succeed and quickly. Only four days. Sandra had seen the photos of the shredded, bloodied remains of Mariom. Less than ninety hours now. She shuddered and threw her watch in the waste bin. Too distracting. She felt a desperate need to move. Somewhere, anywhere. The south coast. Why not? It was just as likely as any other patch of shoreline. Grabbing her car keys, she left the office.

Ford joined his companions at the table.

"Seem to spend my whole life in motels," he muttered.

"I haven't really had a home since I was a kid," Eliza responded wistfully.

"When I'm rich, I'll create a nature park. All the animals living in their natural habitat without people interfering," Locey announced.

Eliza nodded.

"You'll do it. But just now we've got work to do. We've brought you up to date, Ford. Any other questions?"

"I'm a little concerned that only you know where the two orbs are hidden. If you're captured, they could get both of them. Maybe you should let me take them now?"

"I agree in principle but now there's a bigger risk in me returning to their hiding places. I could be followed."

"At least you should give us an idea of where they are. If something happened to you, we'd have nothing."

"They are in a location where they will not be found."

"Secret places are fascinating. I think they're on a desert island," Locey observed.

"I'll just say that they are somewhere on the planet."

Ford didn't look too pleased.

"We'll talk again about them. Question is, what to do now about the third one?"

"Eliza's really good at plans. My best idea is to sit and meditate until a place pops into my brain. Somewhere near the sea, of course," said Locey.

"That's probably better than my proposal," Eliza responded.

"Tell us anyway," said Ford.

"I'm sure all the Trysse now know that I'm the one who hid the two spheres. That makes me a target and I'm sure they'll be sending people after me. People and maybe creatures. So it makes sense for you two to work separately."

"I suppose that's logical," he said dubiously.

"The next thing is where to look and I've thought of a possible lead for you to follow. The woman who originally hid it in 1850. Before she left with the orb, she had to give the general location of where she would hide it. She just said England but must have had somewhere more exact in mind."

Ford nodded.

"Right, I see. She had to have some knowledge of the area and the favourite would be the locality where she lived. Did the records tell us her full name?"

"It's not in the Book of Codue but John told me that when he was in their library at the place by the Thames, he saw lots of other original manuscripts and found it on one of them. Her name was Firma Roding."

Ford smiled.

"Great. A little genealogy detective work is called for. So what are your plans while Locey and I are doing that?"

"I'll be looking for the Joiner."

Locey looked up, wide-eyed.

"You'll have to be careful. I think it's a creature from the vampire lands underground," she said.

"I'll keep my neck covered."

A look passed between Eliza and Ford. A look containing something more than visual contact. Then he spoke.

"We'll need to keep in closer touch this time. I'll buy new mobile phones for us all as an extra precaution."

"What about John?" Locey asked.

Eliza shrugged.

"What can we do? He seems to have switched to their side. Maybe we can help him later but our other tasks are more urgent."

Eliza left a few hours later in the recently delivered hire car. A new mobile phone was in her pocket.

"She'll need to be careful. Very careful," Ford remarked.

"If she phones, we'll go help her fight those neck biters," Locey affirmed.

"Okay. I'll do some research. Firma Roding. Fortunately, the name is unusual. Let's see what we can find on the internet."

It didn't take too long to find the first reference. Much longer to confirm it was the only one. A woman in Rutfordshire, north east centre of England. Birth dated 1811 in a small town called Upper Vultswine.

"Here's our destination," said Ford, pointing at a map.

"Wherever. No bears anywhere in England," Locey responded.

It seemed a slow journey at the beginning, with heavy traffic on the motorway. Eventually they turned on to the side roads and progress was swifter. Rutfordshire retains vestiges of rural life although nearly crushed by the destructive weapons of greed and selfishness. Those residents that were not involved in crime revered the double headed god of righteous rapaciousness behind their shuttered windows.

Ford parked in the centre of Upper Vultswine, a town of under a thousand inhabitants.

"Why don't we split up? You can try the church and library for old records and I'll check out the inn."

"Pub. They're called pubs in England. Short for Public Houses, places with a licence to sell alcohol," Locey advised.

A couple of minutes later, Ford entered the typical cosy English country pub. Ear cracking pop music, imitation wooden panels and various plastic replica historic ornaments scattered around the walls. Two couples at tables, morosely tipping glasses to their mouths. A small, wiry man leaning against the bar. All five stared at him with distaste. If there had been any conversation, it would have stopped. A mean faced woman stood behind the bar and began a conversation with the small man as soon she saw him approach. The subject of discussion was a scene in the previous nights TV soap.

Ford leant against the bar and waited. After a couple of minutes, the woman turned with a sigh.

"With you in a minute," she muttered without looking at him.

"That's okay."

Two minutes later she ran out of soap conversation and grudgingly moved to Ford.

"Yes?"

"A pint of country ale, please," he asked cordially.

She grunted and filled three quarters of a glass with Scandinavian beer. Slopping the glass on the counter, she grabbed a note he offered and scattered a few coins change next to the glass. Then she turned back to the man at the bar to discuss another TV programme. The nearest unspeaking couple began to talk about the rudeness of visitors to the town.

Ford drank some of the tasteless alcohol, pulled out his mobile phone and jabbed some keys. He used an American accent.

"Hello, Richard. I'm in Upper Vultswine but don't think it's the best place for the filming. People here don't seem too amenable. Pity, we were going to offer them ten grand each for a few days of inconvenience. I'll try somewhere else."

He clicked off the imaginary call and left the pub quickly, closing the door on the little man who had begun to follow him with an ingratiating smile. He saw Locey, walking back from the church.

"Any luck?" he asked.

"Spinster. Isn't that lovely sounding word. Spinster," she responded.

"Right. Old name for unmarried woman."

"Spin-ster." Locey dragged it out this time, savouring the sound.

"So you found a record?"

"It's on her death certificate."

"Then I don't think she's the one. That woman was born and died here but the story says the one who hid the sphere was a scientist and I wouldn't expect her to return to this place at the end of her life."

"A scientist? Then we should be checking the universities."

Ford looked at her for a second.

"Darn. I should have thought of that. Let's get back to the car and I'll connect the laptop to the web."

It took forty nine minutes and three telephone calls to verify. Success.

"University of Crakeston. Firma Roding. Involved in biological research. Remained at the University after her degree. She was there from 1842 to 1867. It's got to be her."

"Is Crakeston by the sea?" asked Locey.

"No it isn't but I've been thinking about that. Rhythmic water could also be a river cascading across a rocky bed. I think Sandra missed that possibility. Crakeston is west of London and most of the area is covered by buildings but there could be a river somewhere nearby."

Sandra didn't feel too good. She had returned from her unsuccessful visit to the coast. Haranguing her people and increasing their working hours had proved pointless. Under nineteen hours before death. She needed a miracle. What she didn't need was to be summoned to Perl's office on this bleak morning.

"Come on in," Perl called brightly from her desk. Tung Hot's secretary was standing beside her. Presumably she was employing him in a similar capacity. Sandra entered and took one of the padded white leather chairs.

"You wanted to see me?"

Perl smiled.

"You're looking very tired, Sandra. Not well at all. Still, that won't matter this time tomorrow, will it?"

"This visit is not helping. I could be out searching instead of wasting time here."

"A little edgy. That's understandable. My advice would be to get your favourite man and go to bed. At least you would die satisfied."

"Am I here just to be taunted?"

"No, you're here to give me your pyramid."

Sandra instinctively clasped at the sphere pendant round her neck.

"What? You can't have this. I need its strength more than ever now. It is necessary to control my people."

"You have no people. I am the leader of the Trysse and all are subject to my command. I have Wander's pyramid and find that my powers of influence are significantly enhanced with two of them. I therefore want yours. Do not refuse me."

Sandra's chin set firm.

"It was a gift from the Joiner. I am keeping it."

Perl sighed. As if this was a signal, the door opens and two muscular women entered. They grabbed Sandra's arms and lifted her to her feet. Perl approached them and gripped the pendant. Then she pulled sharply, snapping the gold chain. She returned to her desk with a satisfied smile.

"You're very fortunate that I didn't cut off your head to get it."

Sandra made no attempt to disguise the look of hatred on her face but the woman at the desk completely ignored it.

"You may go now," she said, nodding to the two heavies and they dragged Sandra from the room.

Crakeston wasn't the biggest university in England. Founded in 1782, it attempted to preserve a quality over quantity reputation with considerable success and had long maintained a top five position among the most sought after establishments.

Ford and Locey had presented a postgraduate research scenario to the receptive rector. They were now alone in a restricted area of the library, thumbing through a pile of books and documents that contained the history of the University and its students.

"Found another one," Locey remarked.

"Another what?"

"Spin-ster. So what did they used to call a man with no wife?"

"Gay or lucky? The real answer is no special name. It was a man's world then, before women's suffrage."

"That's why they were always fighting then. Like little boys. It's surprising that they hadn't already invented football to watch all the time. What did they ever talk about in the early 1800s?"

Ford didn't answer the question.

"Hey, found something. Short bios of staff members, including Firma Roding. She was born in a little village called Bakkilsfield," he said.

"I saw it on the map. It's just ten miles away."

"Okay. The nearest decent river is a good distance from here but there are a few streams. We'll go slowly and watch for any sign of water."

They soon saw a sign. A couple of minutes drive and raindrops spattered the windscreen. It got heavier until the grey sky poured it down like it had plans to become a waterfall.

Ford grimaced.

"Change of plan. We'll slog through this to Bakkilsfield, get a coffee and wait till it's blown over," he muttered.

"Rain is nature's way of feeding the planet and keeping animals clean. Look, a pond!"

"Right, it's just a pool of water in a meadow. Can't be any rhythm to it. I guess the water we need must be moving in some way. Hello, we're here."

Here was a bunch of houses huddled together, round a single main street. They couldn't have sheltered more than 150 people. Ford drove past them all in a few seconds then turned and came back. He parked opposite the small general store.

"I wonder where Firma used to live?" Locey mused.

"Doesn't matter. I'm sure she wouldn't have hidden the orb in her back garden. Don't forget something else. We found in Grestwick that everyone was super intelligent and this certainly doesn't look like a high IQ sort of place."

Locey put her hand to her forehead.

"Then perhaps we should postulate an isolated environment. A significant pattern of communal elevated intellect would have unquestionably become apparent over more than a century. Restricted accessibility commensurate with that existing in Grestwick would be functionally impracticable in a locale with high density population. My consequent hypothesis is to locate an unfrequented location within the area and subsequently research the presence of water."

Ford grinned widely.

"What can I say? Brilliant. Let's get coffee."

No cafe but they obtained a paper cup of coffee from a machine along with local maps in the general store and returned to the car. Ford took a gulp before speaking.

"We don't know for sure what the radius of influence is. From the Grestwick example, I'd estimate no more than five miles. So we need to look for a ten mile circle with virtually no habitations. That's unusual anywhere in England and certainly this close to London."

They studied detailed maps of the area for fourteen minutes.

"I can only see one possibility," he said, pointing at an area that began three miles north of the village.

"Maybe Firma knew the place when she was a little girl. She probably went there to play with the badgers," Locey observed thoughtfully.

"A good possibility. The downside is that I don't see too much water on the map, just a few streams. I think it's stopped raining so we can go see."

He drove off North without noticing the other car that had arrived just after them and had parked some distance behind. The sole occupant left the vehicle and walked to the store. Two minutes later, the individual emerged and visited a house further down the main street, remaining inside over an hour before returning to the car. The person glanced in the direction taken by Ford and Locey and then smiled, with a slight shake of the head, before driving off rapidly to the south.

18

The Joiner operated independently of the body it had created to occupy. The human container was capable of continuing conversations, eating, washing, driving, walking and most other basic activities while the entity inside concurrently performed its true tasks. These included communication to the pyramid holders and controlling the Akur and Fuffax. The little fluffy creatures were cunning killers but it knew that Locey had somehow found a way to control them. That surprised the Joiner. It had not believed that any inhabitant of this planet was capable of that and the usefulness of the Fuffax could now be at an end. The Akur were different. They could be described as cyber creatures in earthly terms. During their creation, the Joiner had programmed their brains to uniquely align to its commands. It could communicate with any of them instantly, become part of them and able to see through their unreal yellow eyes. That allowed it to participate in the hunt and even more enjoyable, the kill.

It knew Sandra didn't have to be eradicated but she had failed to find the orb and her time limit had now expired. The Joiner's human servants must be shown that punishment was carried out. But it was very aware that the real reason to kill her was a shaft of excitement running through its human brain. The pursuit and slaughter were so pleasurable, intense and fulfilling. The Akur were unequalled in these skills. The ripping, shredding and the warm, crimson blood.

The human shell of the Joiner was engaged in talking and other activities but its other brain now directed itself to the first Akur. It felt the creature respond, stirring its body and opening its eyes. The Akur had been hiding in a thicket in bushes during the daylight but now the night was here and it could see perfectly in the darkness. Sandra Inkell, the target.

She was still in the office building. Must be sleeping there, tossing and turning in her bed in the knowledge that death was approaching. Slightly disappointing. The Joiner had hoped she would run, try to escape.

It guided the creature, flashing within the shadows at the edges of pavements and passing through dark alleyways. Now it had reached the building. The room of the target was five floors up but that presented no difficulty. The twin claws on the front legs could easily pierce brick and concrete. It climbed rapidly to the fifth level and looked through the double layer of glass. A bedroom. Two figures on the bed, hidden by the duvet. The Joiner paused for a second. The woman should be alone, panicking and quivering with fear. Continue. The twin claws could easily cut the glass and do it in virtual silence but there was no pleasure in that. It told the creature to smash the window with both forelegs.

The two figures sprang from the bed. Not Sandra. The Perl woman with a man. Then the Joiner knew. It had homed in on Sandra's pyramid and Perl must have it. That was a presumption of power that would be remembered. But now, the lust for blood could not be restrained.

The man screamed as the yellow eyed creature turned towards him. Ignoring his nakedness, he ran for the door. Not fast enough. No normal human was fast enough. Twin claws ripped open his back from shoulder to waist and then the Akur was upon him.

Perl looked on, displaying no emotion. Her face and body quickly became coated with spatters of crimson. Finally, the creature finished its gory activity, looking briefly at her before disappearing through the window. She felt warm blood dribbling down her cheek, across her mouth and she began to laugh, softly and without humour.

Sandra was driving well, all things considered. Her target was Coventry airport, not one of the largest in the country. They would check the major ones first. She planned to go to Brussels and then on to central Africa. Somewhere where the Trysse was not so well represented. A place to hide. A sanctuary.

The Caballini motored smoothly but annoyingly, she now needed a toilet. Pulling over at the next motorway service area, she jogged to the women's facilities, looking around as she moved. Bladder relieved, she left the cubicle. A tall, lean woman stood by the washbasins. Hagg Snowmine.

"I hear you are to be killed today," Hagg remarked casually.

Sandra glanced towards the door but the tall woman shook her head.

"Locked, with a 'not in service' sign outside. You know the Akur have been sent to kill you?"

"Let me go, Hagg."

"Sorry, you didn't give my man that chance."

"Very well. What you want?"

Sandra spoke with resignation but her hand was already on the pistol in her jacket pocket. The tall woman sensed the move and jumped towards her. Wet patch on the floor. She slipped, her lean body prostrate for a second. The first bullet hit her then, followed by three more.

Still she tried to rise but Sandra was now aiming directly at her forehead. As she squeezed the trigger, she saw Hagg's arm move in a blur and then a brief shimmer of reflection in the light. The knife embedded deep, directly in her heart. Just a gasp and Sandra collapsed. No life. A corpse.

The bullet missed its exact target by a centimetre but still drilled through Hagg's skull and into her brain.

"Perl still lives. Somebody kill her," she whispered. Then death also took her with silent finality.

A women's toilet near the motorway wasn't the worst place to die but it took some beating.

Ford stopped the car and scratched his head. They had travelled to the only isolated area on the map and were now in a country lane just about in the centre of the ten mile circle. It was raining heavily. Not at all conducive to travel and there were no vehicles in sight.

"Let's get out and look for watery places," Locey suggested as the rain bucketed down in torrents.

"We can't see much from the car in this weather but I guess we'll get soggy pretty quickly."

"Sog-gy. Sounds lovely. I want soggy."

"Okay but I don't know how we'll get dry again."

The instant they opened the car doors, the rain stopped and shafts of bright sunlight shot across the country.

"Shame. I needed a good sog," said Locey with disappointment.

"I see two buildings to the south. Big farmhouse and what looks like a water mill."

"Water mill!" Locey shouted.

"That's got to be it. Let's go."

The only route appeared to be directly over the sodden fields, their feet squelching deep into the soil. Ford found it difficult to keep up as Locey bounded forward.

"Soon be there," she called from five yards ahead.

Soon was twenty four minutes and several squelching fields later. They were both caked in slimy mud up to their knees when they finally reached the structure.

"Look, a river," said Locey, walking over to an average sized stream and paddling in the waters.

Ford didn't bother to sluice the mud from his legs and approached the entrance to the building. An old construction but the water wheel still churned happily under the power of the gushing stream. It was obviously disused and holes abounded in the brickwork where plants had found a multitude of places to seed and prosper.

"Can't go in there," a voice shouted.

He turned. A heavily built, florid faced man with thick jacket and trousers and carrying a shotgun. Ford put on a big smile.

"Hello there. I'm from America and studying historic architecture. Couldn't resist this lovely old building."

"You're trespassing. I shoot trespassers," the man responded, waving the shotgun.

"Hey, I'm real sorry about that. We'd like to pay you to have a look at this place."

"We? Where are the others? I don't reckon you're a historian. Drug runners more like. I shoot them too."

"Coooeee!" Locey called as she returned from the stream. She had apparently fallen into it as her clothes were now sopping wet and clung tightly to her. Revealingly tightly. The man's eyes opened wider and she walked across to him with an inviting smile.

"You're a farmer," she announced happily.

He grunted, eyes fixed lower than her face.

"Do you have any badgers or otters?" she continued.

"Eh? No otters here and I hope I've shot all those damned badgers. Bloody vermin they are."

Everyone says the completely wrong thing several times each year and this was one of his times. Within ten seconds, the man was flat on his back with Locey kneeling on his chest, squashing his nose with the barrel of the shotgun.

"What did you say?" She shouted the question.

Ford raced across.

"Leave it. He doesn't understand," he shouted and swung a fist at the man's jaw. It connected perfectly and unconsciousness followed immediately.

"He said he murdered badgers," Locey squealed wrestling with Ford for the shotgun.

"Forget it, Locey. The guy is just ignorant. Let's check the water mill and get the sphere."

She released the shotgun and rose to her feet. Then a sudden smile crossed her face.

"I'm taking his trousers."

"What?"

"Trousers and underpants. That'll teach him."

She produced a knife and sliced off the designated garments, leaving the man fully exposed below the waist. Then Ford led her into the mill.

He had expected it to be crammed full of old machinery but it was empty. The building was just a shell.

"Could be under the floor somewhere?" Ford muttered.

It was nineteen minutes later before he saw the foundation stone, set into the front wall. The mill had been built in 1879, over twenty years too late. He'd expected it after the farmer had given no indication of learning and certainly no wisdom.

Ford followed Locey back to the car.

Pyttscoven, near Los Angeles.

John Smith strode forward confidently alongside his mother. He had parked in an elegant, tree-lined avenue and they were now approaching one of the impressive houses.

He had learnt of the deaths of Mariom and Sandra. Perl had announced that Hagg had murdered them both but Sandra had managed to kill the mad woman before dying. John had then begged Perl to be allowed to conduct his own search for the three saboteurs, Ford, Locey and Eliza. She had agreed, on condition that he was accompanied by his mother. He was unaware that Perl still didn't trust him or that she was relying upon unlimited maternal punishment, if it became necessary.

John had known where to begin. He had never divulged Eliza's background to anyone, for reasons he didn't fully understand. The same reasons that caused him to say that Ford, not Eliza, had hidden the first two spheres. John was the only one aware of an important link. When he had first met Eliza, she had told him her sister was married to a computer expert and lived near Los Angeles. He had searched for anything about Eliza on the internet without success but found a reference to her sister. She was Mrs Still, living in Pyttscoven, a small but exclusive commuter town near Los Angeles.

Now they were there. Before travelling, he had deliberately withheld the reason for the journey from his mother, much to her great annoyance. He had only revealed the details a few seconds earlier, as they sat in the parked car.

John rang the doorbell and it was answered thirty seconds later by a dishevelled woman in baggy clothes. Must be a cleaner.

"We're looking for Mrs Still?" he enquired.

"That's me."

Her voice was slurred and the smell of alcohol unmistakable.

"Right, okay. I wanted to ask about your sister."

A pause.

"Why?"

"Well, I met her earlier this year and we were good friends. I've lost touch and was trying to locate her again."

"Get lost, scumbag."

The woman moved to slam the door but John's mother stopped it and then grabbed her by the collar.

"Listen, you drunken cow. Answer the question or I'll cut you up."

The point was emphasised by the production of a slim stiletto.

"Help me!" Still screamed, staggering backwards.

Help arrived immediately. A big man, carrying a pistol, rushed into the hallway. The reek of alcohol increased with his presence.

"Leave her and back off," he shouted.

John backed off but his mother wasn't so amenable.

"Don't threaten me, you slug. I'm from the Trysse, the future of the Earth. Slime like you will be exterminated when we take over."

The man didn't mean to squeeze the trigger but the alcohol had infected his muscular control. John understood that but it didn't help the pain as the bullet slammed into the side of his stomach, buckling him on to his knees.

"Shoot again and I'll cut her throat," his mother screamed, the knife now held tight against Still's neck. The woman seemed to have fainted, her head lolling to one side.

"If you harm her, I'll kill you," he yelled.

John grimaced as the pain intensified. He clasped his stomach and felt blood dribble over his fingers.

"This is stupid. I only wanted to know where her sister was."

"Bloody sicko," the man responded.

The words filtered slowly into John's brain. He was beginning to lose consciousness as he heard his mother speaking.

"I think you've killed the boy anyway. I'll offer a deal. Tell me where this woman's sister is and I'll let her go. Give me five minutes and then tell the police that this man came here alone."

John turned his head painfully. His mother. She was ignoring him, just like when he had been a child. Endured and never loved.

"Okay, a deal."

He heard the man's words and saw his mother drop the senseless woman to the floor. The man raised his gun and fired four times, two for the head and two for the body. John couldn't scream, the pain was too great. He saw his mother fall and knew she would never rise again.

The man bent over Still as she was regaining consciousness. Police sirens. Ambulance sirens. Uniformed men came followed by medics. John saw his mother removed in a body bag while Mrs Still was conveyed upstairs. A detective began to quiz the man and he was very ready to talk.

"I'm just a neighbour who came round to chat. Lucky really. These perverts could've done anything. Kept asking about her sister."

"Sister?" asked the uniform.

"Yeah, Eliza."

"Is she here?"

"No, man. She's dead. Killed thirteen years ago when she was nine. Murdered by a psycho."

John felt himself finally descending into unconsciousness.

Perl had set the trap. It was time to capture and subjugate the Joiner. The killing of her bed companion by the Akur had triggered the action. The man was of no consequence, just another sexual adventure but the creature had come too close. She had sensed its sterile devotion to the kill, the joyless relish of annihilating a human body.

That feeling was afterwards. At the time, she had experienced another emotion, something so powerful, so wonderful that even now her body trembled in recollection. An engulfing wave of climactic fulfilment, far greater than anything she had ever known. The flesh ripped apart as she watched, the organs torn from the body and cast aside. And the blood, so much blood. It had showered, fresh and warm, across her body and face. Dribbling across her lips. Sweet, sweet taste. Perl gasped as a tiny orgasm surged through her body.

Mariom and Sandra were now disposed of and the only barrier to her ultimate power was the Joiner. Perl was already convinced that possession of all three orbs would give her total control over most people on the planet. She was also certain that the spheres had additional powers. Powers she needed to explore and learn. Now she would capture the Joiner and prise out its secrets, force it to reveal all. Perl had no doubt of its identity, the human body it had created to jointly inhabit.

She was in the newly constructed underground section, below the London office of the Trysse. The entrance chamber was generously furnished with desks, sofas and bookshelves. Perl faced the door with Kin Tuk just behind along with six specially selected fighters from her team of guards. All completely obedient, tough and merciless.

The door opened and two people entered.

Lord Feltspen with one of the maids, a blonde and still in uniform. They looked more than surprised to see the group in front of him.

"I thought you just wanted us to visit for a chat," Feltspen said uncomfortably.

"Yes, a chat. No need to worry," Perl replied with a smile.

The blonde looked petrified.

"I've done everything the tutor, I mean the late Sandra Inkell, instructed. Absolutely everything," she whined appealingly.

Perl ignored her and turned to the secretary.

"Kin Tuk, please search her," she instructed and the small man walked quickly to the maid. Then he hesitated, peering uncertainly at her tiny dress.

"No. Search her thoroughly. Take off her clothes and look everywhere."

Perl's voice was more intense now. Kin Tuk looked at her for a moment and then began to fumble with the fittings on the dress while the girl stood rigidly still, petrified with fear. The garment finally fell to the floor and the small man began to tentatively examine the brief underwear.

"No, no. Show him how to search."

The order was directed at the six standing behind her, two women and four men. They moved forward rapidly. Then Perl clicked her fingers.

The six leapt upon their target and he screamed with the unexpected assault.

"Quickly, before he summons his creatures," Perl shouted and the body was carried rapidly through the inner door, into a small room then on to the next. This one resembled a bank safe. Massive thick steel door, metal lined walls and fluorescent lights. The furniture comprised a desk, chairs and raised, padded table. The table could have been transferred from a hospital operating theatre but was fitted with a series of steel shackles. Within seconds, the captive was stripped naked and clamped to the table. When she was certain there was no possibility of movement, Perl gestured to the six guards.

"Wait outside. Twenty four hour watch. I am the only person allowed to enter. No exceptions. Do you understand?"

They nodded and left, swinging the heavy door closed.

Perl smiled as she looked down at the squirming figure of Kin Tuk.

"Not so mighty now, Joiner?"

He shook his head.

"No, not me. Not Joiner."

Her expression changed for the worse.

"You are the Joiner. Only you could have monitored our activities. I checked the background you gave us. Your papers were fake."

"Yes, yes. That's true. I was forced to get forged documents after I escaped from prison. I was convicted in the Japanese stock market case, five years ago. I was innocent. Real criminals twisted the evidence to point at me."

Perl laughed and then spat in the man's face.

"Ridiculous. Strange that the mighty Joiner chose to create such a puny little body to occupy. I fully appreciate that you can mentally communicate with the Fuffax and more importantly, the Akur. I would just like you to be aware of the consequences of doing that."

She reached under the table and produced a metal construction, somewhat larger than palm size. It was roughly oval in shape with razor sharp metal blades around the edges with a small electronic box mounted on top. Perl fitted it carefully around the very private parts of his body and locked it in place.

"There. A little large for you but it will do the job. You will understand that the mechanism is radio controlled from a tiny box that I always keep with me. If I open the box and press the switch inside, those blades start cutting repeatedly. Cut, cut, cut until there is nothing left to chop off. I would imagine it will be extremely painful, not to mention bloody. If one Akur appears anywhere in this vicinity, I will press the switch. I hope that's clear."

"I'm not the Joiner. It's not me," Kin Tuk squealed, face contorted.

"I have plenty of time. You'll be surprised how many organs and areas of flesh can be severely damaged before death ensues. I have medical people here who can keep you alive with only parts of your body still functioning. I'll leave you to consider for a while. If you still resist, I think I will begin with the eyes."

Perl started for the door but the urge was irresistible. She took a scalpel from the wall rack and returned to him. A surge of pleasure shivered through her as he screamed. Perl sliced the blade lightly across his thigh, leaving a ribbon of blood. Then she bent down to run her tongue over it.

Her eyes closed a few seconds and then she left the room, securing the door and confirming that the guards were correctly posted outside.

19

Ford slumped back in the passenger seat. His legs were still covered in mud from the water mill episode but the discomfort was negligible compared to his disappointment. He had been so certain the orb would be in the mill. So very certain.

He looked across at Locey who was humming as she drove. Her clothes were still wet but it didn't seem to bother her.

"Now we have no idea where it is," he said with frustration.

"Where what is?" she responded.

This tested his patience but it held out.

"The sphere. That water mill seemed a sure bet."

"Well, it was best to check that possibility first."

"Right."

A pause before he spoke again.

"First before what?"

"Before the second choice, of course."

"Okay, what's the second choice?"

"We were looking around where she was born. It made sense to do that first. Next, we need to find out if she had any favourite places. Maybe for holidays or a boyfriend's home. For that, we have to talk to people in the village."

Ford brightened.

"Yes. Stupid of me. We should've checked last time."

Back to the village and the general store. The woman there looked mildly surprised by the question and directed them immediately to a house further down the main street. Ford sensed her gazing after them as they hurried towards it.

The door was answered by a thick skirted, woollen jumpered woman. He attempted the smiling approach that had failed so miserably on the farmer.

"Hello. We're archivists working with Crakeston University and tracking down some of the famous people who studied or worked there. Firma Roding was one of the first women to reach a high level at the University and the lady in the store told us to come here for more information."

"Your trousers are very muddy, young man."

"Ah, sorry. Got stuck in the mud along one of the back lanes."

"You can't come in covered in that stuff."

Ford briefly considered an offer to remove the offending garments but correctly thought better of it.

"Look at me. I'm very wet," Locey announced, pirouetting on a heel.

The woman smiled maternally.

"You poor girl. Come on inside and dry your clothes by the fire. A hot cup of tea is what you need."

Her expression changed as she turned back to Ford.

"You'll have to wait and preferably not on my doorstep, dropping bits of mud everywhere," she said icily.

He held up a hand.

"Okay. I'll go back to the car."

Locey didn't seem to hear, engaging herself in conversation with the woman.

"English tea. I love it. Do you like badgers?"

The door slammed shut and Ford meandered to the car. Forty minutes before Locey emerged and he scurried to the house to meet her as she stood talking on the doorstep. Thick skirt gave him a disapproving look and continued the conversation.

"Locey, it's been lovely to have you. Please come and visit any time."

"The tea was delicious and I'm all dry now. Thanks for everything."

"Well, as I told the other lady, Firma Roding was really the heroine of our family. We are very proud to have her in our bloodline."

They were back in the car before Ford was able to ask.

"What other lady?"

"I didn't ask. Someone who visited her before."

Ford gave it up.

"Any clues to the location?"

"Oh yes, a very likely place."

"Yes?"

"Yes."

"What's the place, Locey?"

"Given Head."

"What?"

"I'm driving there now."

"Where is it?"

"On the coast, of course. It'll take at least two hours. She used to go there all the time. Her father took her on his horse and cart when she was young and she still visited when she was grown up."

"To Given Head?"

"Yes."

"I'll find it on the map."

He found it. Promontory in an unusually isolated area of coastline.

"It's all rocky and lashed by the sea with the rough caresses of loving nature who takes you to her bosom but chastises with loving cruelty."

"Right, Locey."

"There's also a lighthouse there," she added.

138 minutes later they were looking at the lighthouse, a lone erection amid miles of rough terrain. The only habitation anywhere in view was a small farmhouse. No people visible but a flock of sheep dozed in the field next to the building. Locey parked in the grassy lane leading to the farm and they trudged towards it, trying to keep upright in the furious wind that blasted across the craggy waste.

"Lovely breeze!" Locey enthused, hair flying back horizontally.

"Certainly fills the lungs. Our problem now is where to look. I guess we should ask at the farm first."

The wind dropped as they approached the farmhouse and Locey began to laugh.

"Clever little woollies," she giggled.

"Sorry?"

"It's a rabbit," she yelled.

He followed the direction of her shout. Sheep. Peacefully sleeping. Then he saw it as well.

"I'll be damned."

The animals were not in random positions. They were lying in the shape of a rabbit's head with gaps for eyes and mouth and five sheep forming each ear. Locey waved at the nearest.

"You made a bunny," she called.

The sheep stirred and looked at her. Then it closed and opened one eye.

"Hey, it winked at you. Didn't think they could do that," he said.

"I love woollies. They're nearly as cuddly as bears."

"That confirms we must be in the right place. The animals must have absorbed the power of the orb," Ford observed.

They reached the farmhouse. Compact and unprepossessing but clean and tidy. A white bearded old man sat outside in an area sheltered by the walls. He was lounging back in a rocking chair and smoking a pipe.

"That's interesting. Another one was here yesterday," he said.

Ford smiled benignly. The old man was obviously rambling.

"I'm Ford and this is Locey. We're with Crakeston University, studying wildlife and coastal formations."

"I'd begin with the lighthouse. That was her favourite."

"Yes, thank you. We are also researching the biography of a woman called Firma Roding who lived around the mid-1800s. I don't suppose you'd know where her favourite places would be around here?"

"I'd enjoy that. We can have it in the kitchen," said the bearded one.

Locey stepped forward.

"Would you like to make passionate love to me?" she asked.

Ford scratched his head as the other two screamed with laughter. Then Locey grabbed the man by the arm and kissed his cheek warmly.

"Come on in, Ford," she called, accompanying the man into the building with an arm around him.

He followed them into a picture book kitchen and they sat with steaming mugs of tea.

"I'm lost here, Locey. Did you offer to make love to this guy?"

"I just said tea would be nice and it was kind of him to invite us. Then again, I do like beards. They're sort of ruggedy."

The old man grinned.

"Rugged comes from an old Norse word, rugg. Shaggy matting. Its use in describing a person is much more recent, certainly in the last hundred years."

"Shag-gy, spin-ster, sog-gy. I think I've developed a fetish for S words."

"Speaking psychiatrically, I wouldn't worry. Empirical research indicates a natural human predilection for soft sounding syllables that frequently involve the letter S. One may postulate a relationship with the saliva glands and consequent food intake. Natural emotion to favour that."

Locey smiled knowingly.

"Fet-ish," she said.

Ford caught up and jumped on the conversation train, albeit in the rear carriage.

"Hold on. You said someone already asked about Firma Roding?"

The man nodded, eyes twinkling.

"Like you, she pretended to be a researcher. I don't know the answer to your next question."

"You don't know exactly where she went to look?"

"If you tell me what Firma left here, maybe I can help."

Ford took the chance.

"Okay, it's an ancient artefact. Probably in a wooden box about so big."

He used his hands to demonstrate size.

"Critical question although I've already assumed the answer. Did she mean it to be found?"

"Only by specific people she knew. Why is that critical?"

The bearded one didn't reply, just looked at Locey.

"Because it would be impossible for anyone to find in this big area," she said emphatically.

"Wasn't that the idea? She'd give the exact place to the people who needed to know."

"Ford, that would be impossible. How could you give a precise location amongst all these rocks. The people she told might not be looking for ages afterwards when some things could have changed. You couldn't put it under a particular bush or stone, for example."

The old man chuckled.

"You said it exactly. Also, it couldn't be in too prominent a place where anyone could come across it. The solution has an eighty seven percent probability."

Locey rushed forwards to hug him.

"And we know where that is," she cried happily.

"I did tell you much earlier."

He paused for a second and then returned her hug.

"If he does, I'll be waiting here."

She kissed his cheek again, grabbed Ford by the arm and led him from the building.

"I'm lost here. Can't grasp anything you're saying," he said.

"Wheeee!" yelled Locey and began to run.

He began to follow and then stopped, mouth open. The sheep had rearranged themselves into a woman's face. Locey's face. If Michelangelo had been forced to use sheep instead of paint, he'd have been hard pushed to do it better. Locey was rapidly proceeding around the reclining animals, giving a hug and kiss to each one. Eventually she returned to Ford, eyes shining.

"Aren't they great? It was a lovely thing to do."

"They did a good job but I'm still confused."

"Put yourself in Firma's shoes. She was in France and had to say a likely place, so she gave this locality, her favourite area. Her plan was to hide the ball somewhere in all the rocks. She couldn't risk someone finding it in the lighthouse, for example and it had to be a place that would still be there for a long time ahead. Then, when it had been hidden and she got back to the monks, how would she tell them exactly where to look amongst all this rocky stuff? Answer is she couldn't. So she must have left a clue here. By far the most likely place for that is the lighthouse."

"Right, I see. So that's where we're heading. But why did he say 'if he does, I'll be waiting here'?"

She grinned.

"If Ford ever leaves me, I'll come back and visit you alone. That's what I didn't say but it was in my mind and he anticipated."

"Okay," he responded dourly but she was already bouncing along ahead of him.

The lighthouse was still operational but with an automatic beacon. No one in residence. However, the door at the base was surprisingly not locked. Ford opened it and they stood in a circular chamber with stone steps leading up.

"Place is falling apart," muttered Ford as he scanned the bare stone room. A block had fallen from the wall and various chips and pieces covered the floor.

"Not fallen. Taken out and recently," Locey commented, walking over to the block. An inscription was etched into one side.

"It's obviously a clue," Ford muttered as he copied the text into a notebook. It wasn't overlong.

'On fourteen occasions, Firma Roding made a point of rising here. May this stone lay one hundred full turns long to prove its worth. By right, she strode the day and understood. X.IV.MDCCCL.'

Locey glanced at it briefly and then wandered back to the doorway.

"Did you like the sheep picture? I forgot to take a photo," she remarked idly.

"Yeah, it was just like you. We'll use the camera on the way back."

"They even got my hair just right."

"Right. Now let's look at these words."

Locey didn't bother to look again.

"It's easy. We just need a compass and a tape measure."

He didn't ask for the solution.

"I've got both in the car. I'll go fetch," he said and left her sitting on the rocks with the brazen sea wallowing at her feet. She was still there when he returned, her eyes in some distant world.

"I've got them. Now what?"

Locey returned to Earth.

"Fourteen points from rising. That's East, rising fourteen degrees to the north."

He took a reading and pointed at an angle across a barren area of coastline. Locey continued.

"Now we need to measure the block. It said a hundred full turns lengthways so we need to double the sum of length and depth and multiply by a hundred. That's how far we go along the line."

"Now I'm with you."

They used the tape to measure out the distance. Progress was slow across sharp and often slippery rocks. Finally, they stood on a relatively flat area about fifty metres from the sea.

"I think I've worked out the last part of the clue," Ford announced.

"You're very clever."

"The words, 'by right she strode the day' means we go ten paces directly to the right of the line we followed. The day is the date at the end of the text, a Roman ten."

He took ten strides and looked down. A square opening had been cut in the side of a massive upright chunk of granite. It was surrounded by a mass of other small slabs that had obviously been covering the aperture until very recently. Ford shouted in annoyance.

"Damn. It's gone. Damn, damn, damn. The old guy said someone came yesterday. They must have taken it."

"I wonder who it was?" Locey mused.

"I could guess but I'll go and check with the man again."

"And I'll take a picture of the sheep this time," Locey exclaimed.

No bearded man outside and the wind was blowing strongly now. Locey took the sheep photo and rejoined Ford as he knocked on the door. A few seconds before it opened.

"Tea's ready Come on in," said John.

Locey squealed with delight and hugged him but Ford was more cautious.

"You're with the Trysse. Is this a trap?"

John turned to him.

"No trap. I don't even know why I'm here. I'm not part of the Trysse now and never will be again. I've learned a few things and I'm stronger for it."

They entered the kitchen and sipped tea at the table while John related the details of his visit to Los Angeles.

"So Eliza is a fake identity. Why would she need that?" asked Ford.

John shrugged.

"I simply don't know. Maybe she's part of the Trysse. Some special agent of Perl?"

"You were shot but you're not dead yet," Locey said with concern.

"I lost consciousness but I really am fine now."

"So you were in the LA hospital. How did you get here?" asked Ford.

"It's weird. I was accused with attempted murder and they kept me under police guard. Two nights ago, someone woke me up in the middle of the night."

"Who?"

"I never found out. It was dark and the figure wore an all-over blue uniform, including a mask. I only know it was a man because he spoke to me. He came to the bed and whispered 'please come'. Then he helped me dress and led me from hospital."

"Didn't someone stop you?"

"That's the strangest part. Everyone seemed to be asleep. We just walked straight past the policeman on guard then down the stairs and out through reception. There were loads of people there but they all had their eyes closed, even the ones standing up. It was just like a dream."

"I dreamt something like that once," Locey interrupted.

"Yes, well I followed the man to a car and he drove to the airport. Didn't speak a word. Then he put me on a private plane, a small jetliner. The cabin was completely empty but there was food and drink in front of me. All the doors were locked except the toilets. The man must have been up front because he came into the cabin just before we landed. He helped me out and then into a car. No customs, no officials. The car was parked just next to the plane."

"Recognise the airport?" enquired Ford.

"I think it might have been Birmingham but I'm not sure. We were on a runway right at the edge. The car had dark windows at the back and I just sat there while the man drove. We stopped at a house in the middle of nowhere. With the time difference, it was still dark and he guided me to a bedroom and provided a hot drink. I'm sure it was drugged as I slept immediately. When I woke, broad daylight was shining around the edges of the drawn curtains. The man came again with food and another hot drink. I couldn't resist consuming it, don't know why. Of course, I fell asleep straight away and the next thing I knew, the curtains were drawn and I could see the sun had just risen."

"Quite an ordeal for an injured guy," remarked Ford.

"It was initially but when I got up, there was no pain at all. The wound had healed completely and I felt fine."

"I went to the bathroom to shave and shower. After I'd finished, the man was waiting in the bedroom with breakfast. For some reason, I felt ravenous and ate like a horse. Then my rescuer whispered 'please come' again. Back in the car with dark windows for a long drive. He finally stopped and opened the door. I was here, outside the farmhouse. He brought me inside and then whispered once more. He said 'get tea ready. Ford and Locey will be here soon'. Then he left and I heard the car drive away. Really weird but it's the truth. What about you two?"

Ford recounted the details of the fruitless search.

John listened intently and spoke as he finished.

"So Eliza said she was going to look for the Joiner. I wonder where she is."

"Here I am."

Eliza entered the kitchen looking fresh and happy. She returned Locey's hug and greeted the men.

"What's happening here?" Ford asked her, rising from his chair.

"Let's all sit down and I'll tell you what I know," she responded brightly, ignoring his lack of warmth.

John prepared more tea and they sat with eyes fixed on her.

"As you will have guessed, I have the orb that was concealed near here."

"So you've got all three then," Ford remarked, his eyes hardening further.

"That's one of two reasons why I'm here."

"What reasons?" John enquired.

"First, I haven't got all three spheres."

A silence before Ford spoke.

"You must have them all. You took the one from Brazil, Locey gave you the second that we found in Colorado. Then you just said you found the third one here."

Eliza shook her head.

"One of them is a fake."

Ford looked astounded.

"Then it must be the one here. I saw the other two and their powers were well evidenced."

"It looks like the search in England begins again," John observed and saw an agonised look cross Ford's face.

"So what's the second reason you're here?"

"The Joiner is now sitting at this table."

The silence was much longer, eventually broken by Locey.

"Exciting! A whodunnit!"

Ford looked unsurprised.

"I think you're right and I believe I know who it is. There's only one of us who has been working inside the Trysse. That's you, John."

He pulled out his pistol and John raised his hands.

"No, not me. I've suffered more than all of you. Have you all forgotten about my discovery in America? It's obviously Eliza. She doesn't even exist and remember she made sure she took all the spheres. Who else would do that?"

"Yes, my name isn't Eliza but you'll just have to believe me when I say I'm not the Joiner. I think we should be looking for a person who has displayed unnatural powers. Able to control bears as well as Fuffax. It's you Locey, isn't it?"

She giggled.

"I'm really enjoying this. Is it my turn now?"

John looked at her solemnly.

"Eliza said you are the Joiner. You haven't denied it," he said.

She didn't appear too concerned at the statement.

"Whooo! I'm the chief suspect. Shall we play some more or do you want me to spoil the game?"

Eliza looked unamused.

"The fake sphere was not the one I found here. It was from Colorado. It was in your possession for quite a while, certainly long enough to get a copy made."

Locey squirmed delightedly.

"I should have lights shining in my eyes. Grilled by the detectives, just like a film. Well, I'll come clean. I did hide the real one and substituted a fake that an old friend made for me. He's over eighty now but a super craftsman. He reproduced the box exactly and got a crystal ball to put inside."

"Why did you do it?" asked Ford. He had now turned the gun towards her.

"You said it was a big secret to be kept safe. So I hid the real one and carried the fake around with me. Isn't anyone on my side? There's always someone to help a girl in the films."

John raised his voice.

"You killed a lot of people, murdered them savagely. It's not a joke, Locey."

"So I have to finish the game? Okay, the Joiner is Ford. It's a shame because his human side is nice. I suppose that was deliberate when it created the body."

"That's pure fantasy, Locey. If it was true, then he'd have been grabbing the spheres rather than Eliza," observed John.

"I can guarantee it's not me," Ford added.

"Sorry Locey, you've no evidence to offer. I need the real orb that you took. Please tell me where it is."

Eliza wasn't asking, she was demanding.

Locey simply smiled.

"I'll tell you, Eliza. But we need to do something with Ford before the Akur arrive here."

"As she said, you've got no evidence," John said solemnly.

Locey turned to him, still grinning.

"No evidence but witnesses. The bears told me."

He shook his head.

"The bears. Right."

"And of course, the Fuffax," Locey added.

Silence for a few seconds.

"Yeah, right. Of course they did," said Ford.

Locey kissed his cheek quickly.

"I think the Akur will be here soon. Sorry Ford."

She struck his jaw with the edge of her hand and he slumped unconscious across the table.

"The Joiner still operates when his human body is out. You know that, don't you Eliza?" Locey asked, the humour gone from her voice.

"Yes, I know that."

"This building won't stop the Akur. How many are there?"

"Three. They'll be coming fast."

"Maybe we should get a boat?"

"Water is like air to them. They move just as fast and we'd be slower."

John appeared to be in a daze.

"I don't understand anything. What's happening here?" he asked.

Locey put an arm round his shoulder.

"Just do what Eliza tells you," she murmured.

20

John looked quizzically at Eliza.

"Okay, I'll do as you say. What's the first instruction?"

"The means to destroy them is being brought to me but it may not arrive in time."

Eliza spoke softly but there was something in her voice that made John rise to his feet.

"Who are you?" he asked.

As he spoke, there was a mighty crash at the door. It buckled inwards but just held. Then the sound of a smashing window elsewhere in the house. The door was struck again and this time it crashed inwards. Two Akur. They paused for a moment and then edged forward. Another sound of impact as the internal door shattered. A third Akur that had entered through the window.

"John, Locey. Get behind me," Eliza shouted.

John found his legs were shaking. He had looked into the yellow eyes. No horror there, just a basic requirement to kill. No savagery, only perfect competence to do the job. The creatures circled closer, assessing the best method of attack. John glanced at Ford's unconscious body.

"Should we kill him? Would that stop them?" he shouted.

"No and no," Eliza replied with a strangely calm expression on her face.

He turned back but the nearest Akur had taken the opportunity and slashed a claw towards his face. He twisted instinctively and felt pain shoot down his arm. Blood was flowing from twin wounds on his bicep. Locey dragged him backwards.

"Don't be afraid," she said and gave a brief smile. Then her arm shot across him, her fist striking the creature between the eyes. It fell back momentarily but John saw her knuckles were red and bloody from the blow. The other two Akur were now attacking Eliza who moved constantly to avoid the razor sharp claws.

Suddenly the air began to pop.

"Fuffax," yelled Locey.

The room filled with furry bodies that quickly formed into a line, a barrier between the creatures and their human prey. The Akur paused and John realised that the Joiner must be attempting to regain control of the Fuffax. It didn't appear to succeed and the three killers moved forward again. They were immensely larger and more powerful than the little furry things. This should just be a minor delay. But the Fuffax fought bravely, leaping on to the lean bodies of the adversary and attempting to pierce the yellow eyes with their razor claws. Locey had grabbed a broom but was only able to fend off the attacks while Eliza used only her hands and legs that were now dripping with bloody wounds.

A Fuffax fell, cut in two halves. Then another and another. Soon, only three of them remained, their fur soaked with blood that now flowed freely from the three humans.

John did what he could, even though he wasn't a natural fighter but he grabbed ornaments, hurling them as hard as he could. He knew his companions were weakening and the aggressors remained tireless. Knew the kill was imminent. Three kills.

Then he heard a sound from the window. Not aural but in his head. Someone outside he recognised. The blue clad, masked figure who had escorted him from America. John saw him throw something. A tiny, shapeless object that glowed brightly. It curled in a dazzling parabola directly into Eliza's raised and bloody hand, the yellow eyes of the Akur following the curve of the light.

The instant it made contact with her flesh, Eliza changed. Her outline distorted, became jagged. Her limbs merged into her body that was transforming into a perfect vertical oval of white flame.

Nothing moved for a few seconds. The lean killers seemed transfixed by the flickering radiance in front of them. Then they began to step backwards, bodies lowered. Perhaps it was imagination but John felt sure he saw their eyes change. From yellow into the deepest red.

A crack like thunder overhead and the flame shot forward. It didn't strike the first Akur, just enveloped it in a blinding flash. Then the light raced towards the other two, engulfing them in brilliance. John wasn't sure what happened next. The three creatures had vanished and the flame had simply disappeared.

"Eliza!" John shouted but he didn't know why. She wasn't there and the figure at the window had also gone.

He looked at Locey. Tears were streaming down her face as she reached towards the three surviving Fuffax but he could see they were barely clinging to existence. They turned to her for a second, eyes still shining brightly. Then they moved to the unconscious figure slumped at the table.

"No, please no," Locey cried but their bodies were already in position, arms inside his mouth and clenching his nose.

John saw her trying to move to them but knew she couldn't. He knew because he was also paralysed. Muscles refusing contact with the brain. Time passed, as if in a dream and he felt an iciness enter the room, an ethereal chill that gripped the heart and soul.

The Fuffax now seemed to have merged with Ford's body and it began to decay, flesh and bones crumbling to dust that became finer and finer until it was simply invisible.

It was another few seconds before John regained the power to move. The kitchen was like the aftermath of a massacre but without any corpses. Furniture and utensils scattered everywhere and crimson pools of blood shimmered on almost every surface. He looked across at Locey. No tears now.

"Wow. The Fuffax certainly found the right way to go. Were they brave or what?" she asked rhetorically.

"I'm really sorry they didn't survive."

"I knew they couldn't exist here when the Joiner had gone. It's not been boring today, has it?"

John couldn't help returning her grin.

"No but Eliza's gone too and I had become sort of attached to her."

Her smile got wider and she clapped her hands together.

"You fell in love with her. That's so beautiful. A bit sad as well, though."

"Locey, you seem to know what's happening but I'm completely lost."

"I know that's a terrible feeling. I hate to be lost. Now I need to make sure the sheep weren't upset by all the ruckus but we'd better get cleaned up first."

The sheep were fine and had repositioned into a memorial picture of a Fuffax. Locey waved in gratitude.

"So what now?" John asked.

"We're waiting."

"What for?"

"Hmmm. That's a hard one. Obviously for Eliza to come back but maybe Perl will get here first."

"Eliza's coming back?" he exclaimed.

"Yes, of course. I have to tell her where I hid the ball."

"Oh, right. And how do you know Perl is coming?"

"That's easy. Woman's intuition."

Perl arrived seventeen minutes later. Two cars screaming to a halt outside the farm and five armed guards emerged with Perl leading them.

"I got your message, John. You've offered to surrender the three orbs to me in return for your life."

John looked bemused.

"What? I haven't sent you a message."

Locey stepped forward to face the woman.

"You don't like bears, sheep or badgers, do you?"

Perl looked at her with distaste.

"You're madder than the Hagg woman. John didn't include your life in the deal, so I'll just kill you now."

She produced a pistol and aimed carefully at Locey's chest but her potential victim simply smiled.

"Wait, the deal has changed," John shouted.

"You have five seconds to make it impossible for me to refuse. If I don't like it, I will kill her immediately. But before I do, I will allow these men to have her."

John fumbled in his brain for a plan.

"Look, I've got the three spheres. I'll give them to you if you let both of us go free."

"I'm not agreeing yet. I think I'll make you watch while my men enjoy themselves. Where are the orbs?"

"They're hidden near the lighthouse but only I know where. They could be in your hands in a few minutes."

Perl lowered her gun.

"You will take me there now but I'm leaving three guards with this lunatic. If I don't get the orbs or you try anything, she will die."

"Yes, I agree," John replied uncomfortably.

Perl gestured for two men to guard John while she walked to the other three.

"Have the girl as soon as we're gone. We're going to kill them both anyway," she whispered.

The three looked pleased with this bonus and moved in a triangle around Locey. They watched as John led the other three towards the sea and turned to her as soon as they were out of sight.

"We've decided to give you a little treat," said one, saliva wetting the corners of his lips.

Locey didn't speak immediately, as though her mind was elsewhere. Finally, she responded.

"I'm really sorry for you," she said solemnly.

"I'm a bit past moral judgement and my conscience left many years ago," he replied, stretching a hand towards her chest.

It never reached its target. Something hit it, scouring a wide gash across his forearm.

"What the hell was that?" he yelled.

The answer came from the skies. They'd darkened. Not clouds but a massive flock of seagulls. Hundreds, maybe more. And they were coming. Coming fast. Before they could move, the men were hit by a tornado of flashing beaks and claws. Their faces were raked, clothes shredded and flesh ripped open. The attack was incessant. Their guns had fallen in the first assault and they crouched low with arms over their heads. Still the assault continued until their clothes were almost completely gone and their backs displayed a gory canvas to the heavens.

Then it stopped. The men looked up, brushing streams of blood from their eyes. The seagulls had disappeared but the sky wasn't empty. A smaller number of birds. Much larger birds. The ones that feasted on animals. No time to run, no time to hide. The first wave took shards of flesh, the impact of the second knocked the men from their foetal position to lie flat on the ground. Immediately, the third, fourth and fifth were upon them. Ripping at their eyes and vital organs. More than thirty to each man. The huge birds feasted, feasted substantially.

Long before, Locey had walked quietly back inside the farmhouse, shaking her head sadly.

John didn't know what to do. He led Perl and the two guards in a circuitous route to the lighthouse but was just playing for time. They had seen and heard the flock of birds behind them but Perl had just smiled.

"They seem excited. I wonder what they're looking at?" she had said to her men, who responded with knowing grins.

Now John was nearly at the lighthouse. What then? He could go a little further but Perl would soon suspect a trick.

"Just ahead," he said, trying to sound confident.

"For the girl's sake, I hope you're right."

He was near panic now. He had survived the Akur but Locey's life now depended on him and this was not a woman easily fooled.

"Hello Perl," said Eliza. She had emerged from the lighthouse as they passed.

The two guards turned, guns aimed at her while Perl remained calm, sure of her superiority.

"Well, well. If it isn't little Eliza. Last time we met, you were pretending to be a novelist. I really hope you haven't been inventing stories with your friend here."

She pushed John forward and he slipped on the sharp rocks.

"You have no future, Perl. The Joiner has gone," Eliza said.

"It's not dead. I need a lot of information before I kill it."

"That's rubbish. I saw it die," John shouted, rising to his feet. The rocks had sliced open one of his leg wounds and blood was flowing anew.

Eliza looked at him briefly.

"She captured the wrong person."

Perl looked scornfully at her.

"I am quite certain that I am holding the Joiner. It is very uncomfortable but safe. Now I want the orbs and I think you possess all three. Perhaps I will start cutting pieces off John until you show me where they are."

Producing a stiletto from her waistband, she walked towards him.

"Okay, but I'll need the pyramids first," Eliza said firmly.

Perl pulled her jacket open. A necklace with three gold spheres. She opened one to display a pyramid and then refastened it.

"I have all three now and I'm certainly not stupid enough to give them to you. With them, I can control the vast majority of people, including this apology for a man. Let me demonstrate, little Eliza."

She turned to John who was attempting to staunch the blood on his leg.

"Kneel in front of me," she instructed.

"Not bloody likely," he responded, without lifting his head.

The slightest uncertainty crossed Perl's face.

"On your knees. Now!" she shouted but he simply ignored her.

Eliza shook her head.

"As I told you, the Joiner has gone. The pyramids have no power now."

Perl's assurance was diminishing rapidly but she gave an icy smile.

"Then it's back to the first plan."

She swung the knife towards John's face but he grabbed her arm and twisted the blade from her grasp.

"Kill them. Kill them both," she screamed at her men but they didn't seem to hear, their eyes fixed on some distant point out at sea.

Eliza held out a hand.

"I'll offer you one chance. You must realise now that Kin Tuk is not the Joiner. Release him and you will leave here unharmed."

Perl paused before responding.

"Very well. I agree. I just have to send a signal to my people and they'll let him go."

She pulled a little box with the switch. Even if he wasn't the Joiner, he was very unlikely to survive and if he did, he certainly wouldn't be a man any more.

"I'll do it now."

She flicked the switch, still smiling. Then her face twisted into an agonised grimace, her mouth falling open and her eyes bulging. The necklace of the three spheres had suddenly tightened around her neck, blood dribbling out as it cut into her flesh. Tighter and tighter. She clawed at it with her nails, scraping more bloody lacerations into the skin. A staccato sound from her throat as she fell to her knees. Finally, she toppled forward, her skull cracking against a sharp rock. That didn't kill her, she was already dead.

John stood rigidly, horror etched on his features. Then he fell to his knees, retching violently. He was barely conscious as he felt his arms gripped by the two guards and they half carried him to the farmhouse. He vaguely sensed them walking away and heard a car departing.

After that, consciousness left him completely.

The next thing he heard was the sound of Locey's voice.

"Scientists don't say that tea is the very best thing when you've fainted. Then again, what do they know?" she said, thrusting a hot mug into his hand.

He opened his eyes and checked his surroundings. He was in a deep armchair in the lounge of the farmhouse.

"Thanks Locey," he mumbled automatically.

"I'll drive you to your place in Devon as soon as you feel okay. I've already said goodbye to the woollies and the birdie feathers."

"Oh, right. That's really kind of you. Sorry I'm a bit shaken up."

"Cadaver Wincepole. Hmmm. Wince-pole. It's not you, John. You're not made to be a detective. Why don't you start a business selling old books? You can work with your friend, Colwyn Bayers and the Wormgraspers will help."

He looked up in surprise, brain active again.

"I've been thinking about that for a while. How did you know?"

"Eliza told me."

"Yes, Eliza. Where is she?"

"Gone now and never coming back."

Locey bent down and kissed him, long and soft.

"That's from Eliza. She said pass it on."

John's awareness was now improving rapidly.

"Locey, you're terrific. I don't suppose you'd like to stay with me in Devon?"

"Mmmm. No. I don't turn your litmus paper the right colour. Anyway, Eliza said there's someone who wants to offer me a job."

She held up a business card and John could just see the words 'Omasor Agency' printed at the top.

"Sorry, I'm completely confused but you seem to know what's going on," he mumbled.

"Well, I had a nice girly chat with Eliza before she went but I think I already knew most of it."

"Perl said she'd believed her secretary was the Joiner and was holding him prisoner."

"She was a silly woman. He wasn't the Joiner. Eliza told me that her friend had already released him without Perl's knowledge. He's fully recovered and will be in China soon, living next door to Tung Hot."

"Eliza's friend?"

"The one who took you from the hospital and brought you here."

"As Ford was the Joiner, why was he fighting the Trysse?"

"Eliza said you'd ask that and she told me a lovely little story of how it all began. The three orbs were being kept safe until the right time."

"Kept where?"

"Not on earth, of course. Anyway, they were stolen by something very evil. To stop the good guys getting them back, the baddies sent six of their lower ranks to stash them away on this planet until the heat died down. That was about 1850 in our time."

"What did the evil lot plan to do with them?" John asked.

"The orbs have lots of different powers. Their purpose really was to raise the wisdom of humanity when the time was right. But the one who took them planned to use another of their functions."

"Which was?"

Locey made an explosion noise.

"Bang! Blow up the planet, all in little pieces."

"What? Why?"

"Because the evil one knew the Earth was precious to the owner of the spheres and wanted to destroy something important to them. All part of a bigger battle."

"So the Earth could have been destroyed," John remarked.

"That was the original plan but the robber got here soon after and changed its mind."

"Soon after? It was over 150 years later."

"Oh, that's Earth time. Just a few seconds on clocks in other places. Anyway, the so-called Joiner had worked out that the orbs could make people obey whoever possessed them. It decided it would be much more vindictive to convert everyone here to their ways rather than killing them all. But when the Joiner arrived, it found the six baddies guarding the orbs had all died. That was a nasty surprise but something in the Earth's atmosphere made them age much quicker than normal. It was also a shock to discover the balls had gone and this Trysse group had been set up to find them."

"I understand. So the Joiner wasn't involved in setting up the Trysse. That just happened before it arrived."

"Yes. It created a human body to inhabit on earth, Ford's body. Obviously it needed to get the orbs as fast as it could. In the beginning, Ford tried to do that using the Trysse and gave three pyramids to Hagg Snowmine to help her and her two sidekicks in their search. That gave them extra power and vastly increased the number of people under their influence but still they had no success."

"If the Joiner could make the pyramids, why didn't it just create more orbs?"

"That's silly. It's like throwing a coin in the air and comparing it to a jumbo jet. The Joiner didn't have the ability to create anything like them. The orbs are super powerful in all sorts of ways but the pyramids just have a sort of hypnotic effect and act as communicators."

"Okay, I see. So what happened next?"

"Ford decided to replace Hagg and got Mariom and Sandra to get rid of her. He had come across Perl who was a ruthless hit woman for the gangs in Hong Kong. He made her leader and told her to get a front man to allow her to work more efficiently, out of the limelight. With the Joiner's approval, she chose Tung Hot."

John retained a puzzled look.

"That still doesn't explain why Ford joined the opposition."

"Ford saw that the Trysse were hopeless, even after killing some of them for incompetence. So he decided to start his own search in addition to their efforts.

He joined up with you, me and Eliza and found he was making progress at last but had to convince us he was anti-Trysse."

"I was thinking about the Trysse symbol. It was in places that had no connection with the organisation, like that old building in Brazil."

"The symbol wasn't invented by that Codue guy. The design came from the spheres and got into the brains of anyone who came near them."

"What about the Trysse now?"

"Oh, that's all finished. The authorities will soon be selling off all their properties and stuff. They'll have a big bonfire to burn all their stupid books and papers."

"But they had lots of people in the organisation. All those maids, for example."

Locey giggled.

"You're a naughty boy, thinking about them. Remember that they were influenced through the pyramids. But the three spheres together are a zillion times more powerful and Eliza just reversed everything. All the people who were in the Trysse now don't remember anything about it. They've become normal people, like us."

John was tempted to dispute half that statement but asked another question.

"Where are the spheres now?"

"I told Eliza where to find the real one I took. It was in the bottom of the undies drawer of a friend of mine."

"That sounds a risky place to hide something."

"You wouldn't say that if you knew him. Anyway, all the balls have gone. No more talking bears," she said wistfully.

"Yes, the animals. You can communicate with them, Locey. Are you some sort of visitor from outer space?"

She didn't stop laughing for fifty two seconds and the time included a session rolling about on the floor.

"John, you're so funny sometimes," she gasped eventually.

"Yes but you're…special."

He hunted hard for the last word.

"You mean not normal. That's true and it's wonderful. I simply get on with animals. Haven't you ever heard of horse whisperers? I can do that," she announced, still giggling.

"You're definitely special and I think you're great. But Eliza wasn't human, was she?"

"No, of course not. The whole thing was planned from the day you interviewed her. She was sent by the original owner of the spheres to get them back."

"Then who was she? And what was the Joiner?"

"How am I supposed to know that? It's not important."

John looked mystified.

"Not important? Of course it is. I need to know."

"Why?"

He hesitated.

"Because, well, I just do."

"There's a story about the sparrow and the parrot. The sparrow couldn't make out how the parrot was able to speak English. He flew over to her and asked. Kept asking, again and again without reply. After twenty minutes, the parrot spoke. 'I can't understand a word you're saying', she said. I think that should answer your question."

www.ingramcontent.com/pod-product-compliance
Lightning Source LLC
Chambersburg PA
CBHW030540030726
47495CB00004B/1073